THE JUMP

KIRON CROKE

To and because of Lolo,
my fun-size muse

For Joseph and Theodore,
my real world magic

CHAPTER ONE

As she walked from the woods that separated their homes and through the field that surrounded her father's, Maven could feel Liam's presence as she approached his house. Picking up on his good mood, she smiled. His happiness was contagious, even through the walls. Still smiling as she reached the front door, she let herself inside. More of a country cottage, the house was small but suited the needs of one person. A nearly identical layout of her own, there were two bedrooms upstairs, a small library off of the front room, and kitchen, dining, and sunroom off the back. With Maven as the only neighbor around for miles, it was a very quaint setting.

Also sensing her presence as she arrived, Liam's deep voice sounded before she had spoken a word.

"In the kitchen," he hollered out.

After sliding off her shoes near the door, she crossed the unoccupied living room and rounded the short corner into the kitchen. She found him stirring a pot on the stove. Savory scents wafted through the room while a trumpet levitated in the far corner playing its music soft and slow in the background. Walking across the cold floor tile, she sidled next to Liam. A foot taller than Maven, she had to stretch on her tiptoes as he bent sideways to offer her his cheek on which she planted a kiss.

"Happy birthday, Pop. Lunch smells good." She spoke the words as she pulled most of her short, blonde hair back into a ponytail.

"Thanks, kid." He smiled brightly at her.

She then pushed herself up to sit on the counter and glanced inside the pot. Looking to her dad, his young face appeared to be only a couple of years older than Maven's, but it held a wisdom that only comes from age. Standing over six and a half feet tall, he had a strong, broad build that was topped off with a shaggy mop of loose, black curls. His square jaw and wide nose differed from his daughter's heart-shaped face and narrow, pointed nose. Still, their up-turned, emerald green eyes were unmistakably similar.

"Trumpet music?" Maven pointed to the instrument.

"Yes," Liam peeked at her from the corner of his eye. "It was a gift from—"

"I remember," she quietly interrupted.

Turning the heat down on the stove, he could feel her silent reverie through a distant time.

"You know you'll have to put that away before everyone gets here," she stated flatly.

Quick to explain himself, Liam made a move to speak, but Maven spoke first.

"So, remind me. How old are we telling people you are these days?" she teased, changing the subject as she helped herself to the green grapes beside her on the countertop.

"Eight hundred and seven years young," he answered, understanding that the topic was closed and continued to stir.

Maven tilted her head and arched an eyebrow as she chewed.

"What?" Liam questioned her expression.

"Do you really think you can pull that off?" she ribbed.

"Hey, I look good for my age," Liam feigned a scoff.

"You look good for your *real* age," she replied with a humorous smile.

"For any age, ya brat." He pulled up his shirt and pointed to his stomach. "Look at these abs. Do you know many 200-year-olds with abs like these?"

"Oh, my Gods, Dad." Maven rolled her eyes and climbed off the counter. "Yes, I do. Please put your shirt down."

With her back to her father, she still felt his amusement rebound through the room. Gathering spoons and napkins, she began setting the table. Opening the cupboard that held the bowls, Maven strained to reach the top shelf where they sat but was unable to grab the dishes. Placing her feet flatly on the floor again, she instead guided her hand in a small arch on the counter. As she did, a faint twinkle of light emitted from her palm. From nothingness, two deep bowls appeared that matched those sitting high above her head. Turning to place them on the table, she was met with her father's incredulous expression.

"Instead of simply asking for help or any other possible solution, you Created new dishes?" he asked flatly. "That's just lazy."

"Well, honestly. Who puts bowls up that high anyway?" she countered as she finished setting their places.

"Probably someone tall enough to reach them would be my guess," Liam answered sarcastically and brought the soup to the table.

"We all can't be Gargans," she bantered.

"I'm nowhere near as tall as a Gargan. You're just short, Mavey," he teased.

They sat down across from the other at the table, and Liam served them both as they continued their raillery.

"Once again, 5' 8" is pretty tall for a girl," she replied while blowing on her spoonful of steaming food.

"Nah. You're a shrimp just like your mom." Liam smiled both at the mention of his wife and the presence of his daughter.

Maven could feel his bittersweet pain nearly every time her father looked at her.

"Gods, you look so much like your mother," he commented, reading her mind. "Well, except for this blonde hair."

"I wish she could be here, Dad," Maven responded sadly.

"Me, too, kid. Her and..." he let out a weighted sigh, "many, many others."

"You'd think after so many years it'd get easier, but it just doesn't." Maven stared down at her bowl. She stirred through the floating vegetables while her thoughts once more waded through the past.

"It never hurts less to have lost those we love." His heart tore for his daughter, sharing the losses they both had suffered. Reaching his wide hand across the table, he grabbed her arm and gave it a light squeeze. "I know," was all he added.

Looking up into her father's adoring face, she was reminded of the many happy things to be grateful for in her life. She patted his fingers with her free hand.

"Well, enough of this," Maven stated with a grin. "Let's talk party!"

Liam straightened in his seat with the subject change and returned her smile.

"Yes, let's."

———

MAVEN CLEARED their lunch dishes and placed them in the sink.

"Are you sure you don't want me to make you a cake?" she questioned as she rinsed their bowls under the warm water.

She waited for a response but was instead met with silence.

"Dad?" she asked again while scraping the walls of the dish clean of the soup residue.

When he still didn't answer, Maven turned the faucet off and looked to her father. Liam was frozen for a split second, projecting a tiny spike of anxiety, then swiftly recovered himself and relaxed.

"What was that about?" she asked, concerned while drying her hands on the towel from the counter.

"Nothing," Liam waved it off nonchalantly. "Party jitters, I suppose."

Maven knew her father well enough to know he wasn't telling the truth, but he also wasn't going to share.

"Okay," she continued, semi-annoyed with his secrecy. "So, how 'bout it?"

"How 'bout what?" he inquired, confused.

"Cake." Maven eyed him suspiciously. "Are you sure you don't want me to make you one?"

"Oh, right. Yes, I'm sure, but thank you. I don't want you to have to go out of your way," he replied kindly.

"That's a very sweet way of saying you don't like my baking," Maven chuckled softly as she leaned against the counter and folded her arms.

Liam laughed along with her. "It's not that I don't like your baking, it's that you don't actually *bake*. You snap your fingers, food blossoms out of thin air, and you've somehow convinced yourself it tastes the same."

"It tastes exactly the same," she moaned as an old disagreement resurfaced.

"No, kid, it doesn't," he smirked.

Standing from the dining table and pushing in his chair, Liam stretched exaggeratedly and followed that with a lengthy yawn.

"Hot food on a warm day does sit heavy, huh?"

Maven breathed through a small yawn of her own while patting her full stomach.

"It sure does. Actually, I was thinking we should push dinner back a little. Why don't you all get here after sunset instead? That'll give me time to get a nap in before the festivities," he suggested and walked towards the living room.

"That works for me. I'll let the others know," she agreed while following him out of the kitchen. "Do you want me to help decorate before I head out?"

"No, no. That's alright. I'm just going to set the table later. Not much else to do," he spoke quickly.

"You're not trying to get rid of me, are you?" She scrutinized his face.

"Yes, I am... because the sooner you leave, the sooner I can sleep," he retorted mockingly. "According to someone I know, they think I need all the help I can get to pull off the big eight-oh-seven."

"Well, fine then," Maven laughed. "I wouldn't dream of coming between you and your beauty sleep. Gods know you need it."

Liam laughed his deep, hearty laugh while escorting her to the door.

"Thanks for lunch," she spoke as she slipped her sandals back on her feet.

Stepping onto the front portion of the wrap-around porch, they both took a moment to enjoy the view of the scene before them. The warm sun shone brightly in a nearly cloudless sky down onto the wide field encircling the home. The surrounding woods rustled and swayed slightly as a light wind blew through. Glancing down at his daughter, Maven could feel Liam's appreciation and love for her. She beamed a sweet smile back up to him.

"You know how much I love you, right?" he questioned sincerely.

"Beyond the moons in the red sky of the Last Kingdom," she recited from a lifetime of being told.

"And back," Liam said as he pulled her into a tight hug and gently held the side of her head against his chest.

"I love you, too, old man," Maven quipped and squeezed a little tighter.

"'Old man,' huh?" he chuckled and shoved her out of their embrace. "Okay, get outta here. You're stinking up my clean house."

Giggling, she started making her way across the crunchy, green grass back in the direction of her own home.

She turned and shouted from a few yards away, "See you later tonight, Birthday Boy."

"Bye, Mavey," Liam waved as he yelled back.

CHAPTER TWO

A few hours later, Maven sat still while kneeling in the large garden at the back of her house. Nestled in a clearing encompassed by trees similar to Liam's, nature was at its finest, which meant Maven was as well. Closing her eyes, she took in the ambiance. The breeze softly blew her hair to one side and rustled through the freshly bloomed flowers. Birds were singing to one another in the branches of the nearby woods. Tilting her head toward the sky, she absorbed the warm rays from the afternoon sun. The spring day was turning out to be more than perfect, she thought, and Maven felt a sense of peace.

Looking back down and opening her eyes, she cut several tulips from their bases near the ground. The white petals seemed extra bright in contrast to their green leaves. After cutting a dozen, Maven collected the flowers, stood, and stretched her long, lean limbs. Dusting the dirt from the bottom half of her legs and wiping off her muddy feet at the top of the step, she made her way through the sunroom and into the kitchen from the back door.

After washing the stems in her basin sink, she placed the flowers on the counter and tied them together with a simple white string. Drying her hands and noticing the sun was another tick farther down in the sky, Maven decided to go upstairs to start getting ready for the dinner at her father's. As she made her way to the stairs, she caught her tall reflection in the mirror at the base of the steps. Moving her head from side to side and meeting her bright green-eyed gaze, she gave herself a smirk. She placed her hands at the top of her forehead, and an almost imperceptible light came from her palms. She swiped them down to the back of her head, over her shoulders, and in front of her chest. Where her short, blonde locks had just been, laid long, wavy, burgundy red hair. With a satisfying nod to herself, Maven climbed the staircase to her bedroom.

Dressed in a white sleeveless blouse with a keyhole back and wide-legged, black slacks, Maven was almost finished getting ready for dinner. Standing in front of the large, framed floor-length mirror, she straightened her posture and tweaked her new hair. She liked the contrast it gave to her coloring.

Before she heard the knock at her door or the laughter that accompanied it, she felt the amusement of the two women who had arrived on her porch. Sensing a tap at her mind as well, she allowed one of the women to Read her.

Are you decent?

Maven smiled. She could hear Sabine in her mind as clearly as if she had been standing in the room with her.

Come on in. I'll be down in just a second, Maven thought back in reply.

Giving herself a last once-over in the mirror, Maven noticed she had gotten a small sunburn on her cheeks and shoulders from being in the garden earlier. Gently wiping her hands across her face and arms, the soft pink disappeared, and her skin returned to normal. Slipping on her strappy, gold sandals, she was finished and took the stairs down.

Meeting her at the bottom of the steps were Lila and Sabine, each with a bottle of wine in hand. Lila had waist-length, thick, blonde hair tied in a braid that laid over one shoulder and bright, sea-blue eyes. Her fair complexion made it even easier to read her moods. They all knew the darker the red in her cheeks, the wider the birth to give her. The shortest of the three, and with the slightest build, Lila was wearing a light-weight sleeveless dress that cinched at the waist. The dark grey fabric reflected well against her tone.

Next to her was Sabine. She was taller than Lila by a few inches but shorter than Maven by a couple more. Her long, brightly colored floral print romper would have felt ridiculous on either of the other two, but paired perfectly with her athletic build, Islander tan skin, straight, shoulder-length black hair, and exotic dark brown eyes. Her full lips were a constant source of half-joking jealousy between the others. Each of them were beautiful in their own right, and their fresh faces held a grace of maturity.

"Oh, my Gods! I am loving this red, Mave," Lila shouted as she reached out for Maven's new hair.

"It's super fun," agreed Sabine.

"Thank you. I needed a change, plus I thought it'd be fun to surprise my dad," she replied with a smile, happy her friends liked her new look. "You both look pretty foxy yourselves tonight."

"Hey, it's Liam's birthday, and you know I like to look good for him," Lila winked at Sabine.

"It will never, and I mean never, stop being gross that you have a crush on my dad," Maven said with a crinkled nose. "Knock it off, or I'll tell Talmadge you've been drooling. Again."

"Look, I will love Talmadge until the very moment this world stops spinning, but that doesn't mean I can't appreciate *all* the beauty around me." Lila grinned mischievously.

"In her defense, your dad really has kept it tight," Sabine joined in.

"Oh, woof. Neither of you even knows how old he is," Maven said, rolling her eyes.

"Early 800s, right?" Lila asked, still laughing. "No big deal."

"You have no issue with age?" Maven stared at them.

The two women looked at each other. "No," they answered in unison.

"Like I said, 'tight,'" Sabine replied.

"I hate you both," Maven got out before all three erupted with laughter. Each could feel the others' amusement, which only egged them on louder.

"Are the guys meeting us here?" Maven inquired after they calmed down a bit.

"Eldon said if they weren't here by sundown that they would meet us at Liam's," Sabine replied, wiping a tear from the corner of her eye from laughing.

Looking out the window, they could see the sun slowly creeping towards the tops of the trees.

"Where are they now?" Maven wondered.

Sabine shrugged. "Sniff 'em out, would ya?" she asked, looking at Lila.

Lila closed her eyes in response. Her eyes moved back and forth rapidly beneath her lids.

"Talmadge is still at our house," she answered after a moment of Searching. "I bet he's waiting for Eldon to meet up with him."

"Okay, then they can meet us at my dad's. He said he didn't need help setting up, but I want to get there early anyway. I just need to grab the flowers, and we can get going," Maven said as she walked into the kitchen. "Oh, please help me remember to re-grow the tulips when we get back."

They each gathered their party gifts. Maven led the way out the front door and straight on towards a path through the woods.

Halfway to the tree line, Sabine glanced back at the house. "Mave, you left on the lights."

Without turning around or missing a step, Maven ran her thumb across the tips of her fingers, and the house went dark.

The three of them fed off of the others' good humor, laughing and joking through the short walk on the path. Once on the other side of the thick trees, Maven's father's house came into distant view. With the sun nearer to setting, the home looked smaller than usual, with only one hazy light lit inside. Walking across the opening, Maven was confused by the quiet of the house. Despite arriving early, she still expected music and movement. Sensing Maven's growing apprehension, Lila and Sabine started feeling their own.

Before any of them could voice their unease, a blinding light shot out through every opening in the entire house. The women averted their faces as they covered their eyes. Thick, murky grey clouds swallowed the clear blue sky. A low rumble started to build in the distance and quickly turned into a blaring roar. Suddenly, the flowers fell from her weakened grip as the wind was knocked from her chest. Maven dropped to her knees. She could feel a stabbing pain starting in her left hand that burned like a hot iron traveling up her wrist and arm and into her heart. Lila and Sabine felt a portion of her anguish, and panic set in all around. Just as Maven felt herself about to blackout from pain, a giant blast came from within the home, shattering every window and shaking the ground. Then, as quickly as it happened, the light was gone, and silence again came from the house.

Sabine and Lila were at Maven's side immediately.

"Are you okay?" Sabine asked, trying to help Maven to stand.

"What the hell was that?" Lila was grabbing Maven's other arm.

The air filled her lungs again, and the pain slowly

drained from her chest and arm, leaving an echo of the heat. "Dad," Maven barely whispered. The moment she could climb to her feet, she sprinted to the house. Lila and Sabine trailed behind her, failing to keep up.

Thunder rolled angrily overhead as Maven reached the front door, which was barely hanging on its hinges. Hardly slowing down, she threw it open and ran inside. The entire home looked as if a bomb had exploded. Everything was burned and torn apart. She inhaled a deep breath of char. Maven looked from room to room but couldn't find her father. Standing completely still in the kitchen, she strained with her whole heart to feel for him in the house. Lila and Sabine burst into the home, stopping short at the hall. Maven held up her hand to silence them. Lila slammed her eyes shut to Search.

Maven felt it. There. A flicker of agony.

At the same moment, Lila's eyes shot open. "Upstairs," she said.

Before Lila got out the full word, Maven was taking the stairs two at a time. Following the thread of pain in the air, she bolted for the open bedroom door. Stopping cold in her tracks, Maven saw her father's long body splayed out face down on the floor. Tripping over debris, she was quickly kneeling beside him.

"Dad?" she breathed, gently rolling him onto his back. His face looked lifeless. "Dad?" she whispered again as she patted his cheek, which felt cold beneath her hand.

A small groan escaped his lips. Hovering both hands an inch above his skin, she started near the top of his head and worked her way down his body. Maven explored for any physical injury she might place. To her shock, she found nothing. His face was drained of all color, and Maven could feel what little connection she had left to him slipping quickly.

"Dad?" she said louder. "Dad!" she all but screamed.

His eyelids fluttered. It took him a moment before his eyes focused on Maven's face. His breathing was slow and labored.

"Mavey," his voice struggled against the word.

Fear began to grip her heart harder, but she tried to maintain a calmness for her father to feel.

"Family, Mavey. Family," he stammered. Maven's breath was becoming more burdensome as she sensed her father's doing the same.

"It's okay, Dad. I'm fine. I just need you to tell me what happened. I can Heal you, but you have to tell me what to fix," she could barely choke out the words while fighting the tears.

A familiar resolve crossed his face. "Not this time, kid," he said, looking deep into her eyes. He grabbed her hand tightly, and another white-hot stab entered her same palm. "Mavey... families. You have to Jump."

Without a second to try to comprehend what her father had said, his grip loosened on her fingers. Panic made her pulse quicken. "No, no, no. Dad, stay with me. Stay right here," she pled.

As Liam looked into his daughter's face, Maven could feel his projected wave of love and pride and adoration flood over her replacing her panic. Then, as her father closed his eyes and exhaled his last breath, she felt nothing. An instant aching void threatened to crush her. Tears began to flow heavily through her closed lids and down her cheeks.

She held the back of his hand to her face and failed to catch a solid breath. When she opened her eyes, she was shocked to see his skin drying out before her. Maven let go of his hand and shot backwards across the floor into the debris, but his arm was frozen in place where she had released it. In just those few seconds, his body looked like grey, dehydrated, warped wood. Right in front of her eyes, she witnessed his body rapidly deplete and cave in on itself. He shrunk and withered to not even half his original size. As it continued, there were sickening cracks as his body twisted and bent and folded in on itself. The ball of dried, ashen body parts desperately pulled toward its own center, creaking as it broke down smaller and smaller until it finally snapped. He collapsed into a puff, leaving nothing but flakes and dust particles to linger a moment in the air before floating down onto the charred carpet.

Maven sat horrified into perfect stillness.

"Oh, my Gods." The hardly audible words came from Sabine but weren't enough to shake Maven from her stupor.

"Maven," Lila whispered. Her tone was spoken plainly, but the fear and confusion she projected exposed her feigned calmness. "I'm so sorry."

Lila and Sabine were again on either side of Maven, helping her to her feet.

Let's get her outside. She shouldn't be in this room ever again, Sabine Read to Lila.

Nodding in agreement, the two friends helped walk Maven down the stairs and back through the opened front door. As their feet touched the grass, the dark clouds dumped out a heavy rain. Maven shrugged off their supporting hands. She couldn't bear to be touched. Even the falling shower felt like a sharp assault on her skin. She walked several feet away from the other two keeping her back to the house. Every sense she had was reeling and propelled by her raw, throbbing loss, and she didn't want an immediate, vivid reminder of what she had just seen. Her mind swirled dizzyingly. Grabbing her hair in one hand and her knee with the other, Maven bent over and threw up on the grass.

"I don't understand what just happened," Sabine said, shaking her head, taking on part of Maven's benumbed horror. "I've never seen anyone expire like that."

"Is that what you think happened?" Lila sincerely asked. "But he wasn't due. He still had almost 200 years until then."

"What else could it have been?" Sabine questioned, not knowing of any other possible answer.

Maven spat over and over onto the ground, trying to clean out her mouth. She then placed her forehead into her palm and lifted her face toward the sky. The rain made it unnecessary to wipe the wet tracks of the tears from her face. Her own questions were running through her mind. *How could this have happened? What caused this? Why now?* Each question brought on another. She dropped her hands to her sides and continued to welcome the rain as camouflage to her tears. Staring off into the trees, something caught her attention. She held her hand against her forehead to shield her eyes and squinted, but the dim sky of the almost set sun hidden behind the storming weather offered little clarity. Snapping her fingers together caused an orb of light to form in her hand. Behind her, Lila and Sabine went silent. Without a gesture, the orb flew off her open palm towards the woods. As it got closer, she saw definite movement. The light followed her line of sight. Before it disappeared, Maven caught a glimpse of what had caused the stirring in the trees: the back of a person heading deep into the woods at an incredible speed.

"My dad didn't expire," she said. Turning around, Maven looked back and forth between Lila's and Sabine's faces and her father's nearly destroyed house. Her heart fell flat. "He was murdered. And now, whoever that was," she gestured towards the forest, "knows they have three witnesses."

CHAPTER THREE

"**M**urdered?" Sabine, putting a hand to her mouth, looked like she might be sick, too.

"But..." Lila shook her head, "that's impossible."

"No, it's not impossible. It just hasn't happened in a very, very long time," Maven commented almost offhandedly. Her mind was racing.

"Are you sure? I mean, how can you be certain that..." but Lila trailed off, knowing that Maven was right. Beyond sensing Maven's resolve of the fact, she had seen Liam's death with her own eyes. She knew that no part of that had been a natural end.

Maven started walking. "We can't stay here. It's too dangerous," she declared.

"Where are you going?" Lila questioned as she and Sabine fell in line behind her.

Maven ignored her. Reaching the back of the

home, she kept going. She led them away from her father's house and in the opposite direction of her own. Her intense mood kept them following her.

"What do we do?" asked Sabine with her hand again, covering her mouth. Her eyes were wide with alarm. "Who do we go to with this? Maven, where are we going?"

Maven, lost in her own thought, still didn't respond. She guided them through the unkempt, tall grass at the edge of the yard and back into the trees. There was no path to follow, but Maven held to a specific direction. As the downpour relented into breaking sprinkles, the women trudged on not speaking a word, but their exposed emotions left nothing unsaid. Each was picking up on a mingling of fear, anxiety, and determination, thanks to the others.

The sun was setting, and their surroundings grew darker by the minute. Deep into the woods, the underbrush grew thick and gnarly. Branches swiped at their hair and snagged their clothes, but even with the lack of light, none of the women stumbled. The energy emitted from the trees allowed them to make their way around the roots and limbs safely.

Several feet short of the edge of the tree line, Maven finally stopped. Lila and Sabine recognized the small meadow in front of them. They were near the far right of a small semi-circle opening of just a couple hundred feet. In the twilight, innumerous fireflies blinked in waves in midair. At the edge of the meadow was a sharp cutoff of a high cliff. Maven turned around. She closed her eyes, reaching for the right words.

"I'm sorry," she spoke with her eyes still clinched.

"Sorry? You have *nothing* to apologize for," Lila insisted. She wanted more than anything to reach out and hug her friend, but she knew from Maven's stiff demeanor that it wouldn't be well received. It was clear to see that there would be no consoling her anytime soon. Lila's heart ached for her.

"Please stop," Maven said quietly. "I can't handle pity right now." She wiped a tear forming at the corner of her eye.

"Why are we here? Shouldn't we be warning people? Getting help? Calling to the Elders? *Something*?" Sabine, normally so sweet and calm, was about to come apart at the seams.

"No, Sabine. An Elders Circle hasn't dealt with any real conflict for well over three millennia, and when they did, they handled it poorly. The ones now are nothing more than historians." Maven's eyes were glancing at the ground, the trees, the clearing. Anywhere except their faces.

"So, what do we do?" Lila spoke up. "We can't possibly do nothing."

"For the time being, that's exactly what we do," Maven replied curtly.

"What? No. No, other people could be in danger," Lila was shocked by her reply. "What about *our* families? You're being selfish."

Lila's words poured like vinegar in an open wound. Maven's hands clenched into fists. As her already raw emotions started to heat and twist, the trees began to moan and reluctantly sway. Creatures in the woods scurried away. Sabine and Lila backed away from Maven. They had never seen the forest react in such a way, nor had they ever witnessed anyone with those emotions before. The anger she was emitting scared both of the girls near tears.

"I'm sorry," Lila spoke. "I didn't mean..." but fright stole the rest of her sentence.

Maven saw the fear written on their faces and realized it was directed towards her. She closed her eyes and focused on slowing her breathing. As she unclenched her fists, the trees gave out a collective creak as they settled back into the soil. For the first time in her long life, Maven hadn't sensed what those not only near her but loved by her were feeling. And she had frightened them. That, coupled with the very present memory of watching her father turn into nothingness, put a sorrow deep into Maven's heart. She leaned against the tree nearest her, unable to stand on her own anymore.

Silence stayed between them until, finally, Lila spoke. "I am so sorry. I shouldn't have said that. I can't believe I said that." Her regret was broadcast almost louder than Maven's heartache.

"No," Maven waved her words off. "I'm sorry. I know you're only concerned about keeping others safe, but my only concern now is keeping you two safe. This isn't a matter of selfishness, Li." Maven stood up from the tree and shook her head to silence another apology from Lila. Her words were bereft of emotion as she continued. "This is literally life or death. We have no idea who that was in the woods. It could have been anyone. Outside of the three of us, we don't know who to trust, and until I figure out what is happening, we have to get out of here."

Recognition colored Sabine's face. "'Jump.' Liam said," she paused momentarily as she felt Maven's pang with the mention of her father's name, but continued, "He said to Jump. That's what you mean by get out of here, don't you?" She asked. "You intend to Jump realms."

"Yes," Maven replied matter-of-factly. She wasn't sure if she was going to be met with resistance, but she braced for it regardless.

"When?" Sabine questioned. Her initial shock had

begun to thaw, and she was starting to understand the dangers fully if they remained there.

"Now," Maven answered. "We need to leave now."

"But what about Talmadge? Eldon? We *cannot* leave Loremara without them." Lila urged. She turned towards Maven with a desperate, pleading look.

"I can't ask you to leave your partners. I couldn't, and I won't. But know that as of now, they are safer without us. Eldon and Talmadge are ignorant to all of this. The moment they become aware, they will be in just as much danger as we are," Maven's voice became increasingly somber. "Whether to involve them or not is up to you, but it is a decision that needs to be made immediately." The pain in her heart rang loudly as she spoke.

Lila searched Sabine's face for solidarity but only found resolve.

"She's right, Li," Sabine spoke softly, reaching out her hand to comfort the building angst in Lila's gut. "I know it feels impossible to leave them behind, but if it means keeping them safe and alive, what choice do we have?"

Lila's mind was reeling. Her brain was rapidly firing through every scenario of Jumping with them, leaving them behind, placing herself in the reverse situation if it were Talmadge who was in trouble, trying to make sense out of something, anything. Each time she quickly came to the same conclusion.

Wiping the tears in her eyes and with a shaky voice, Lila said, "Okay. Just us. We keep them safe."

An avalanche of compassion and understanding from Maven blanketed Lila and Sabine. Their hearts went out to her in return, in their minds recounting the unbelievable loss of her father.

"We need a Jump site and a destination," Lila said, faking more confidence than she thought possible.

"The closest Jump to here is, what? Twenty miles?" Sabine asked, hoping she was wrong. "And what about the sentries at the sites?"

"Wait. Do you think whoever that was will be expecting us to do just this?" Lila questioned anxiously.

"Yes. I think that's exactly what they'd be expecting," Maven confirmed.

"Oh, my Gods. What are we going to do? We can't stay here. We can't be out in the open. We can't Jump." Sabine's resolve was quickly unraveling.

"Calm down. I have a Jump," Maven responded. "Here."

"What are you talking about? All of the sites are catalogued, and there aren't any sentries stationed here. We've been in these woods a thousand times, and I've never seen it. What do you mean you have one here?" a confused Lila questioned her friend.

"Look, my dad... Liam was paranoid, for lack of a better term. He built an unregistered site close to home in case of an emergency. In case of something like this happening." Maven felt their complete lack of comprehension.

"How could he possibly ever expect something this horrible?" Sabine was truly saddened at the thought of Liam believing that something so tragic was ever possible, that any person could ever be capable of intentionally causing that kind of pain.

Noticing the impending blackness of night, Lila changed the subject. "The question still remains, though: where is it?" she reiterated.

Maven hesitated before she answered. "It's over the cliff."

Lila sucked in her next breath between her teeth. "We have to jump off the top of a 100 foot ledge to hit the site?"

"Yes. Well, we have to get a running start first because it's a ways out, but yes," she replied.

"Sounds about right," Lila snorted.

"How's that?" Maven asked, confused.

"It just seems like the perfect ending to today would be to throw ourselves off a cliff." Lila couldn't help but smile.

Sabine grinned despite herself. Maven shook her head, grateful for her friends.

"We need to get going." Maven brought them back to the present. "We need to get to the farthest, central point in the trees opposite the cliff. From there, we'll be able to get a big enough running start to reach the barrier. It's a ways off the edge, but the lead will launch us far enough," Maven informed them as she pointed to the spot she referred to about 150 feet away.

"Which realm are we going to..."

A loud snap in the distance, high above the trees, cut off Lila's question.

Sabine looked to Lila, who shut her eyes to Search for whoever was near, but Maven kept her gaze on the sky. Scanning the upper darkness, she didn't turn until she heard a gasp.

"Oh, no," Lila whispered, her eyes open.

Maven, hands somewhat raised, sidestepped in front of Sabine and Lila. Before either one could ask what or whom she had found, a large object flew through the sky above and landed heavily on the ground, not twenty feet in front of them, causing a small circle of mud to rise around it.

Just as quickly as landing, he stood up straight and briskly ran his long fingers through his windblown dirty blond hair. He was well over six feet with an athletic build, wide shoulders that narrowed to his waist, and dressed entirely in black. His muted silver eyes were instantly on them, knowing precisely where they were located. Without saying a word, he raised his left palm upwards. Another man raced towards the ground next to him. Moments before crashing into the earth, the first man eased his index finger and thumb together, slowing his descent.

Nowhere near as gracefully, the second man found his footing and stood next to the other. Half a head shorter than the blonde, the other man seemed small in comparison, but Maven knew he was still several inches taller than her. His shoulders were much broader, and his strong body was easy to see through his thin suit jacket. The dark brown hair on top of his head was both the same color and short length as his beard, one growing into the other. His blue eyes gleamed brightly against his tan skin and freckles, even in the fading light.

Without hesitation, the men walked straight towards them, and Maven knew it was pointless to fight. She put her hands down to her sides and stepped away from Lila and Sabine. All three shared a fleeting understanding glance. They each accepted the absoluteness of what came next.

Without taking his eyes off of Maven, the tall blond reached for Lila and engulfed her small frame wrapping his arms around her. The top of her head barely met his chest.

"What the hell is going on, Maven?" Talmadge's eyes were somewhat small and hooded, but she had never known any that were as expressive.

Eldon also embraced Sabine tightly. "Are you okay?" he asked her.

Despite the fact that they had made the decision to leave their partners behind for their wellbeing, both Lila and Sabine were beaming nothing but relief at the presence of the two men.

"We have been everywhere looking for you three," Talmadge shouted. He loosened his grip on Lila just enough that she could tilt her head back and meet his look. Although his voice was loud, he wasn't angry. He had been scared and concerned for all of them, Lila especially. "I felt your terror from miles away! When we landed at Maven's house, it was empty. We go to Liam's, find it destroyed, and can't find him either. And then we're flitting around the area just *hoping* for a trace of any of you anywhere! I'll ask again, Maven. What is going on? And where is your dad?"

CHAPTER FOUR

Talmadge's eyes remained locked on Maven's as he awaited her explanation. Soaking in all three of the girls' shockingly painful reactions to the question, Eldon and Talmadge began to emit apprehension. When Maven didn't respond, both men looked expectantly at their partners.

Do we tell them? Sabine was in both Lila's and Maven's heads at once.

How could we possibly avoid it now? Lila answered.

Both girls turned to Maven. She gave a small nod in response.

Talmadge was getting impatient. He put his hands on Lila's shoulders. "Li, what happened?"

"Here," Sabine stepped forward.

Although she was no longer Reading her, Maven

could tell that Sabine was showing the guys her memories of the last hour. For once, she was grateful to be left out of the conversation. Maven turned her back towards the group and slowly crept a few feet deeper into the woods. It would take much more than a couple of yards to avoid their reactions, but she wanted the space nonetheless.

In that brief reprieve from attention, she noticed for the first time how cool the temperature had gotten since the sun had set. It felt nice against what she then realized was her dried sweat-soaked skin. She took stock of her body: her head was thumping, and her ears were ringing; her mouth was dry; her stomach was turning inside of her so fiercely, she thought she might heave again. In an attempt to still herself, she took deep, quiet breaths in through her nose and out her mouth. Tears pricked behind her eyes.

Then, with her back still to the group, it hit her. Within a moment, Maven was flooded with each person's overwhelming myriad of emotions. Pity, sorrow, grief, anger, suspicion, fear, anxiety, care, panic, and on and on. Wave after wave lapped over her. Each amplified emotion a heavier weight than the last. She could not endure it.

"Enough," Maven spun around and threw her hands up as she spoke. "Please. Enough. There will be a time to mourn, but it is not this moment." She swallowed hard. The tears she had been continually fighting back were threatening to loose once more.

In just a couple of long strides, Talmadge stood beside Maven. She had to crane her neck to see his face. His eyes, no longer demanding but still intense then portrayed an earnest concern, but he said nothing. Placing his hand on the small of her back, he led her again to their little gathering. Looking from him to the others, she stared into four faces of sheer disarray. Every single one was at a loss, never having experienced anything close to what they were going through in that instant. Since watching her father's home be destroyed, her heart had yet to slow its pace. Then, it felt as if it might sink altogether.

"Show them the rest of it," Maven urged Sabine.

Hesitantly, Sabine caught the men up to the point in which they landed.

"You were going to leave me?" Eldon spoke, stunned at the revelation. He took Sabine's hands in his. *What would I do without you?* he Read to her privately.

I only wanted to keep you safe, Eldon, she implored. *To keep you out of harm's way. I'm sorry.*

Promise me you won't ever consider that again. Please. Without you, I am nothing. I won't exist, He pleaded in return. Though their words were unheard by the others, Eldon's desperation was plain to all.

A few feet apart from them, Lila and Talmadge had their own discreet exchange. Neither one a Reader nor uttering a syllable, they still communicated perfectly with one another through silence. Having been partners for more than a hundred years, they each understood the other's mind and heart so well that an explanation of Lila's motives or Talmadge's despair at the thought of losing her was unnecessary. After their brief, wordless exchange, Talmadge pulled Lila against his chest once more. He bent down and kissed the top of her head. A firm determination seeped through his limbs.

"We need to Jump this instant," Talmadge declared while releasing Lila from his clasp.

"Where to?" was all Eldon asked, still holding tightly to one of Sabine's hands.

Maven was amazed by the love and commitment that was echoing through the woods. At that moment, the heavy reality sank in for her. She was responsible for those four lives. Responsible for putting them in danger. Responsible for safely guiding them. Responsible for keeping them protected. Her mouth again went dry, and her palms started to sweat.

"What about Faelin?" Sabine suggested. "I have relatives in that realm who would take us in."

"No, a Searcher would check any place we have known connections to. We need to go somewhere without ties. No families, no friends, no obvious associations," Maven spoke quickly.

"Raemorn would be the safest," Eldon suggested.

"Tartooc," Talmadge stated, plainly ignoring Eldon.

"The Human realm?" Eldon questioned, almost repulsed at the suggestion.

"Yes," answered Talmadge. "It's the farthest domain from here and the last any of us would ever want to go. None of our kin live there, nor have any of us ever crossed its threshold before." His eyes surveyed their faces.

"Maven has been there," Sabine whispered timidly. She didn't want to out her friend's thoughts, but Maven wasn't speaking up, and she felt it wasn't the time for secrets.

"Get out of my head, Sabine," was Maven's only reply. She hadn't been conscious of her wandering mind.

"You've been to Tartooc? When?" Lila was surprised at hearing that news. It made her wonder what else she may not know about her friend.

"Yes. Once," she answered, offering nothing else.

"Is it safe for us to go there, Maven? Would anyone Search for you there?" Talmadge asked, his urgency mounting.

"Yes, it's safe. My dad and I went one time, years

ago. No one even knew we visited much less would think to link us there," she replied.

"Let's go," Talmadge spoke as he turned around to lead them to the launch place Maven had pointed out in Sabine's memory.

They walked in silence as they crept through the woods. Maven fell a few feet behind as she paused at the trunk of a tree that was twice the size of any surrounding it. Briefly, Maven closed her eyes and placed both palms on its damp bark. A weak light escaped her fingertips and sunk into the wood. The tree gave a small shiver rustling its leaves. Eldon walked back to gather her.

"What was that?" he asked.

"Just saying goodbye," she breathed and walked towards the group to catch up.

Eldon noticed a small symbol carved into the wood. Touching the tree curiously with both of his hands, he ran his thumb over the indentations then joined the others as well.

Not midway to the launch, Maven froze. They all did. Not a sound was heard, but the alarm was raised. All five heads swiveled towards the same direction. From a rapidly approaching distance, a presence was felt, and it was coming from the direction of Liam's house. An indistinguishable number of bodies emitted a rampage of intensity mingled with malice. Although the number of bodies could not be counted, there was a singular emotion that easily spearheaded the rest: bloodlust.

Moving as a synchronized unit, all five looked back to each other, and, in one fluid motion, simultaneously fled towards the cliff. Panic fueled their feet. Sprinting as fast as they could, they were out of the forest and in the middle of the clearing before they heard the trees start to tremble and moan at the wicked energy that then inhabited them. Sabine turned her head back to look into the darkness and tripped over herself. Right when she should have hit the ground, she was gripped by air instead. A swift flick of Talmadge's wrist set her upright and in line with the still running group. Maven knew that they were coming up to the ledge from the wrong angle. They wouldn't reach the barrier, but there wasn't any time for an alternative plan.

In what felt like a blink, they were upon the cliff's edge. Without a single hesitation, each friend threw themselves off the rock face. The cold wind whipped at their exposed skin, stung their eyes, and cut through their clothes while their hair was pulled wildly behind them. Arms flailed and legs kicked as they fell faster and faster towards the dark water below. Maven knew Talmadge was the last to leap and twisted her body around on its back to face him behind her as they dropped.

"Tal!" she yelled and caught his attention.

Squinting at her through the burning air, she frantically pointed to the faint shimmer of the Jump until he nodded. Talmadge spread out both arms as far as they would reach. With a barely noticeable effort, he pushed. Already falling at an incredible speed, everyone was launched forward like an explosion had gone off behind them. Maven looked up once more and caught a glimpse of a shadowy crowd starting to form at the top of the cliff before she hit the Jump and all of Loremara disappeared.

CHAPTER FIVE

B reaking through the Jump barrier was like swimming through clear mud while running at the speed of sound. Time sped up and slowed down all at once. Brilliant, white lights shot past them quicker than they could acknowledge they were coming. The awareness of falling remained while coinciding with the sensation of floating midair. And even though they were Jumping down, their directionality was moving forward.

After what felt like both a moment and an eternity, their velocity began to slow, and the brightness of the lights started to dim. All readied themselves. Maven, still falling backward, heard deep ripping noises echo around her as Lila, Sabine, and Eldon exited the Jump. Quickly, she was through as well but continued to fall. The instant she saw Talmadge's fingers peek through the invisible boundary, Maven drove her hands together into a tight clench. A heavy boom and sparks flew from her clasped palms. The transparent edges of the large circular Jump above started to singe and curl like a thin piece of a paper caught on fire.

She hit the ground hard, knocking all the air from her lungs. Talmadge narrowly avoided landing on top of her. He tried to control his landing but still hit awkwardly next to her. Maven, unable to breathe, kept her watering eyes locked on the site above. The Jump shrunk and caved in on itself. With a fizzle and small wisp of smoke, it was gone. She then tried to take a deep breath but only managed a wheeze through her sore, deflated lungs. Unclenching her fingers, she placed one hand on her chest. As the light escaped her hand, her lungs responded to her touch and relaxed as she inhaled deeply. A couple of coughs later, she found her breath again.

Using the brick wall of the tall building to her right, Maven looked around as she climbed to her feet. It took a moment for her eyes to adjust to the poorly lit narrow passage. Noticing how much darker it was, she remembered they lost time during the Jump. She found Eldon and Sabine standing next to the brick wall of another building opposite her. Eldon wiped the blood from a scrape over Sabine's forehead, which showed a large gash on his elbow through the tear on his jacket sleeve. Scattered a few feet from them, Talmadge was kneeling over Lila, who sat on the ground. It appeared that everyone had received some sort of injury. The black concrete beneath them was a vastly different landing from almost every other Jump site.

"Maven," Talmadge got her attention. He gestured his head for her to join them.

Once she reached where he knelt, Maven saw what his long torso had concealed; Lila's right ankle was twisted too far inward, clearly broken. Lila had her eyes closed, and tears silently streamed down her cheeks.

"Oh, Li," Maven muttered.

Nudging Talmadge out of the way, she crouched down at Lila's feet. Very gently she removed Lila's busted, dangling sandal, and then placed her left hand on the outside of the ankle as her right gripped the bottom of the foot. A delicate light flowed from Maven's hands into Lila's skin around the wounded area. Slowly, the foot straightened, and a small crack was heard as it fell back into place. Lila winced slightly but gave a breath of relief. The little color she had returned to her face.

"Thank you," Lila smiled at her.

"Of course," Maven tried to smile back as she stood, but already her mind was tripping over itself back to their current predicament. Walking from one person to the next, Maven placed her hands over their cuts to Heal.

"Where are we?" Eldon wondered, looking around the dark alley.

"And what is that awful smell?" Talmadge, already back to kneeling beside Lila, asked as he covered his mouth and nose.

"The smell is that dumpster," Maven pointed to the large, lidded metal box a few feet away, "and we are in New York. Brooklyn, to be exact."

"I've heard of this place," Eldon commented. He bent his arm, testing the mend at his elbow.

"I think I read about New York once. Isn't it supposed to be dangerous?" Lila questioned. Talmadge helped her to her feet.

Almost on cue, a loud siren blared from a police car on the street. Everyone except Maven startled. For the first time, they noticed people walking past them on the sidewalk at the mouth of the alleyway. Even though it was late into the night, the hustle of the city had not died out. Nervously, the four inadvertently backed up.

"It can be," she nodded, "but we'll be fine. So long as we stick together, I can steer you through."

As the initial shock of the Jump and their spiked adrenalin wore off, a strange surge began. Like an avalanche, the emotions of every single body near them in the crowded city cascaded over their senses. Sabine blanched and recoiled as Lila and Talmadge grimaced. Eldon placed his hands on either side of his head, befuddled.

"What's happening?" Sabine uttered through her teeth. Her knees began to shake.

"Link up," Maven insisted. She took Eldon's hand on her left and Lila's on her right. They followed suit and formed a small circle. The same faint light started in Maven's palms and lit up each consecutive pair of hands through their chain. Once Sabine's and Talmadge's hold shone, the light faded altogether. The relief they all felt was immediate.

Maven shook her head. "I meant to do that before we Jumped." The apology was in her voice as she released her grip.

"What did you do?" Sabine asked wide-eyed.

"I put a Protection over us. It's kind of like a bubble; we can still sense each other, but I blocked out all of *this*," she gestured over her head, emphasizing her last word.

"Amazing," Eldon commented.

Maven only shrugged.

"Well, what now?" Lila asked.

"We need somewhere to take cover, Maven," Talmadge spoke. "Do you know of a safe place near here?"

Before she knew she had done it, Sabine blurted out, "Who's Sam?" Her hand flew to her mouth.

Maven shot Sabine a hard look. She closed her eyes, and her brow slightly furrowed. A second later, Sabine flinched. Maven had shielded her mind from Sabine's ability to Read her. It cut between them like a metal curtain severing the connection of her trespass. Sabine had an exceptionally powerful gift, and that was the first time she couldn't see another's thoughts or speak to someone's mind at will. The quiet from Maven's mental self was eerie.

"I didn't mean to," Sabine offered up apologetically. Wounded from Maven's rebuke, she bit her lower lip and looked to the ground.

"I know you didn't, but you can't help yourself, Sabine. And right now, I'm allowed a little privacy," Maven forced herself to speak calmly. "I'm not mad," she added, sorry to have hurt her.

"Who is Sam, Maven?" Talmadge, again intense, inquired.

"He was an acquaintance I made while I visited here with my dad," she reluctantly answered.

"An acquaintance? Could you trust him now?" Talmadge was obviously anxious to clear away from the collapsed Jump.

Maven knew Sam was trustworthy, and her sentiment of that was enough to convince the others without voicing any confirmation.

"Then, we go there." Talmadge's tone left no room for discussion.

Maven nodded in response. Whatever hesitation she felt was trumped by her need to keep them safe. She could only hope that in keeping her friends out of harm, she wouldn't be putting Sam into danger.

"But keep in mind, he's human. He doesn't know anything about me, or us, or our realm, or that any other realms even exist, for that matter. I need it to stay that way. Whatever explanation given will be given by me. Understood?" She made certain they each felt her importance of that fact, and they agreed.

As she readied to lead the way, Maven noticed Sabine shiver, which caused her to realize she was cold, too.

"I think it might be autumn in Tartooc," she spoke as she eyed each of them and took note that their beautiful clothes were torn and filthy. Most had dried blood showing somewhere.

"I'll be right back." Maven turned and started walking towards the street.

"Maven, wait," Lila called after her.

Maven held up her index finger in reply, continued to the street, and turned the corner.

A few minutes later, Maven returned. "Get behind the dumpster," she stated.

They followed her command. She took a brief glimpse at each member of the group before she closed her eyes and snapped the fingers of both hands. Without realizing what she intended to do, they were surprised at the small flash that came and made them squint. As it vanished, they discovered each other's new outfits before glancing down and realizing they had their own. To save time and avoid standing out, Maven placed them all in some variation of the same outfit: boots, jeans, white t-shirts, and black jackets. Talmadge was also given a red plaid shirt and Eldon a grey beanie. Lila's and Sabine's hair had been fixed to how it was before leaving for Liam's.

"These are... great," Sabine forced out weakly trying to be gracious.

Maven forced a smile in return. "We're trying to blend in. They'll do."

"Let's get at it, shall we?" Talmadge suggested.

"Follow me." With that, Maven swiped her hair over one shoulder, put her jacket's hood over her head, and led the way.

Grateful to be out of the alley, away from the dumpster, and onto the street, Eldon took a deep breath. He was shocked to find that the air was still noxious and polluted.

"How can these humans even breathe?" he asked no one in particular.

With their fears somewhat dissipated and their curiosities piqued, Maven felt that trying to lead her friends down a New York City street in the middle of the night was like trying to herd cats. Every few yards, something shiny caught their attention. Sabine gazed at designer dresses in the showcase windows. Eldon's blue eyes swallowed every tall building and lamppost and street sign he saw. An art gallery front captured Lila's eye. She stopped briefly, amazed at the lit paintings and sculptures. Talmadge, never leaving her side, stood next to her while the other three waited a few feet ahead. A group of girls was walking down the sidewalk, and all stared at his tall frame. Coming closer, one girl let out a long whistle. Lila came out of her reverie and recognized that the whistle was for Talmadge.

"May I help you?" Lila asked loudly as the girls passed by, still staring. Not embarrassed at all, they laughed and walked on.

Lila turned back to Talmadge, who was staring deliberately into the gallery window. Seeing half a smirk on his face and feeling his amusement at her jealousy, she scoffed, albeit humorously. She pushed him with both hands to force him to catch up to the others. Her small frame didn't budge him an inch, which only egged on his amusement further. Talmadge laughed and relaxed slightly for the first time since first feeling her panic hours earlier. Wrapping his arm around Lila's shoulder, he aimed them back to their friends.

Although grateful for the time to prepare before reaching Sam's, Maven was anxious to get off the road.

"No more stops. Please?" she urged.

A little contrite, everyone stayed close and followed Maven as she guided them through the twists and turns of the city. No one said much as they made their way. Lost in their thoughts about what was to come next left them also to remember all that had already happened. A somber note fell over the lot. Their momentarily forgotten nerves and anxiety returned. They kept pace with the rest of the pulsing traffic through the veins of the city. Then, without warning, Maven stopped in front of a high, broad red brick building covered in chipped white paint. Each floor of the building had elevated ceilings with tall, arched windows. A minute passed in silence, and Maven hadn't made a move to walk up the steps to the front entrance.

"Is this it?" Sabine asked. "Do you not remember?"

"No, this is it," Maven muttered. She stared high above at the glass of one of the few apartments with a light still on.

"C'mon." Lila tugged on Maven's sleeve.

They took the few steps to the door. Against the left wall of the frame was a panel of names with buttons next to them.

"It's stuck," Eldon said as he tried to open the door.

"It's not stuck. It's locked to keep people out who either don't live here or aren't invited," Maven explained. "You find the name of the person you're looking for, press the button, and they can buzz you in."

"They lock people out?" Sabine could not comprehend the thought.

"'Buzz you in'?" Lila repeated.

"Unlock the door from upstairs," Maven corrected. Scanning the printed names placed under the panel, Maven found the name S. Ranae. "That's him." She pointed to Sam's name.

"Shouldn't we press it? You know, to get off the street." Talmadge was puzzled by her dawdling. He had never seen her behave so uncertainly before.

After a beat, Maven said, "Tal, why don't you unlock the door? We'll just knock once we get up there." She turned toward the doorknob expectantly and motioned instructions.

"Okay." Talmadge didn't argue. He simply leaned forward, twisted his hand clockwise like Maven had, and unlatched the deadbolt. He held the door open, and they all walked inside.

Once indoors, Maven again led the way. Straight and to the right, she took them to a hallway with three elevators and pressed the "up" button. The others regarded the doors cautiously.

"They're basically boxes that are raised and lowered by cables to whichever floor you choose," Maven explained, sensing the tension. Her explanation didn't seem to calm their nerves. "They're perfectly safe," she continued.

"Perfectly?" Talmadge raised an eyebrow.

"They're nearly perfectly safe," Maven corrected as she shrugged. Talmadge didn't find much comfort in her amendment.

A bell dinged, and the doors opened to the elevator farthest to the right. Maven climbed in, and the rest reluctantly slid in behind her. Pressing the button for the fifth floor, the doors closed, and Maven felt as all four of her friends quietly held their breath. She concealed her amusement. The elevator climbed the floors quickly. As the doors glided open, she could feel them each exhale with their relief. She shook her head, took a right out of the lift, and started down the long hallway.

Their collective shuffle echoed softly in the deserted hall. Each step toward the very last door on the left came a little slower than the one before. The only reason Maven's feet kept moving forward was the fact that she was responsible for lives not her own. Inevitably reaching the apartment, the group formed a small semi-circle around the entry to number 502. With Maven in the middle facing the door, she poised her hand to knock. Then, her hesitation returned. A million thoughts swiftly inundated her. Her heart began to race, and again her mouth went dry. She dropped her frozen fist back to her side.

Not being able to bear feeling her friend under such distress, Lila stepped forward and knocked for Maven. Maven looked to Lila aghast and wide-eyed then not-so-subtly slinked back between Eldon and Sabine. Taken aback by her reaction, Lila did not have time to move before the door swung open.

Lila's eye line barely met the breastbone of the man answering the door. She had to take a step behind her and tilt her head virtually backward to see his imposing face a foot higher than her own. Looking down at her was an exceptionally handsome man with well-defined muscles protruding from underneath every inch of his skin. The worn-through crimson shirt and charcoal grey pajama pants he wore were extremely large but still didn't do much to contain his physique. Underneath his top, the outline of a necklace and several tattoos could be seen. His shaved head only made his amber brown eyes more prominent. A bushy beard that had newly begun to sprinkle with grey framed his mouth.

The man gave an uncomfortable half-smile as he looked around at the group of strangers in front of him.

"Can I help you?" his velvety voice asked.

Lila's jaw dropped. She pointed to the man in front of her, turned to lock eyes with Maven as a shocked choking squeal escaped her throat.

"Oh, my Gods, Maven!" Lila called out.

At that point, Talmadge reached forward, grabbed Lila's shoulder, and pulled her back towards him. "Down, girl," he whispered.

The man's eyebrows stitched together as he again searched their faces and found her. She had been all but hiding behind Eldon's shoulder, but he recognized her eyes.

"Maven?" He asked, disbelievingly.

Stepping forward, she pulled the hood down from her head.

"Hi, Sam," Maven creaked out, her gaze to the floor.

His eyes scanned her face and body up and down several times. His expression quickly changed from disbelief to distaste. "What in God's name did you do to your hair?"

CHAPTER SIX

"My hair?" Confused, Maven examined the new strands she held between her fingers. "Oh."

She had forgotten altogether that she had changed it to red. That afternoon felt like a lifetime ago.

"Not your best look," he grumbled.

As he got a good eyeful of each of them then, he noticed how similar all their clothes were.

"Why are you all dressed the same? Are you in a band or something?" Sam spoke with a quiet venom lacing his bored tone. He pulled a rag he had tucked into the back of his waistband and methodically wiped black paint from his bulky hands. His now-emotionless gaze never left her face.

Words failing her, Maven shrugged her shoulders.

"Excuse me?" Lila's interjection was directed at both Sam and Maven. She could not fathom as to why two supposed friends would behave as they were. His palpable anger and insults, and her... she couldn't place a firm grip on the exact emotion that was coming from Maven. Remorse? Relief? Anxiety? It seemed to be bouncing around, unable to land. Apparently, not even Maven knew what she was feeling.

Talmadge stirred from behind Lila. Her upset with Maven's interaction, or lack thereof, was rippling through the group. They all grew agitated.

"Maybe we should go," Sabine softly suggested. Briefly touching Maven's wrist, she could feel how quickly Maven's heart was beating.

"Maybe that's not such a terrible idea," Sam agreed. He crossed his arms over his wide chest. His stance seemed to take up the entirety of the doorframe.

Maven faced downward. The only part of Sam she dared to glimpse was his bare feet on top of the metal door sill. Her mind pitched and wobbled. Inside of an infinitesimal speck of time, her world had turned to chaos. But even as faulty as her footing felt, she didn't budge a muscle.

"No," Maven croaked. Raising her eyes, she met Sam's harsh stare. "No, we're not going anywhere."

Sam's eyebrows shot up in surprise. "You're not?" he asked.

"No," she said again, finding her voice and standing up straighter. "Look, Sam, I know this is unexpected," his snort interrupted her. She continued, "but I... we... we're in trouble."

"Of course you are," he retorted while rolling his eyes. "What other reason could *possibly* make you show up here?"

Maven ignored him. "We're not just in trouble; we are in flat-out danger. And I know that I have no right to expect, much less ask, but I'm going to. Will you *please* help us?"

She steeled herself for whatever spiteful retaliation he might fling and for his inevitable cold brush-off. She could tell from his contemptible expression and stiff body language that it had been a waste of time showing up there. Their history aside, though, she was accountable for the precious lives behind her, and she refused to leave without having at least tried.

Sam's bitter eyes bore down into Maven's skull. Still, she did not falter.

"Please," Sabine's voice all but sang. She came and stood beside Maven. Forgetting that another person existed in the hallway, Sam pried his eyes off Maven's and rested on Sabine. His attitude visibly softened at seeing the trepidation on her face. He unlocked his arms and placed them at his sides.

"Please," Eldon stepped forward. His hand slipped around Sabine's waist.

Sam looked at both of their troubled surfaces. He

glanced at Lila. Although her eyes flew daggers at the man who held a clear contempt for her friend, her demeanor was also one of unease. Talmadge, about the same height as Sam, evenly met his gaze. His face did not show fear, but his unrelenting hold on his partner could not be ignored. Sam turned again to Maven. Animosity colored his face once more.

"Maven..." Sam started but couldn't finish. As if to steady himself, he gripped one side of the wall. He closed his eyelids and shook his head slowly.

"I understand," Maven spoke sedately. Her words were genuine. She truly did understand his reasoning for turning them away.

"Bye, Sam."

"Wait." Before they could make a move to leave, Sam spoke. "Just... wait." He rubbed his forehead and closed his eyes roughly and pinched the skin at the top of his nose.

They all stayed perfectly still very unaware of how it was to play out. Sam scratched his chin through his beard then let go of his face altogether. Silently, he shook his head again and glanced heavenward. Giving a deep, heavy sigh, Sam took a step backward. He held the door open and gestured for them to come inside.

Skepticism resounded. Quietly, Maven ushered her friends inside. They cautiously filed over the threshold one by one.

"Thank you," said Sabine sweetly. The sincerity in her dark brown eyes chipped away a little of Sam's icy exterior.

"You're welcome," he brusquely replied and cleared his throat. "Nice beard," he commented as Eldon passed.

Lila walked through sporting a tight, strained smile but avoided Sam directly. He watched her stride away and mentally noted to avoid the tiny blonde at all costs. He had been bitten by an overly protective dog as a child and felt a strong connection between Lila and the memory. Looking up from watching Lila, he saw Talmadge fixed on him with clenched teeth. Sam raised a disgruntled eyebrow but then put his hands up in a yielding manner. Talmadge continued inside, and, again, Sam shook his head.

"Living room is there on the right," he pointed as they accumulated in the middle of the hall. They were impressed with the vaulted ceilings and enormous paintings staggered all along the length of the walls.

Maven entered the apartment as the others followed Sam's direction and emptied from view. She stood off to the left next to the open door of a large utility closet. It was dark, but she could see it was filled with boxes and unused furniture. He closed and locked the front door behind him. A small quiet sat between them.

"I--" Maven began.

"Let's join your friends." Sam ambled into the living room before Maven had even shut her mouth. Eating her unspoken words, she shoved her hands into her jacket pockets and trailed the others down the hall.

Even in the small room, the ceilings were hung high. Two columns on either side supported beams at their tops. A brown leather sectional couch laid snug in the far right corner. Two broken-in matching armchairs sat across from it with a rectangular glass coffee table set between them. A short bookshelf hid behind the door. Besides a lamp, no other decorations were adorned.

"No paintings in this room?" Maven snuck a peek at Sam out of the corner of her eye as she joined her friends standing in front of the couch.

"Nope," Sam replied and pursed his lips. He plopped down into one of the chairs.

"Sam, this is Talmadge, Lila, Sabine, and Eldon," Maven pointed down the line to each, respectively. "Everyone, this is Sam."

After a jumble of "hellos," an awkward pause initiated as five sets of expectant eyes fell on Sam.

"Why are you all standing?" Sam questioned.

"You haven't invited us to sit," Lila mumbled, continuing to avoid his face.

"Oh, won't you please sit?" Sam dumped out

sardonically. "While you're making yourselves comfortable, how about someone tells me why you're all here? In the middle of the night. In danger. And, better yet, why your hair is so God-awful," he shot at Maven.

Ignoring his dig, Maven perched on the arm of the couch.

"You're sure showing your age, Maven," Sam spouted another attempted insult.

"I think we both know that's not true," Maven replied calmly to his additional derision. She guardedly began to answer his initial question, "We're here because we need somewhere to lay low."

"And?" Both of Sam's eyebrows rose. "Lay low from what? Or whom?"

"The less you know, the better," Maven countered.

"What? No. You can't show up out of nowhere after nearly a decade, expect to use my apartment as a safe house, and for me to stay ignorant of the cause. Get serious," Sam asserted loudly.

The tension in the room was starting to build, but, to their credit, Maven's friends stayed quiet.

"Lila, Sabine, and I saw a crime being committed. We didn't see who did it, but we know for a fact that they saw us. We left as fast and got as far as we could," Maven stated matter-of-factly. Her voice shook towards the end as she felt her friends' compassion once more at recounting the events. She avoided their looks and kept her head aimed at Sam.

"When was this?" he questioned.

"A couple of hours ago," Maven replied.

Sam's eyes widened with that information, but he didn't comment.

"What crime?" he asked.

Maven shook her head.

"What crime?" Sam repeated. When Maven didn't respond, he looked to Lila and Sabine expectantly, but their attention was on their friend.

"I need some time here. Enough to figure out what the next safest step is for us," Maven continued.

"Maven, what crime? What did you see?" Sam questioned again, his tone a mix of irritation and impatience. He was anxiously sitting forward in his seat.

"I think no more than a day or two, and we'll be gone." Maven disregarded his question once more, and Sam's face began to seethe.

"Fine. Then, answer my first question: what in the world is going on on top of your head?" Sam piled on.

"Are you seriously giving me grief about my hair?" Maven felt her cheeks begin to flush. She could see that he looked pleased to finally have gotten a rise out of her, which only made her angrier. "*My* hair, Sam? It's a different color, but at least I have some left. From what I can tell, all the hair that was on top of your head migrated to your chin."

Sam laughed at her. That was it. That was all it took for what remained of Maven's poorly hinged control to splinter and break. Without a thought, Maven stood, took a step towards Sam, and wiped her hands over the red hair. In its place fell black, tightly curled hair that nearly touched below her shoulders. Sam stopped laughing.

"... the hell!" Sam yelled and leaped up and behind his chair in one swift movement. His eyes bugged out as he regarded them all dangerously. "What did you just do?"

"There," Maven stated. "Is this better? This was how you knew it, yes?" She asked as she pointed to her hair. Her temper stormed.

"How? How did you do that?" Sam asked, still yelling.

Maven's hands balled into fists. The corners of her mouth turned upwards as she started to enjoy the sight of a scared, cowering Sam. A myriad of ideas began to dance through her mind of what else she might do to shut his smart mouth. She heard Talmadge stand and could feel his entertainment. On the other side of him, Eldon promptly joined, failing to hide a hateful snicker. She glanced at Lila and Sabine, still sitting. When she saw their faces turn up as they gained pleasure from Sam's panic on the other side of the room, Maven's delight dispelled. She knew she had gone too far.

"Stop." Maven spoke to her friends, but no one paid her any attention. "Stop!" she shouted.

They all turned to her compliantly. Using the same methods that she had utilized in the woods, Maven closed her eyes and focused on her breathing. She tried to calm herself and relax her body, but she felt sick. In all her years, she had never lost control so badly. She wasn't even aware that she could. The recently pent-up tears stabbed at the backs of her eyes, but she refused their passage. She stood, counting with her eyes closed until someone spoke.

"What was that?" Sabine whispered.

Maven opened her clenched eyelids. She saw that Talmadge and Eldon were again seated. Sam had his back pressed against the wall. All eyes were on her.

"I'm so sorry," Maven choked out as she wiped the flush in her cheeks away with the back of her fingers. "That's never happened before, but none of this has." She continued to pat her face until the heat subsided.

"What?" Talmadge asked. "What just happened?" His grip on Lila's hand looked painful, but she didn't dare budge.

"We're, we're feeding off of each other," Maven sputtered, still calming herself.

"But we've always done that," Eldon spoke up from farthest away. His face was ashen.

"Yes, but it's always been positivity and happiness bolstering up honesty and good intentions. Here, now, we're radiating fear, and anger, grief, and panic. It's like blood in the water. And I'm the main source of that." Maven's heart wrenched at the realization. "I'm sorry."

"We're just as guilty," Lila consoled, but they all knew it was only partly true.

"What do we do?" Talmadge asked.

"I have to pair you off," Maven advised. Her anger had ebbed as she felt their new wave of apprehension.

"This is exactly what she means," Sabine insisted. She physically tried to shake off the other's exposed emotions. "We can't function properly with these feelings. We aren't built for this type of disharmony, and my soul cannot take it much longer." As she spoke, a single teardrop fell down her cheek.

Facing Sam, Maven saw he was still frozen in place behind the chair. "Would you please wait for me in your bedroom," she requested as normally as she could manage.

He nodded and inched out of the living room. It was the slowest she had ever seen him move. She was sure it would have been funny at any other time but only felt more heartache at its presence in that moment. Returning to her friends, she made quick work of pairing off the couples.

"You're going to sense a kind of emptiness, but you'll still have each other. Whatever you're feeling at all, you need to discuss it with one another. Don't let things fester," Maven explained.

"What about you?" Sabine's worried eyes scanned Maven's. "You'll be all alone."

Looking out the opening of the living room, Maven could see Sam's closed bedroom door across the hall. "I'm okay, Sabine. Thank you. Right now, though, I need to go talk to him."

"I'll go with you," Talmadge stood to accompany her.

"Thanks, Tal, but I really think I should talk to him by myself." She appreciated his offer, but there were some things she and Sam needed to discuss in private.

Talmadge had no idea how to respond to that. He very much did not want to leave Maven alone. "What if he tries something? We wouldn't know to help."

"He won't hurt me. He never has. The first time he even insulted me was just now. I promise I will be fine across the hall. Besides, we know I can take care of myself." She gave what was meant to be a reassuring smile, but it only came off as sad.

To give them at least a feigned sense of privacy, Maven shut the door to the living room behind her. As she crossed the hall and tapped on the bedroom, she realized that just as every other time she imagined it, she had no idea what to say to Sam. The door opened only enough to show a sliver of his face. He said nothing.

"May I come in?" Maven nervously asked.

"Could I stop you, even if I wanted to?" He questioned through the small crack.

Maven didn't answer.

"Thought so." Sam opened the door the rest of the way and stepped backward, giving her a wide berth. He watched her suspiciously as she shut and leaned against the door behind her. She unconsciously inhaled the familiar scent of his cologne and clean laundry. He reversed until his bed was at his heels, and he sat.

Although much wider, that room, unlike the one opposite it, had a lowered ceiling not much more than a foot and a half higher than Sam's head. Even sitting, he seemed too big for the space.

"Please don't be scared of me. I'm not sure I could handle that," Maven pleaded weakly.

"You haven't given me a lot of options of what to feel about you over the years," Sam replied.

To that, Maven could only nod.

"Who are you?" he asked, enunciating each word carefully.

"I'm me, Sam. I am the same person I've always

been." She took a step closer, but he scooted back. She leaned against the door again.

"Speaking of being the same person," he pointed to her face. "How do you look *exactly* the same as the last time I saw you?"

"Good genes," she tried a smile.

"If you're only going to lie to me, I don't need to waste my time," he spoke with more boldness, which Maven took to be a good sign.

"That was a genuine answer," she said, not wanting the conversation to end so quickly. "It really is genetic."

"What are you?" Sam's words were caked in curiosity and fear. "Alien?" he proffered.

"No, I'm not an alien," she shook her head. "At least, not in the sense you mean."

"Then what?" He leaned forward with his question.

"I can't get into this with you, Sam. I really can't." She sighed and knew he was furious.

"Are you kidding me? You can't get into it?" he barked out, but there was no question. "After ruining a part of my life, you want to come into my house, unannounced, ask me for favors, flaunt some voodoo that you should never have shown me just to freak me out, not answer my questions and give me a couple of half-truths? Do I have this right? Did I catch it all?" He yelled as he stood and paced.

"Seems like you mentioned everything," she breathed out stoically.

He gave her a fiercely annoyed look. "Your buddies out there, they're the same as you? Your best friends, right?" he wondered loudly.

"Yes," she answered hesitantly.

"Did they know about me? Because it sure didn't look like there was any recognition when you showed up at my door or mentioned my name." His tone was terse.

"They found out about you today. After we... Once we got here. I told them you were a friend from before," she whispered.

"So, the people who love you the most don't really know much about you at all, huh?" He paused his pacing to ask.

She took a few steps forward to reply, but Maven had no defense against his question.

"Hmm. Sounds vaguely familiar," He stood still long enough to drive his response home.

Talmadge rushed through the door with Lila hot on his heels. Their faces were charged with concern and confusion. They looked surprised not to have walked in on a bloody brawl.

"Get out!" Sam's deep voice screamed.

Talmadge and Sam stepped at one another challengingly, but Maven wedged herself between them, placing a glowing hand on each of their chests. Oblivious to her in the middle, the men dwarfed her as they stood and snarled at each other.

"Talmadge, I am fine. Thank you. Please, calm down," Maven asked politely, but neither man made a move to back off. "Guys, I'm asking you both to act like adults."

With that, Talmadge scoffed, "Adults? He's a child!"

Sam looked down at Maven even more perplexed. Noticing her lit palm on his chest, though, he backed away from all of them. His hand brushed at the trace of where hers had sat. Maven looked to Lila for help with the other tower of a man.

"Come on, Tal," Lila swooped in and took him by the elbow.

Begrudgingly retreating into the hallway, Sam and Maven heard Talmadge say, "I really hate Tartooc, Li. A lot."

"Tartooc?" Sam, again puzzled, looked to Maven. Maven, though, was still not offering any answers. Frustrated and tired, Sam rubbed his face with his hands. "Why did you even come here, Maven? It's been *eight years*. What purpose do I serve in your sick, little game now?"

"Game? Sam, there's no game. You're not some stupid pawn." She was offended. Hurt. But then again, so was he.

He looked down at her. "Tell me the truth, then. What is going on? What happened? And if I can help, tell me how." His eyes softened and pled.

"Can you please trust me that I'm trying to help you by not telling you?" Maven's tone begged as well.

"*Trust* you? Trust *you*?" He was stunned and angry at her suggestion. "No," he stated flatly as he stared her in the eye.

Maven went cold. After everything the day had brought, that simple, small word hurt more than a slap across the face.

"I..." She tried to think of the words, blinking excessively. "I'm sorry that I--"

He held his hand up to block her words. "Mavey baby, I don't want to hear it," he said and walked passed her to leave.

"Sam," she spoke reluctantly as he reached for the handle of the ajar door. He stopped but didn't turn around. "Someone killed Liam."

Sam gently spun around. "Liam? Your brother?" he asked.

"Liam was actually my dad. Someone murdered my dad last night," she barely got out before attempting to choke down more tears.

"Your... Your dad?" he faltered. "I'm sorry, Maven. Liam was a great guy," he offered, not knowing the right thing to say. He made a motion to walk over to her, but he stopped himself.

"I know you're mad at me for a lot of incredibly valid reasons, but if you could please stay in the building, I'd appreciate it," she said as she turned her back to him.

"Yeah. Yes. I'll, uh, give you a minute."

Maven did nothing as she listened to him walk out of the room. Statue still, she heard another door open and close. The air in the room tingled with the leftover hostile negativity from their argument. She left, too, unable to bear it and made her way back into the living room. It wasn't until she saw Sabine's and Lila's faces looking up at her from the couch that Maven realized they most likely overheard her conversation with Sam.

"Where are the guys?" she asked, almost too exasperated to care.

"Outside. They found a balcony," Lila answered. Their eyes were wide with concern and watched every step she took as she crossed to the armchair.

"What did they hear?" Maven questioned as she slouched into the armchair Sam lunged out of not too much earlier.

"Everything that we did," Sabine replied honestly.

With her elbows on her knees, Maven started

massaging her forehead. Her head pounded, but it was also working at shielding her eyes.

"Mave?" Lila tentatively asked after a moment.

"What?" was all Maven could muster.

Lila softly asked, "Did you Bond with him? With Sam?"

Maven stopped rubbing her temples but still covered her eyes. After a long pause, she answered the question she knew was inevitable by showing up at Sam's, "Yes. I did." She glanced up to gauge their reactions.

"Oh, my Gods. Why didn't you tell us?" Sabine's emotions were cast all over her face. Incredulity and burden crossed her nearly infallible features. Maven had never seen her beautiful skin creased with worry lines before. She was grateful to have blocked their connection before the conversation took place.

"I wasn't sure if you two, if anyone, could or would understand," Maven said.

"When we were in the woods, before we Jumped, you empathized with our choice to leave our partners, with our loss," Lila spoke the words aloud but was merely piecing things together.

"He and I... We..." Maven trailed off, resting her face in her palms, unwilling to finish the thought.

"You loved him," Lila stated plainly.

"Very much," she quietly replied.

"Do you still?" Sabine asked, even quieter.

"Can we not talk about this here? Please?" Maven spoke, remembering they weren't exactly alone but also not wanting to have that particular conversation at all. She scanned the open door to her right, paranoid.

Sabine and Lila gave each other a sideways glance.

"Spit it out," Maven said, knowing they were Reading each other and not appreciating their silent conversation.

"We were wondering," Sabine began, "since you and Sam are Bonded, why does he seem so lost and angry? Didn't he feel your regret for whatever happened at the time? Doesn't he feel it now like we do? Well, did."

"He doesn't feel it, because I don't want him to," Maven stated.

"What do you mean?" Lila questioned.

"I mean that I built a Protection for him."

"Only for him?" Lila pushed, her confusion blatant.

"Yes," Maven curtly responded. A heat was beginning to build in her chest. She knew what they were steering the conversation towards.

"That's why you sit here tortured, and he can walk away, not even aware of how you ache." Sabine was shocked.

"It's not his problem to know, Sabine," Maven's

intonation was a warning. She could feel herself ready to snap at her friends. Again.

"But you could show him!" Sabine urged. "You could easily allow him all the pain and suffering and angst and..."

"No," Maven sharply cut her off. "Look, I know it's difficult for you to understand. But after what I did, everything I'm doing now, I will not put him through anything else. If I can spare him a single twinge, I'm going to. Everything he felt then and everything he's feeling now, I've earned. I've earned his hatred, and I won't rob him of that. So, hear me when I say this: drop it."

CHAPTER SEVEN

Not long after Maven and Sam's altercation, the scene in the apartment was a stark contrast from when they first arrived. Reining in the emotions of the couples had helped to speedily smooth tensions. Everyone eventually lied down from pure exhaustion. Only able to keep her eyes shut for a couple of hours, Maven was awakened by haunting dreams. Lying in the soundless calm, she could swear she smelled the faint singe of her father's house. Frustrated with her subconscious, she rubbed her nose and mouth.

Sitting up, she let her eyes adjust to the dim light. She had forgotten she fell asleep on the carpet in the wide loft area that sat outside the upstairs bedroom and restroom. Someone had given her a blanket and pillow while she slept. She hoped it was Sam, but her inclination led her to Sabine. Her sight acclimated; Maven rose and walked the few feet into the restroom, locking the door behind her.

Flipping on the light, she caught her reflection in the mirror. She noticed that she had fallen asleep with her makeup still on. Raising her hands towards her face, a hazy glow emitted from her palms. As she readied to clean the makeup off in a quick swipe, the memory of Liam's disapproving look and comment on her laziness sprung to mind. The light in her hands vanished. She closed her eyes and took a steadying breath. Maven twisted the sink faucet handle until the water ran tepid. Leaning at the counter, she brought handfuls of water to her face and slowly, methodically began washing off the makeup.

With every touch of her skin beneath her fingers and new splash of water, the reality of her father's death sunk deeper as did her guilt for not being able to save him. Maven rubbed her eyes angrily as the eyeliner and mascara ran down her cheeks. Her breathing grew stuttered and more difficult, and then the dam of tears she had fought all night burst. She placed her soaking wet hands on the sink's cool rim to support her overwhelmed frame. Her weeping was soon accompanied by uncontrollable convulsing, and she tightly gripped her mouth to stifle her sobs, not wanting anyone to wake and hear.

Stepping away from the counter, Maven's back met the wall. Sliding to the floor, she buried her face in her hands. Her thoughts spiraled in a chaotic frenzy. Even in a home filled with many who loved and supported her, she had never felt more alone. With her father dead, the last of her family was gone. The realization destroyed her. Wiping her hot tears away only made space for the new ones to fall. Leaning her head against the wall, she quit fighting the tears and let them flow freely down her cheeks and neck while her mind tripped over its agony into abysmal despair she never fathomed possible.

Several minutes later, her crying eventually began to subside. She had never been more grateful to be disconnected from those around her, but it was the thought of her friends at that moment that allowed her reprieve from her dark anguish. Not remembering the responsibility she felt for their lives, but her gratitude and love for them was her escape. A vivid memory of Liam came to her mind. After losing someone close to her when she was younger, her father had told her:

Mavey, bad things happen. All the time, every day, in every realm. You can't let it ruin the life you have left. Being sad is easy; it's something you don't have to lift a finger to have. Being happy can be hard work at times, especially when you have a genuine reason not to be. But happiness is worth the effort, kid. Don't let what happens to you define who you are. Don't be a victim. Be a person who is known for the amazing legacy you chose to create, not the person who existed in the circumstances given.

Maven could hear every word perfectly in Liam's voice. Looking up, she grabbed the towel hanging on the rod above her head. Drying her face, she took a couple of deep breaths and smiled at the memory. Her father had been her foundation of support in every difficulty throughout her past, and it was of great comfort to her to know he still had that capability for her then. Realizing that the water was still running, Maven stood and finished washing her face. That time, she felt as if a thin layer of her residual pain was cleaned as well.

Leaving the restroom, a chill ran down her spine. She picked up her blanket from the floor and wrapped it around her shoulders. Maven was reminded that Sam always kept his home at a low temperature. He attributed it to what he had called "having an internal furnace." Glancing around, she saw that the door to the bedroom was cracked open. She spied on Lila and Talmadge asleep on the spare bed. Even under the covers, she could see Talmadge holding Lila.

Creeping down the wrought iron spiral staircase, Maven stayed silent.

If anyone deserves a rest, it's this household, she thought to herself.

At the bottom of the steps was a large, open area that met the one hallway on the right and a kitchen to the left. The farthest wall from the front door boasted four wide, arched floor-to-ceiling windows, which were even more impressive because of the high, vaulted ceilings. The very leftmost window had a separately framed panel that was hidden access to the balcony. Hugging the windows was the same red brick and chipped white paint from the exterior of the building.

Where most people placed a combined dining and living room, Sam had fit a studio. Drop cloths covered most of the stained concrete floors. Paintings and sculptures were sprinkled all across the expanse. A memory came to Maven of her and a younger Sam in the room when it was still empty. He spoke animatedly about how much he loved the light that shone through the tremendous panes and how he, for once, wouldn't feel the need to be constantly ducking. That was the day he bought the loft. It was a nice memory. Simple. Uncomplicated. Very unlike this day.

Maven turned and stepped away from the room and the past. The cold of the floor seeped through the bottoms of her bare feet. Down the hall, she noticed a light casting out of the half-opened door of the living room. First, she stopped in front of Sam's sealed off bedroom and lightly pressed her ear against the door. Expecting snoring at some volume, she heard nothing. She hoped he'd sleep at some point that night.

Pivoting around, Maven noiselessly opened the living room entrance. The lamp was on. On the couch, Sabine lay sprawled out with her head on Eldon's lap. Eldon, lightly stroking Sabine's hair, was reading a book. Apparently, one he had found on Sam's shelf. He looked up to Maven and squinted. His eyes were clearly tired. Maven waved from the doorframe. He gave a friendly, crooked smile. She then felt a well-known tap on her mind. Eldon, also a Reader, was nowhere near as powerful as Sabine. He had to request permission to enter someone's mind. For that reason, she hadn't removed herself from his reach.

Can't sleep? She asked, granting him access.

No, I could crash easily, but she, nodding to Sabine, *was pretty worked up earlier. I told her I'd stay up for a while to kind of watch over,* he explained. *You?*

I caught a couple of hours, but the rest got away, she kidded.

Well, come in. Keep me company for a minute, he yawned as he beckoned for her to take a seat.

Maven obliged. She tiptoed across the floor and softly sank into a chair, gathering her knees to her chest. She fixed her blanket to cover her legs, too.

So, Eldon chimed. His azure eyes sparkled with what appeared to be playfulness.

So, Maven did her best to echo his attitude.

Come up with any genius plans to save us all, yet? He chaffed.

Of course, she mocked. *I have at least a dozen, and each is even more dazzlingly brilliant than the last.*

Ohhh, I see. You have nothing? he smiled.

If it's possible to have less than nothing, I have that, she replied only half-kidding.

Change of subject? he asked.

Yes, please, she nodded.

You Bonded with a human, huh? He asked the personal question incredibly matter-of-factly. *I don't mean to pry. Well, yes, I do actually,* he laughed.

Although they had never been the closest friendship in their group, Maven had always highly regarded Eldon's candor. It didn't occur to her to be offended because that was never his intent.

You heard that, did you? She raised her eyebrows and cocked her head to the side.

I'm fairly certain that most of Tartooc heard that, he quipped, *but Sabine filled me in on the rest.*

I am sorry about all that, she scrunched up her face. *For the arguing and negativity and all.*

Quit blaming yourself, Maven. There are a lot of fingers to point, and none of them aim your direction. Even with their general connection severed, she could appreciate Eldon's sincerity. *So, our Maven is Bonded,* he repeated as he gestured towards Sam's room.

I honestly don't know what to say, Eldon. Maven hugged herself tighter with the blanket.

I'm not trying to hassle you about it. Our lives are our own, and we do what we feel to be right at the time we make our decisions. No one can fault you that. But let me give you one bit of advice? His eyes were careful to measure her response, trying not to upset her.

I'm all ears, she replied. At that point, she didn't think she could mishandle the situation any worse than she already had.

Tell him what's going on. Eldon's eyes implored her. *This is a man you chose to Bond with — the same man you are entrusting our lives to. You've already involved him past any invisible line you think you've drawn to keep him safe. The less you tell him now, the greater the danger he'll be in. Let him know what he's up against. Tell him everything, and I think in doing so, you might even find a couple of answers for yourself.*

Maven gaped at Eldon and said nothing.

I wasn't trying to ruffle any feathers, Mave, Eldon started to backpedal.

No, Eldon. You are right. How did you get so smart? She teased

Honestly, in the past, I haven't always been as forth-coming in my relationships as I should or could have been. I've had some regrets about it, but as I said before: we all do what we feel to be right in the moment. But whatever this thing is that's going on between the two of you, you've been given a second chance to set it right. You shouldn't waste that, ya know? he shrugged.

Why don't you talk more? Maven joked, but she truly meant it. *You really are such an insightful guy.*

Oh, I am smart. Yeah, and wise. And, Gods, just so sage, he bantered.

Don't forget humble, she teased.

Maven, I would never. *My humility is the thing I'm most proud of!* He got out with a straight face.

At that, they both tried to suppress their laughter. Maven wasn't sure if it was the late hour, the lack of sleep, the fact that they were trying to stay silent, the sheer relief of a blithe moment, or any combination of it all. Still, she was absolutely tickled at the sight of Eldon, eyes squeezed, grasping his mouth shut with one hand while he attempted to steady himself on the arm of the couch with the other and failing at both as his body shook while Sabine's head still rested in his lap. The harder they tried to smother their laughter, the louder it grew. Sabine stirred. Maven jumped up and ran out of the room. In the hallway, she spun around. Eldon's jaw hung open.

Traitor! He called as he shook a fist at her.

She winked and left him to fend for himself. Effort-lessly, she took the stairs back to her makeshift bed.

CHAPTER EIGHT

A loud crash from below startled Maven awake. Another clangorous clatter was followed by a hushed, "Dang it." Rubbing her eyes and stretching as she stood, she poked her head over the edge of the loft's banister. Through weary, puffy eyes, she found Eldon and Talmadge ransacking the cupboards in the kitchen. She yawned before she could ask what was going on. The men glanced up as they heard her.

"Sorry, Mave. Didn't mean to wake you," Talmadge grinned sheepishly, then went back to searching the shelves.

"I'm not sorry," Eldon gave her an amused, annoyed look. He hadn't forgiven her from abandoning him with Sabine earlier.

Maven smiled and dragged her tired feet to the bathroom.

"I'm not sorry, Maven!" Eldon called out again.

The sun had hardly slunk itself halfway up the horizon by the time Maven and her four friends had gathered in the corner kitchen and its island. They rummaged through Sam's fridge and pantry for breakfast. For a brief instant, they almost felt normal as they lightheartedly laughed and joked and prepared their breakfast together. Sam's stern face came around the corner and annihilated their pleasant atmosphere.

"Could you, please, for the love of God, keep it down to a low rumble? Most of my neighbors don't get up at sunrise," he sneered, turned the corner, and slammed his bedroom door.

"Such a charmer. No wonder you couldn't resist him," Talmadge muttered under his breath as he chopped onions.

Maven knew the dig was meant for Sam, but that didn't make it sting any less. She stood from the stool she perched on. She dusted her hands and started for the balcony, opening and closing the glass door without another word from anyone. Leaning on the railing, Maven closed her eyes and took a deep breath. She focused on the fraction of nature that was available to her there. A few scattered birds were chirping high on the power lines. A light breeze cut back and forth, unsure of which way to blow. It caused a rustle in the old leaves on the few planted trees that sporadically lined the street. Interrupting her focus was the traffic forming on the streets below. Folding her arms on the ledge, she rested her head on top of them.

A freshly showered and dressed Sam reentered the kitchen while Maven was still outside. He scanned the room.

"Where is she?" he asked promptly.

No one responded.

"Seriously? You're giving me crickets?" he questioned, miffed.

"Actually," Lila spoke, "we wanted to say something to you first. If you wouldn't mind."

Except for Sabine, Sam regarded them all with reservation. "What's up?"

"Just... Thank you," Lila answered. "Truly."

Eldon and Sabine chimed in. Everyone looked at Talmadge, who was chewing on his lower lip. Lila elbowed him. As he started to speak, Sam stopped him.

"Don't bother. I wouldn't believe you anyway," Sam directed to Talmadge. "But to the rest of you, you're welcome."

Eldon picked up a pepper slice and took a bite. "She's on the balcony."

Sam gave him a quick nod of gratitude on his way to the door.

"Busted," Sam declared, closing the glass behind him.

A cloud of smoke escaped Maven's lips.

"When did you even have time to buy cigarettes?" he asked.

"I, uh... I didn't buy them," she responded as she stamped out the butt. She peeked at him from the corner of her eye.

"So, what? You stole them?" Sam didn't understand.

"No," was all she gave in return.

After a short pause, Maven saw him connect the dots. "You can *make* cigarettes," he quietly breathed out the revelation.

She could tell he was both taken aback and impressed.

"I can do a lot more than that, Sam," she replied. She risked enjoying his calm mood.

"I'm learning that," he remarked. "I'm learning a lot about you, actually."

Maven nodded, unsure of how to respond and not wanting to say the wrong thing.

Sam rubbed his hands together and shuddered at the crisp fall air. "Aren't you cold?" he asked, noticing Maven was barefoot and only wearing jeans with a thin white t-shirt.

"No. I can block it. Here," she said, eager to make him even the slightest bit more comfortable around her. She reached up and put her hands on his broad shoulders. Sam stiffened but didn't pull away. Picking up on his uncertainty, Maven avoided his face and focused on her hands. A minute glow came from under her palms. The scent of his soap found her nose and caught her off guard. Resisting the urge to lean in closer, Maven lingered for a moment then looked up, hands still on his shoulders. Sam was looking down at her, cautious and in awe.

"There. That should help." She slowly stepped away.

"Wow," was all he managed to say.

Maven said nothing.

He shifted his body, feeling the warmth spread and the chill disappear. Looking her over again, he was completely taken aback by her appearance.

"What happened to your tattoos?" he asked with a sad confusion. "Did you get them *all* removed?"

"In a fashion," she mumbled.

Annoyed with another brush-off of an answer, his eyes steeled over. "I need answers, Maven."

"I know," she replied.

"You need to be straight with me. No more secrets. At the very least, I deserve your honesty." He stared down at her like a snake poised to strike. His eyes dared her to disagree or, maybe, argue.

"Ask me anything," she acceded more enthusiastically than she intended. Without realizing it, she was craving the sound of his voice. She did not want her time alone with him to end yet.

Sam, relieved to meet no resistance, looked her dead in the eye, "What are you?"

"In layman's terms, the girls are witches, and the guys are wizards," Maven answered.

There was a pause as he let the words sink in. Then, his face slowly turned into a reluctant grin. "Seriously?"

"Yes, seriously." She was utterly unaware of what he found humorous.

"You don't get it?" he couldn't help smiling wider.

"Get what?"

"You three witches saw a crime, and you came to my house to be safe..." he left the air empty for Maven to catch on.

She groaned as she understood where he was going with it. "Oh, Gods, please don't say it."

"You're here under Witchness Protection, Maven." He chuckled at his joke.

"And you said it anyway," she smiled with a grimace. "Very punny, Sam."

Almost like a light being switched off, the grin was wiped from his face. His expression looked guilty like he'd been caught doing something horrible and immediately went back to business.

"So, you're," he struggled to spit the word out, "magical?"

"Magic is a term your ancestors came up with a long time ago to comprehend what we do. To us, it's like breathing," she explained.

"How do you do... what you do?" He wagged his hands around in the air.

"I'm a Creator," she shrugged. "It's kind of a talent I have."

He pounced on the little information she presented. "What does that mean? You can make things? Do things? Just by what? Thinking about it?" The expression on his face was in complete contrast with his tone. He appeared interested and excited, but his voice kept a deliberately even, cool pace.

"Basically. It's a matter of harnessing energy," she stated.

"Wow," Sam said again. "Okay. What about them?" thumbing to everyone inside. "Are they Creators, too?"

Maven shook her head. "No. Lila's a Searcher; they can find almost anyone or anything if they know what to look for. Talmadge is a Flyer. That's close to what you would call a telekinetic here; he can move things around, including himself. And the stronger ones can, ya know..." she trailed.

"Fly," Sam finished for her, astonished.

"Yes." She glanced at his face to see if he was absorbing her delineations. He waved her on, so she continued, "Sabine's a Reader; that means reading thoughts, communicating telepathically, showing you her memories, or watching yours. And Eldon Reads a little, Searches a little. He tries his hand at everything. That's what we can do, but there are other different talents out there."

"You can't all wave your wands and do the same tricks?" he naively inquired.

"We don't use wands," she conquered an urge to roll her eyes. "Here, it would be like singing or being athletic or artistic; everyone has their own gifts that they're born with. Those talents can be developed or squandered, and others still can be taught a skill."

"Okay," he nodded his head as he thought of his next question. "How old are you?"

Maven faintly sighed, preparing to answer, "Witches and wizards have a lifespan of exactly 1,000 years. Talmadge is the oldest in there," she pointed to the kitchen, "and he's nearing three hundred."

"No way. Most of you couldn't pass for more than thirty here," he breathed out as he attempted to digest her explanations. "That's a lot to take in."

"I know."

"I mean, wow," he spoke while his thoughts swirled.

"You keep saying that," Maven lightly kidded.

Sam stiffened again. "It might be a stalling tactic."

"Stalling for what?" Maven's breath tripped in her throat. It was her turn to be unleveled.

"What's a 'Bond'?" His eyes locked on hers.

Surprised at his term, she realized he had, in fact, overheard her conversation with the girls after their fight. Meeting his gaze, she dubiously began, "A Bond is exactly what it sounds like; it's a connection made between two people. But in our realm, it is much, much more intense. It's a fusing of the emotional, mental, and physical, and it is *never* made lightly."

"*Realm?*" Her answer distracted him from his original query.

"There are, as far as my people know, an almost limitless number of realms. Ours is Loremara. We call this one Tartooc," she spoke.

Sam mulled over her response for a moment. "Okay. Realms on the back burner," he rubbed his forehead and continued, "Why are your friends so concerned with our history?" he blurted out.

"Sealing a Bond, it's essentially marriage, and most partners spend decades courting before reaching that kind of commitment," Maven answered equally as blunt.

"So, they... they what? They're upset we skipped a few years?" he asked, genuinely not comprehending.

"No," she swallowed and broke eye contact for the first time.

"Then, what?" he prodded. He could sense the significance of what lay on the other side of his question.

Struggling, she finally replied, "It's because witches and wizards mate for life. We don't do bad breakups or separations or divorce. Once Bonded, a couple is together literally until death do they part." She looked up to see that Sam was then the one avoiding her.

He paused for a long moment, absorbing what had been laid out, "You Bonded with me," was all he said.

"Yes," she replied. Motionless, Maven gave him a moment to grasp the confession.

"But you..." Sam started but didn't complete his thought. He clenched and unclenched his teeth repeatedly.

"Sam?" She reached out to put her hand on his arm.

In a quiet, hostile motion, he jerked his hand away before she could touch him. "You said it's also an emotional connection?" he continued curtly.

Retracting her hand, she whispered, "Yes."

"How so?" His cold tone started to heat up in a terrible way.

"Empathy," she replied calmly. "We can literally

feel what the other is experiencing as they experience it."

Sam nodded in recognition. "I had that with you."

"To an extent, yes," Maven responded.

"Meaning what?" he snapped. He defensively folded his arms.

"Your people's ability to empathize is great, but it's nowhere near as developed as ours," she evenly stated. She tried to explain without talking down to him. "I let you sense my emotions but shielded you from their full degree. I couldn't be sure how overwhelming you'd find it."

"And when you left?" His questions slowly felt more like an interrogation.

With a knot forming in her stomach, Maven answered, "I shielded you completely."

"Like blocking the cold just now?"

"Similar, but different. Bigger," she said.

"Your 'Protection?'" he asked, quoting her again from the eavesdropped conversation.

"Yes," she admitted.

"What did you protect me from?" His voice raised a little.

"I..." she began but noticed his brewing indignation. "Sam, I--"

He talked over her. "No, really. I'd love to know what exactly you think you protected me from."

His face was angry. For the first time since seeing him again, Maven truly noticed his age. She took note of the faint beginnings of creases in his brow and the soft lines at the edges of his mouth. Even in his animosity, she couldn't help but think he was still the most handsome man she had ever known. She made a move to speak, but Sam cut her off before she uttered a syllable.

"It is absurd that you think you protected me from a single damn thing. You left me, Maven. You *left* me. And not only did you leave, you took off hours after I had asked if you would marry me. You just scurried away in the middle of the night like a criminal!" His hands flew wildly as he spoke.

His anger was so palpable she had a hard time forming any words, much less the right ones.

"I am so sorry, Sam," she started. The knot in her stomach was joined by another in the back of her throat. The second one burned and threatened to bring back tears any second. She placed her fingers to her neck to will it away.

"You're sorry! Great. That fixes everything, doesn't it?" He paced his small section of the balcony.

Maven's head drummed like a battlefield. Her guilt and sadness were being jackhammered by Sam's rage. The heart in her chest felt like a sinking ship. Sam, noticing her weakened expression, made a small concentrated effort to calm down.

"You know what? I get it. You didn't love me, so you split. That part is fine. But you know what I still don't understand?" He paused and lowered his voice. "If you were just going to leave, why did you even bother to say 'yes' first?" He asked, shaking his head. "God, Maven, when were you going to tell me about all of this? At our wedding? Twenty years from now? On my deathbed when you still hadn't aged a day? How could you not realize that I should have been told something this huge?"

His anger quickly shifted to the same sadness she was feeling.

"But I guess that didn't matter to you. You knew you weren't going to be sticking around long enough to need to explain yourself, huh?" Sam's brow creased. "When you took off, when you went back to wherever you came from, did that end our Bond?" he questioned.

"No," was all she could muster.

"So, you're still in my head?" he spoke between tight teeth.

"Yes, but it's not like you think," she tried to explain quickly.

"End it," he demanded.

"What?" Shocked, Maven could only hope she misheard him.

"End it," he repeated. "Break it, cut it, whatever you call it. Make it go away. I'm not letting you get the upper hand, and I sure don't need you knowing anything about me that I don't want to tell you myself."

"Do I look like I have the upper hand to you, Sam?" she distraughtly pointed out.

"Do it. Now." His eyes refused mercy.

Unwillingly, Maven placed a weak hand on top of Sam's that was then gripping the railing so tightly that his knuckles blanched. In the sunlight, her usually faint light went unseen, but the effect was noticed immediately. The raw emptiness she had only just grudgingly been forced to acquire from Liam was now echoed voluntarily from Sam.

Deflated, Maven sagged to the opposite side of the balcony, and her brimmed tears finally dropped. Sam heard her sniffle softly as she tried to hide the fact that she was crying, which caused him to look up. Staring at her broke his heart. Maven was unchanged from the day she left. She seemed so young compared to him then. Looking small and pathetic, a part of him wanted to comfort her, but his inflamed ire kept him still.

Before either one said anything else, they were interrupted by the glass door to the balcony swinging open.

"Lila says if you don't come in now..." Talmadge

paused, interpreting the tension. "...we get to eat your food," he finished slowly.

Maven had turned away to wipe her eyes.

"Everything alright out here?" he asked, eyeing Sam with disdain, recollecting the similar scene from the night before.

"Yeah," Maven answered. She cleared her throat and placed a flimsy, disingenuous smile on her lips in an attempt to placate Talmadge.

"Get some breakfast, Mave," Talmadge spoke to her but never took his eyes off Sam.

"Tal, I'm okay. I've just been interpreting Loremara," she petitioned. With many things still left unsaid, and as brutally agonizing as it was, she didn't want her talk with Sam to be over.

"Maven, please," Talmadge said nothing else, but she understood his tone.

Maven crossed the short balcony, and Talmadge patted her shoulder as she went by him through the doorway. She, more sincerely, gave him as much of a half-smile as she could manage. Sam also started inside, but Talmadge grabbed his forearm as he tried to pass and shut the door, leaving them alone outside. Glancing down to where he was being held and looking back up, Sam met Talmadge's boiling stare. About the same height, their usual intimidations were lost on each other.

"You need to get your hand off of me," Sam said coolly.

"And you need to show her a little compassion," Talmadge responded equally as cool as he released his grip on Sam's arm.

"Compassion?" he scoffed. "You have no idea what you're talking about."

"Apparently, neither do you," Talmadge inserted. "What exactly did she explain to you?"

"You really need to get out of my way," Sam ignored his question.

"Did she explain Bonding to you, Sam? Just answer the question," Talmadge pushed.

Sam gave a terse nod.

"Did she give you any inclination what it would take to separate from a Bond? The type of control and strength she must have shown to not only leave but to stay gone? It's unheard of. Until last night, I was certain it wasn't even possible," Talmadge spoke.

"Is that supposed to make it better? The fact that it was harder for her to leave means she had that much more resolve to do so. And," Sam stopped himself before getting even more worked up. "You know what, man? I'm not doing this. It is none of your business."

"You're right. It's not, and I honestly could not care less about you or your limited understanding. But Maven is one of my oldest friends, and I *do* care for her happiness. So, I'll say this: knowing what you do now, do you not wonder why? What could have possibly made her break such a sacred vow of her people by leaving?" Talmadge's words hung in the air.

Sam was quiet, not sure what to make of the newly posed thought.

"What about our empathy?" Talmadge asked. "Did she get to that?"

"Sure," Sam answered.

"The closer you are with someone, the more you feel, and the stronger you feel it," Talmadge explained.

Sam blankly nodded.

"Her father was murdered while she stood fifty yards away," Talmadge's voice cracked as he recalled the memory Sabine had shown him of Maven collapsing to her knees onto the ground.

Sam winced as he understood Talmadge's point.

"Just as she took on the entirety of your hurt when she left, she felt every single ounce of pain and fear and agony that her dad went through. Then, she saw his life drain from his eyes," Talmadge continued. "So, imagine watching, *feeling* the person you love most dying."

Sam held up his hands in defeat. "I get it."

"No, you don't. You couldn't possibly. Maybe now, though, you can at least understand me when I tell you that you need to show her some compassion,"

Talmadge retorted. "You live in this place where you see, hear, touch too much. Your senses are all but screaming from overload, yet you're utterly numb to it all. She's splintering, Sam. It's happening right in front of your face, and you're looking through her like smoke."

Sam was at a loss for words. Unable to return Talmadge's gaze, he turned away.

"I've said my piece."

With that, Talmadge went inside, shutting the door behind him.

CHAPTER NINE

It was afternoon before Maven emerged from the spare bedroom. The scent of whatever was cooking in the kitchen wafted upstairs. Her second clash with Sam had subdued her appetite at breakfast, and she had gone straight upstairs after Talmadge had ushered her inside. Then, though, the aroma she smelled reminded her it had been over 24 hours since she had last eaten. Famished, she descended the stairs. She was a little confounded to see that it was Sam who was at the stove. It was, of course, his house, but the sight still escaped her reasoning. Busy and with his back to her, Maven surreptitiously slipped around the corner. Not ready to face him yet, she found her companions in the living room.

On the couch, Sabine was the one flipping through pages of a book while Eldon's head rested on her legs.

Talmadge was in a chair also reading. Seated snuggled in his lap was Lila. With an arm wrapped around his neck, she laid her head on her shoulder as she absent-mindedly traced his ear. Maven's heart quietly faltered. A small pang of jealousy was swiftly replaced by earnest gratitude that her friends had found such immense love.

Sabine brightened at seeing Maven walk in but then frowned as she got a good look at her face.

"Could you still not sleep?" Sabine asked.

"Do I look that bad?" Maven chuckled as she sat in the unoccupied armchair.

"Your eyes are tired," Sabine's eyebrows creased with worry.

"Don't make that face. I'm fine," she consoled Sabine. "Besides, that's how you get wrinkles."

Sabine put one hand on each eyebrow and smoothed out her forehead, making them all smile right before Sam popped into view. He was surprised to see Maven in the room but didn't address it.

"Lunch is ready," Sam spoke. "If you're hungry," he added. Without waiting for a response, he went back to the kitchen.

Maven recognized his distinctly softened demeanor but wasn't sure of its source. She looked from Sabine to Lila expectantly, but they offered no explanation only vacant expressions. They all stood to follow Sam. In the hall, she turned to Talmadge.

"What did you do?" Maven eyed him suspiciously.

"Me?" Talmadge feigned innocence.

"Of course you," she smirked. "It's always you."

"Don't worry about it," was all he said.

She knew Talmadge wasn't one to offer details. Whatever interaction he had with Sam, she only hoped it would have a lasting effect.

In the studio, Maven saw that most of the art pieces had been scooted to the far right side of the room. A table that she recognized from years ago was set up near the kitchen side. On the island sat an assortment of dishes, each of which happened to be a different favorite of Maven's. She balked at the sight. She was unable to control her gape at Sam.

"What's all this?" Maven asked.

"You didn't eat earlier," he spoke while his face twisted with some guilt. "So, I thought I'd make what I knew you liked. At least, liked before."

Even though she was taken aback with his swift turnaround, Maven wasn't about to question it further. She rolled with it.

"Thank you," she said. "I am starving."

"Well, dish up." Pleased, Sam flashed his flawless, electrifying smile at her, causing the corners of his eyes to crinkle. He spun around to put the rest of the dirty dishes in the sink.

Thrilled and grinning, she looked up at Talmadge. "I love you," she mouthed.

Talmadge rolled his eyes. "Witches," he whispered and walked to the food.

With the girls on one side, they all gathered around the island to serve themselves. Hungry, Eldon and Talmadge fixed their plates and sat down. Maven was explaining each different dish and what was in them when Sam dropped a deep pot into the already filled sink. Dirty water sloshed down his front.

"Gross," Sam grumbled.

He picked off chunks of cooked food from his dripping shirt and flung them back into the sink. Giving up quickly, he put his hands on his shoulders and pulled the shirt off over his head. Watching him, Maven froze, halting her explanations. Lila and Sabine followed her gaze. As Sam twisted and rung out his soaked shirt, the muscles in his back and arms flexed. He shook the wad of fabric a few times to be certain he had gotten the majority of the water out.

His eyebrows climbed upward in surprise when he turned and saw all three women staring at him. He looked to the guys, but they sat at the table with their backs to him. Without a word, Sam awkwardly took off for his bedroom. Maven's eyes followed him across the room. It was then she noticed Sabine and Lila also watching him slack-jawed. She popped Sabine in the back of the head and elbowed Lila in his ribs. They both swatted at her blindly, not taking their eyes off Sam until he was in the hall. Once he was out of sight, they turned back to her.

"Are you kidding me?" Maven faked partial indignant.

"What?" Lila and Sabine asked in unison.

"You 'ladies' need to attempt to stop the gawking," Maven teased.

"Can't," Sabine resigned.

"Try," Maven said.

"Don't want to," Lila shrugged.

"Learn," Maven countered.

"Maven, I don't know what you want from us. We *had* to look. It was physically impossible not to," Sabine joked.

"His bicep is bigger than my head," Lila smiled as they got a rise out of Maven.

"Yeah, but you have a small head to begin with." Maven turned and began serving her food.

"Wait. What's that now?" Lila asked.

"You heard me, Li." Maven kept a straight face.

Sam walked back into the kitchen to the island with a set of clean clothes on. Lila turned to him.

"Do I have a small head?" Lila questioned him.

Confused, Sam blinked. He glanced at the girls' faces trying to gauge their reactions for an indication of how Lila wanted him to answer, but no one gave anything away.

"This... feels like a trick," he confessed.

The whole room erupted with the girls' laughter. Still not sure what was going on, Sam cautiously laughed along with them. The high ceilings ricocheted with their loud chuckles. Lila laughed so hard that no noise came out.

"You two are incorrigible." Maven wiped at her eyes. "First Liam and now Sam, huh?"

The mention of her father's name somewhat flattened the flash of merriment in the room.

Maven sucked in a deep breath. "Wow. I honestly forgot for a minute."

Sabine rubbed her hand across Maven's back.

"Here," Sam picked up a tray from the counter and carried it to the island. On it were six glasses of white wine. Eldon and Talmadge stood and joined them. He passed a glass to each of them.

"Look," Sam started. "I didn't know Liam nearly as well nor as long as the rest of you, but I did know him to be kind and generous and incredibly funny, and it was always easy to see how much he loved and cared for Maven. So, here."

Sam raised his glass, and they all followed suit.

"To Liam," Sam said.

"To Liam," the group toasted. Everyone touched glasses and took a drink.

Maven beamed gratitude at her friends, who smiled in return. Looking at Sam, he winked at her, and, for the first time in over eight years, he put a hand on her shoulder.

CHAPTER TEN

After lunch, they sat around the table, chatting. Since Sam's toast, the unspoken ban on the subject of Maven's father seemed to have lifted. Everyone joined in sharing their favorite stories about Liam. Some were touching, others were thoughtful, but most were hilarious. They all shook with laughter as each memory recalled seemed to escalate the already exaggerated levity in the room. As she wiped the happy tears from her eyes, Maven looked pensive.

"Thank you all," she said. "I wasn't sure how or when I'd be able to deal with my dad's passing, but a makeshift wake seems pretty fitting for Liam." She smiled and took another long drink from her wine glass.

A calm, tipsy lull fell over them. Catty-corner

across the table from Maven, Sam glanced at all their faces.

"I don't mean to change the subject, but I think there's another obvious discussion we all need to have," he spoke quietly, hesitant to ruin the stillness.

"You're right. We do," Talmadge chimed as he placed the napkin that was in his lap onto the top of his empty plate.

With her elbow on the arm of her chair, Maven ran her index finger back and forth across her lips. Her expression turned glum, but Sam didn't acknowledge it.

Clearing his throat, Sam asked, "Earlier Maven touched somewhat on what it is you all can do. What I don't understand is that if you can Search," he motioned to both Lila and Eldon, "what is to stop whoever is after you from doing the same and finding you here?"

"It's nearly impossible to Search cross-realms," Lila spoke. "Once we arrived here, our energies were severed from any connections we had in Loremara."

Relieved to hear that, Sam's shoulders relaxed a little. Every answer they gave only led him to multiple new questions. "How did you get here?"

"We Jumped," Lila stated simply.

Sam's raised eyebrows asked his next question for him.

"A Jump is a portal between worlds. It is virtually an alignment of transdimensional energies tunneled through time and space," Talmadge returned.

"Is there a specific Jump for each realm, then?" Sam questioned.

"No, any site can be used to travel to any other realm that has a site of its own. To Jump, you gear your mind toward the specific realm in which you want to enter. Everything we do and are capable of is linked directly to our energy, or spirit, or life light, or whatever you may call it here. Intention from the soul directs our actions," Talmadge concluded. "Am I explaining myself well enough?" He asked Sam.

Sam slowly bobbed his head in approval. "If Jumping is done through energy as you said, couldn't they follow that? Just chase you through the Jump? Or is that a stupid question?" He knew that if he didn't pursue his inquiry, he'd only get lost in the magnitude of their answers.

"That's actually a very astute perception," Eldon said, surprised at Sam's grasp of all the information he was being slammed with. "You're right; they could have traced our intended destination, but Maven collapsed our site immediately after we landed. It's destroyed."

"Does that destroy it on the other end as well?" he continued.

"No, collapsing a Jump only prevents a link to a trace and from anyone landing at that site again," Eldon explained.

"So, will you Jump again from here to somewhere new? Will you keep running?" Sam inquired.

"We could, but I think our safest move would be to remain here in Tartooc, in New York even. The odds of anyone Jumping to this specific realm in hopes of finding us are beyond infinitesimal. In addition to that, this city is so crowded and overwhelming that we could remain shrouded in the chaos until we know who is, in fact, responsible for Liam's death," Talmadge spoke ardently to the entire group. His desire to have them stay was obvious.

"It makes the most sense to me," Lila agreed.

"I couldn't argue with that, even if I wanted to," Eldon admitted.

Sabine also concurred.

"So, you'll stay?" Sam's question was steeped with a timid hope.

Again, all eyes fell to Maven for her thoughts. Still rubbing her finger across her lips, she took a minute to mull over the recent conversation and points made. Dropping her hand from her mouth, she straightened her slouch in the chair.

"For now, it makes the most sense to stay put. Our chances of being found only greaten by leaving and making our presence known in more realms than necessary. And I very much need some time to figure out who killed Liam," Maven spoke mathematically.

"It's agreed, then," Talmadge affirmed.

"I still don't understand who would have done this. Or why," Lila frowned dismayed.

They sat for a while in absorbed, saddened silence. Most of them racked their brains for any kind of a solution or suggestion.

"Maven, did you ever consider the warlocks?" Sabine asked facetiously in an attempt to lighten the mood.

Everyone, including Sabine, chuckled softly at the suggestion except for Sam.

"Why is that funny?" he asked. "And *what* is a warlock?"

"It's not funny so much as absurd," Talmadge grinned. "Warlocks used to be witches and wizards, but they both evolved and regressed simultaneously. Without any known explanation, their powers grew at a tremendous rate within a single generation. Instead of having one or two prominent gifts like we still do now, each member of this specific class was born with almost every single known talent, including ones that have died out over the millennia. But because of their excessive powers coming into place, something had to be given up to make room.

Their nature had chosen to remove their reasoning and empathy. Imagine an all-powerful group of beings with no compassion for anyone or any living thing."

"I am, and I'm not sure I see what's funny yet," Sam spoke wide-eyed.

"The warlocks got greedy. They decided that having their own boundless power wasn't enough, and they somehow learned a way to siphon off the talents of helpless witches and wizards. They started The War, the only discord to have ever existed in Loremara. Long story short, the Elders Circle came together. They made every attempt possible to save them but were eventually forced to eradicate the entire population of warlocks," Talmadge finished.

"Talmadge is actually a direct descendant of one of the Elders from that time's Circle," Lila spoke proudly.

"It was a very long time ago, Sam," Maven offered. She noticed his still widened eyes. "It would be like you discussing The Thirty Years' War."

"Which I, also, know nothing about," Sam understood. "Wait, how do you know what that is? And how did the warlocks siphon the others' gifts?"

"I read a lot while I was here." Maven shrugged, answering only his first question.

"That's something else no one knows. The Elders found out how they did it, but, in an attempt to thwart future powerlust, they took the secret to their graves," Eldon answered.

"Nowadays, warlocks are only spoken of in scary children's stories to keep the young in line as they learn to develop their empathy. Kind of like your Santa, I think," Sabine offered a comparison.

"That is *nothing* like our Santa, but I do understand what you're saying," Sam laughed. Without skipping a beat, he stood. "Better get these on to soak," he said.

"I'll help," Maven also stood and started gathering dishes. As she reached out her left hand to pick up Sabine's plate, Sabine grabbed her wrist so hard it almost hurt. "Ow," she yelped.

"What is that?" Sabine ignored Maven's protest and did not release her grip.

With her other hand, she held Maven's fingers and splayed her hand open. In the center of Maven's palm was a near-perfect circular, scorched, black burn. The skin was severely charred but fully intact.

"Oh, my Gods, Maven! When did you get that?" Lila was leaning halfway over the table to get a better look.

"Is that from collapsing the Jump?" Eldon was also careening his neck to see.

Maven ripped her hand out of Sabine's firm grasp and sighed. "I got it at Liam's," she spoke. "I first noticed it when you took me outside after..." she didn't need to complete her sentence for them.

"It looks painful," Sabine's face creased.

"Why don't you mend it?" Talmadge questioned.

"It is painful, but it'll heal in its own time," Maven said quietly as she gathered up the plates once more.

Only Sam picked up on the poetry in her words.

CHAPTER ELEVEN

Outside, the evening onset of darkness had begun. With all the doors shut, everyone had earlier retreated to their respective corners. Sam went to his room, Sabine and Eldon were in the living room, and Lila and Talmadge took the upstairs bedroom. Alone, Maven was still at the table. She sat silently in the fading light with her eyes closed and palms flat on the table's cool surface. Other than her evenly spaced breath raising and lowering her chest, she did not move. Caught up in her thoughts, she didn't notice when Sam entered the kitchen. Watching her in the dimness, he flipped a switch on the wall illuminating a light overhead. Maven's lids shot open.

"Sorry," he said. "I didn't mean to startle you, but I didn't think you'd want to be sitting in the dark soon."

"It's okay," she smiled sleepily at him and twirled one of her long curls around her finger.

"It looked like you were meditating," he spoke as he leaned against the counter near the sink.

"Something like that. Just trying to find some answers up here." She pointed to her head with the finger wrapped in her hair.

He smiled at her silly movement. Since his talk with Talmadge earlier, Sam's countenance had been beyond favorable, but right then, his face held a tiny hint of affection for the girl in front of him. Maven knew that Sam could never forget what she had done, but her heart fluttered at the inkling that he could, maybe, one day learn to forgive her.

"C'mon." He pushed off the countertop and motioned for her to follow him.

Sensing his enthusiasm, Maven complied and trailed after him into his bedroom. He shut the door behind them, and she inhaled the room's ever-familiar scent. Leaning on the far wall were four covered canvases that hadn't been there the previous night. Sam walked over and unsheathed one after the other. Maven gasped quietly through the hand over her mouth. Bright colors and bold brushstrokes looked back at her from the four abstract landscape paintings that used to hang in the living room.

"You kept these?" Maven was shocked. She had painted them for Sam after he had moved into the loft.

"They weren't mine to get rid of," he shrugged.

Maven's eyes were glued to the last painting he uncovered. "That's Liam's house in Loremara," she whispered. "All of these are of home."

"Tell me about it," Sam gently requested.

Maven smiled just thinking about her realm.

"Loremara is incredibly different from here," she began. "There are no cars or big machines, no pollution. There's not much development; we try to disturb the land as little as possible. Mountains, beaches, deserts, forests... Everywhere you look, there is natural, untouched beauty. We don't do a lot of excess. Most accommodations are just big enough for the families living in them. Although there are a few older, grandiose buildings, and they are truly beautiful. They're mostly used as meeting places for councils, or gatherings for Bonding celebrations, or any of the annual balls."

Maven stared at the paintings as she described Loremara.

"We're connected to the land, the animals, to all of nature. There's a sense of clarity in the air that I've never found in any other realm. Everyone has a garden to grow their food, and what we don't have, we trade for. There's no crime or violence or fear. Children can run free without parents having to worry about their safety. And there is such an amazing, sincere sense of community; we take care of each other. It's made certain that none go without."

Sam stood silently and listened intently to every word she spoke.

"It's peaceful. Uncomplicated. To me, it is perfection. It's home," she concluded somewhat somberly.

"Sounds like a dream," Sam replied.

"It was," she whispered, "and I feel like I just woke up."

Unsure of how to respond, Sam didn't comment. "This is also your stuff," he said after a moment, pointing to a cardboard box at the foot of his bed.

Maven pulled herself away from the paintings and dug through the box. Inside, she found every single picture that she and Sam had taken, either together or of each other. She flipped through the photos until she found her favorite one. In it, Sam was younger, with hair on his head and a clean-shaven face. Their arms were wrapped around each other. His huge, happy smile took up most of his face that was looking down lovingly and unbeknownst to Maven. Her smile was equally as bright as she looked at the camera head-on.

"Ya know, I bet you'd still look this young if you shaved," she joked.

"Are you telling me I look old?" he smirked.

"I wouldn't dare. I'm sure I will get used it," she grinned.

"Will you?" he asked.

"Probably not," she laughed.

Shuffling through the last of the pictures, Maven halted. She stared at the moment she had captured of Sam and Liam. It was from a decade earlier of Liam's birthday. He had just opened Sam's gift to him, and he was holding the polished trumpet in the photo. The two stood together as Liam puffed out his cheeks, pretending to blow on the horn next to Sam's head while Sam covered his ears in feigned pain. Sam leaned over Maven's shoulder to see which picture had stopped her.

"Did he ever learn to play? I know he talked about it enough. That was the reason I bought it for him," he told her even though he had disclosed the same reason to her years earlier when he initially bought the instrument.

"I'm not sure. I honestly didn't even know he still had it until yesterday. He had it out when I was there for lunch..." Maven shook her head slightly, lost in thought.

Putting her attention back to the box, she found her favorite Cornell t-shirt of Sam's that she had often slept in. Near the bottom was every note, and card, and letter that Maven had ever written to him. Underneath all of that, at the very bottom, sat a small, black, leather box. She lifted it out of the cardboard as if it might shatter. Very carefully, and with trembling fingers, she opened the hinged lid. Looking up at her was the vintage diamond ring Sam had used to propose those years ago. Glancing up, she saw Sam staring down at her.

"You kept *this*?" she whispered.

"Also wasn't mine to get rid of," he spoke very composed.

Her emotions battled for priority. Before being able to grasp any one of them fully, Sam interrupted her thoughts.

"Maven," he took a step closer to her, "there isn't one memory that I have of us that isn't happy. I spent years replaying every conversation, every look, and wondering if there was something I did wrong. Why did you leave? What happened to change your mind about us?" His eyes, his face, his entire body begged for an answer, an ending to his self-doubt.

Her heart about jerked out of her chest. She took a deep breath.

"One of my dad's talents was called Seeing. It's one of the gifts that have all but faded out of existence. Because of that, no one was ever able to teach him how to control it fully. He would get snippets and fragments of the future as visions during the day or dreams while he was sleeping. As haphazard and completely out of context as they were, they were always accurate and absolutely assured." Her voice rattled as she explained.

"What did he See?" Sam prodded quietly. He was hell-bent on hearing the rest.

"He Saw you," Maven swallowed hard, "on the ground. He said there was blood all over, and I was hovering over you, hysterical, because... you were dead. And he said it all happened because you had tried to protect me."

Sam, with his jaw slightly ajar, stood utterly frozen.

"He called immediately after he Saw it, which wasn't even half an hour after I agreed to marry you," she continued. "I could only assume that one thing was directly linked to the other."

"So, instead, you left," Sam breathed out, "to protect me."

"I also think he Saw me coming back here. To you. I think that's why he brought the trumpet out. And... he must have seen his death. That's why he sent me away in a hurry yesterday. Why he pushed back the time the others and I were supposed to arrive at his house that evening..." she finally spoke aloud the conclusions she'd pieced together earlier.

"To protect you all from whoever came for him," Sam explicated.

Maven nodded and again swallowed hard at the

memories they both were reliving. Sam said nothing more as he sat on the edge of his bed. Watching him take in all the new information, she suddenly felt like she was spying. Uncomfortable, she walked to the door. Opening it to leave, she paused.

"Sam, just so you know, I never, not once, not even close, changed my mind about you or us. The only thing I was more certain of was that if I *had* to live without you, it needed to be because you were alive somewhere without me," she uttered, then closed the door behind her.

CHAPTER TWELVE

Nothing more than a thin slab of wood was between them, but Maven still felt as separated from Sam as if she were realms away. She forced herself away from the door and back into the kitchen. She needed something to distract her. Looking out the window, she saw the last of the light licking at the horizon.

Dinner, she thought, then rummaged through every pantry, fridge shelf, and cupboard. Finding most of the ingredients she wanted, she covered the counters with them. Maven Created the last couple missing components from her recipe then began.

Not a full hour later, Sabine entered the kitchen and saw Maven busy chopping vegetables. "Need some help?" she asked.

Maven sniffled as she turned to see her.

"Are you crying?" Sabine hurried across the floor to Maven.

"No," Maven laughed. "Onions," she said, pointing to the cutting board.

"Oh. Right," Sabine smiled, but she wasn't sure she believed her friend.

"What can I do?" Sam's voice came as he rounded the corner from the hallway.

Grateful he was out of his room, Maven opened her mouth to reply to them both. Seeing Sam, though, her jaw refused to form a word or even close.

"What's wrong?" Sabine wondered as her eyes bounced back and forth from each of their faces.

"No, um," Maven, dazed, shook her head, "nothing's wrong. I was just taking in Sam's new look." She smiled.

"Ohhh!" Sabine realized what Maven meant. "You look really good without facial hair, Sam. You look a lot younger, too."

His laugh matched Maven's at Sabine's comment.

"Can we help at all?" Sabine happily ignored their inside joke.

"Actually, I'm almost done with the prep work. Now, it just needs to cook. But while I get it in the oven, Sabine, will you please get Eldon? And Sam, will you get Lila and Talmadge? I need to talk to everyone,"

Maven spoke as she piled the food into two large casserole pans.

"Of course," Sabine replied with a smile and left.

Sam nodded and started climbing the stairs.

"Hey, Sam," Maven called out.

"Yeah?" he spoke from midway up the steps.

"I like your face," she grinned broadly.

Smiling and shaking his head, he continued ascending the stairs.

"Sam," she called again.

"Yes?" he asked cautiously.

"Make sure you knock," she warned with an even wider smile.

He groaned because he knew she wasn't joking.

At the top of the staircase, Sam was only twenty feet from the bedroom. Having slept in that room a lot after Maven left, he knew that almost every sound in the apartment carried up into the loft, which meant they had to hear him coming. Walking slowly to the door, he waited a full minute before he knocked. Nothing. He knocked again, a little louder. No reply. Knocking again, and still receiving no answer, Sam got anxious. He opened the door, nervous about what he might find.

"You must be kidding me," Sam griped.

Although both were fully clothed, Sam averted his

eyes. Sitting on the bed was Talmadge, but Lila was straddling his lap, facing him as they kissed.

"Did you not hear me knocking?" Sam asked, supremely annoyed as they stood.

"I heard you," Talmadge spoke unapologetically.

"And still, you thought it was an appropriate time to keep making out?" Sam's dissipating dislike for Talmadge halted.

Lila discreetly slid past their argument and headed downstairs. Talmadge walked to Sam and slapped him on the shoulder.

"It's always the right time to kiss your girl," he winked and ambled down after Lila.

Irked, Sam also went back down the steps. Once there, he found the kitchen to be already spotless, the table set, and the food in the oven. He was about to ask how that was possible, but he stopped himself. Anything was possible with those people.

"Did you shave?" Eldon asked as Sam took the last seat at the table.

"Yes," Sam answered shortly.

"Yeah, I thought you looked a bit more boyish," Talmadge added without the hint of a smile.

"Guys," Maven spoke, silencing their would-be squabble, "I have a favor to ask."

"Of course. Anything," Sabine replied.

"I need you two," Maven pointed at Eldon and Lila, "to Search as many Jumps as you can. Not just the close ones, but as far as your reach extends. And I need you two," she then pointed to Sabine and Talmadge, "to boost their range as far and as wide as you can."

"Absolutely," Eldon responded. "What are we looking for?"

"You're looking for any and every Jump you can find. If someone has come through anywhere near here since we've arrived, I want us to know about it. I sincerely doubt anyone has, but we don't want to be caught unaware," Maven asserted.

"But there are sentries posted at the Jumps at home," Sabine questioned. "They wouldn't let anyone through who intended to cause harm."

"As I said before, Sabine, just because they are guards doesn't make them trustworthy," Maven countered before remembering Eldon had been a sentry for several decades. "I'm sorry, Eldon. I wasn't implying anything."

"Don't think on it," Eldon shrugged it off, knowing full well that she didn't actually suspect him of being untrustworthy. "I'll Search all of the closest sites if you take the outlying ones," Eldon spoke to Lila, acknowledging that her talent exceeded his own.

Lila nodded.

"How will they 'boost' their ranges?" Sam questioned.

"We can lend our energies," Maven answered.

"Can you see what they do as they Search?" Sam asked.

"No," Sabine replied. "Our focus is inward as the other's goes outward."

"I see," Sam spoke. He understood what they were saying, yet he still felt at a total loss. "Is there anything I can do?"

"I'd appreciate it if you would watch the food for me, please," Maven said genuinely.

Talmadge smirked.

"And where will you be?" Sam was more concerned with Maven's phrasing than Talmadge's subtle jab.

"I really need some time alone," Maven sighed, and her face pinched. "I am beyond exhausted, and my brain hasn't paused for a second for days. I need some space for myself and fresh air. I was thinking about going to the roof until dinner is ready."

Sam looked to the oven at the timer set on the dash. It flashed a neon "00:54." Almost an hour.

"Like I said, I'll be back when it's ready," she spoke to all their worried faces, but she awaited Sam's reply.

"I'll get your jacket," he acquiesced.

Lila and Talmadge retook the spare bedroom at the

insistence of Sabine. She and Eldon took the living room to Search. Sam reluctantly walked Maven to the front door. As they passed the living room in the hallway, he stopped for a moment to watch as Sabine and Eldon sat on the couch, holding hands with their eyes closed and a light flowing from Sabine's body directly into Eldon's. Sam shook his head. He couldn't believe what he was seeing.

Maven cleared her throat at the front door bringing Sam's attention back to her. He joined her as she retrieved her jacket from the closet. Even knowing she didn't need it against the chilly weather, he took the jacket from her and held it out until she let him help her into the sleeves. He handed her his keychain, at her insistence that the door be locked behind her.

"Are you pouting," Maven kidded as she put the key into her pant pocket.

"I am *not* pouting, and I'm not the only one who doesn't think it's a safe idea for you to separate from the herd. That's how you get eaten by the predators," he contended.

"You're all being ridiculous. It's not even a full hour, and I very much need this time, Sam," she replied earnestly.

"I know," he spoke. He hadn't understood much since they had arrived, but he did get that she had been through a lot and had worried for every other person there more than herself.

He opened the apartment door and kept an eye on her as she met the elevators and pressed the "up" button. Quickly, the middle lift arrived and slid its doors open. Smiling back, Maven waved and stepped inside.

Locking the door, Sam rambled through his apartment. The clock on the oven flashed "00:47" when he checked next. With nothing to do and no way to contribute, he went out on the balcony. Leaning against the railing, he glanced up towards the roof. He knew it wasn't a ludicrous request from Maven to have a sliver of time by herself, but he couldn't help thinking it was asking for trouble. She should have been on the top of the building by then, and he wondered if he'd be able to hear her up there. Shaking his head at the notion, Sam glanced downward. Shivering against the cold, he then decided to go back inside.

Something caught his eye, though, causing him to do a double-take. Squinting from the dark and the height, it came into view underneath a lit lamppost. There, on the street, was Maven hurrying down the sidewalk.

CHAPTER THIRTEEN

Maven tried not to run, but she had a hard time controlling her feet. Reaching the corner, she waved to a car that stopped as she hustled across the street. Pushing up her jacket sleeve, she looked at the watch she had Created. It didn't tell time but kept a countdown in sync with the timer back in the loft. She had 44 minutes until she was expected back. With that, she picked up the pace and started jogging through the night air.

A few minutes later, Maven arrived in front of a large cemetery. The tall stone walls were attached by an even taller iron gate. The two enormous doors were wrapped with a thick, heavy chain and fastened with a padlock bigger than her fist. Placing her palms on either side of the lock, it disintegrated between her fingers. She dusted her hands on her pants. Loosening the chains just enough to separate the gates, she squeezed through.

Inside the silent cemetery, the field of the dead seemed endless. She did the best she could to stave off her thoughts of Liam. Maven ran to the farthest row of burials at the back of the cemetery. Resting there were the first and oldest memorials. Briskly making her way through the headstones that met the encompassing trees, she explored each grave marker in the line. She stalled in front of the largest, most impressive one. On top of a faded, three-foot-tall, carved, white marble slab was an angel sculpture of the same material. The angel kneeled behind the headstone, and her head was laid facedown in sorrow atop one bent arm, while the other fell loosely in front. Even her immense, divine wings that hugged both her and the sides of the marker hung despondently. Maven's heart slumped at the sight of the angel without hope.

Squatting in front of the guardian, she couldn't make out the name on the marble. Wiping the dried, caked dirt from the stone, the worn carvings came into view:

SHEPHERD

If you seek
you shall find
One in me
if you are mine

That was the one. Maven stood and looked at her watch. She had 24 minutes left. Hurrying, she walked in a perfectly straight line from the back of the angel into the sparse surrounding woods until a grand oak fell directly in her path. It wasn't the largest of the trees, but it was the oldest. The same small symbol that had been carved into the body of the tree Maven touched in Loremara was also etched into the oak. She placed her hands firmly on its bark. Focusing, she closed her eyes. A fine shimmer flowed out of her fingers and was readily absorbed into the wood. As before, the tree trembled lightly then straightened.

Opening her eyes, she checked the ever-retreating numbers on her watch. Speedily, Maven turned to flat-out run towards the front of the cemetery. Instead, she ran head-on into Sam. Ricocheting off his chest, she stumbled backward only to be caught by his hands on both her arms. Placing her on her feet, she took in his face. Fury stared down at her.

"What are you doing here?" she shot out impatiently in a breathless voice as she shook her arms from his hold.

"What am *I* doing here?" Sam shouted appalled.

"Shhh!" Maven hushed him while she swiftly led them in the direction of the gate.

"I followed you after I saw you sneak out, again, like the nefarious, wicked witch that you are. I'm here because I'm not going to let you run out on people who love you. Again. What the hell are *you* doing here?" Sam's volume was quieter, but his thoughts were rabid.

"Really, Sam? I'm a wicked witch?" She was surprised at how miffed she was over his word choice. "Clever."

He stopped walking. With his legs shoulder-width apart, he locked his knees and folded his arms.

"Is that truly all you heard me say?" he asked, firmly planted to the ground.

"No. No, no, no. I heard everything you said, and I will gladly address it, and explain, and listen to every angry insult you come up with, but not until we're back at the apartment," Maven tried to assuage his temper and usher him to the exit.

"How 'bout you explain it to me, now," he wasn't asking a question.

"It's not safe..." she began.

"You are so full of crap, Maven. I mean, you could not have picked a creepier place to run to, but that doesn't mean we're unsafe. You don't think anyone else Jumped here. You sent everyone Searching on some wild goose chase to keep busy so you could skip out on them, and we both know it. You're just a coward, and we both know that, too," Sam spat.

"You know *nothing*, Sam!" Frustrated beyond restraint, she raised her voice, "I get it: I hurt you. You'll never trust me again, and I will forever be the villain in the story of us. I was the monster who left a ring on the dresser in the middle of the night *to save your life*. And now I'm the coward who snuck out on her friends to run a secret errand in an attempt *to save theirs*! Again, I get it: I'm the worst. You're a victim. Life is hard."

Maven didn't need a Bond to feel the intensity of Sam's boiling rage radiating from every pore in his skin. Her own blazing fury served well as a barometer. Their bitter stares collided midair.

"Now, are you going to walk back to the apartment? Or are you going to keep behaving like a bratty, obstinate child throwing a tantrum? Either is fine with me, but know this: if you don't start placing one foot in front of the other, I will make you move. And you will not like how I go about it," her threat sizzled with promise.

After what seemed to them both to be a very long stretch frozen in their anger, Sam moved at an achingly slow pace towards the front of the cemetery. Maven hardly cared that all of the progress she and Sam had made up to that point had been thrashed. What mattered most right then was getting them both home safely. She inwardly acknowledged that she needed to find somewhere else for her and her friends to stay while they were stuck in the Human realm. Getting Sam involved was a mistake, she thought, but she was still glad it had happened. At least she had been able to provide him with some answers, and this time he'd be happy to watch her go.

Absentmindedly, Maven ran her fingers over her palm. Surprised she didn't feel any twinge, she looked at her hand. Before her eyes, the very last of her burn finished healing itself. She open and closed her fist to make sure there was no soreness. It seemed fitting to her that it was at that moment the mend culminated.

Glancing at her watch, the time had ticked down to only a few remaining minutes. Still only halfway to the gates, Maven knew that Sam was deliberately going slowly so the rest of the group would realize she had, in fact, left. Irritated, she went to tell Sam to move it along, but could only articulate a cry of anguish as a searing explosion of pain erupted in her head. Every neuron in her brain felt like it was being coated with lava. With her eyes closed and hands clenching at her hair, she fell to the ground and writhed. Without warning, the burning disappeared. Maven barely opened her eyelids before she slammed them shut again as a blinding light stole her sight. She flung an arm over her eyes to defend them, but the light was emitting from within.

Abruptly, all of her senses failed. In total blackness, she felt nothing, heard nothing. Even her emotions ceased. Silent, sudden bursts of colors started to flash before her. Blurry at first, they came into focus. Hung low between his shoulders as he sat, the top of Sam's head came into view. She thought he might be sad but couldn't tell exactly. Someone reached over, placed a hand under his chin, and lifted his face to her. Maven wanted to gasp but couldn't. His eyes were bruised and nearly swollen shut. Cuts were scattered over his cheeks, and nose, and lips, and blood ran from each wound down his neck to his chest. His head had been hanging because he was on the cusp of unconsciousness.

In a dizzying 180 degree spin, Maven's own face came into view. Also sitting, her body appeared physically unharmed, but hot, angry tears had fallen down her cheeks. She had, apparently, been forced to watch on as Sam took the beating. Only a mouth and a tip of a nose came into view as it slid in close to the side of her face. The lips were speaking, but Maven heard no words. Trying to focus harder, static crackled and buzzed in her ears. Concentrating all of her energy on the mouth's two moving lips, its tongue as it touched its teeth while it spoke, she heard a man's voice.

"Remember, Maven, *you* are choosing to let him die," he spoke calmly.

Her viewed whipped back to Sam as two large hands snaked around and firmly gripped either side of his face.

"Do it," the voice commanded.

In the instant the second man's arms flexed to twist, the same blinding light brought Maven back to reality.

"Seriously, Maven, come on," Sam's tone dripped with disdain.

She opened her eyes to find herself still in the graveyard. Not huddled on the damp grass in pain, she was surprised to be still standing. Checking her watch, the number of minutes was unchanged. Her stun did not register with Sam.

"Run," she whispered.

"What? No," Sam flatly refused.

"Run!" Maven yelled as she grabbed Sam's hand in a grip so tight it shocked him.

Her strength jolted him forward, and he had a hard time keeping up with her. Their locked clasp between him caught his attention. Looking down, he noticed the normally faint light she produced was glaringly bright.

"Maven!" he yelled, but she didn't reply. "Maven!"

She glanced at him as they ran, but her face immediately shut him up. Her eyes glowed brighter than the light coming from their hands. They continued at a full sprint. A moment before meeting the gate, something hit the back of Sam's head so hard it knocked his entire body to the ground releasing the grip on their hands. Maven's head swiveled around to see from where it came. Three men landed from seemingly nowhere. Glancing down at Sam's body, confused and scared, there was no time to defend against a set of hands from behind on either side of her head. Darkness fell instantly through her eyes.

THE TIMER on the stove had sounded for a while before Talmadge came out to tell Sam how distracting it was from their Searching, only to find that Sam was no longer in the apartment. On the roof, Maven was also nowhere to be found. The two couples gathered in the kitchen to formulate a plan.

"Let's give them a minute to show up," Talmadge insisted. "For all we know, they're off rekindling their Bond."

"They wouldn't have just left us without warning," Sabine insisted loudly.

"I agree with Sabine, Tal. This doesn't feel right," Lila said.

Then, unprompted, every one of their hands illuminated. Bewildered, they looked to each other for some form of explanation. None had any to offer.

They're here. They have us. RUN.

They all startled at the sound of Maven in their heads.

CHAPTER FOURTEEN

The assault on their brains resulted in a throbbing that rebounded through their skulls. Even the veins in their eyeballs pulsed heavily, causing biting discomfort. Sitting in utter darkness may have been a play at fear from their captors, but both Sam and Maven were grateful there were no lights to irritate their already aching heads. The black room smelled musty and sour. Still deeply dazed, they had no idea how long they had been out cold before waking. Not knowing who or what may be observing, Maven didn't dare cast even the dimmest of glows to appraise their surroundings. Neither broke the silence, but they were each aware of the other's presence across from them.

Eventually, there was a muffled shuffling and short, muted conversation on the far side of one wall. They both turned towards the noise in anticipation, and the door burst open. The sudden light made them squint and avert their eyes. To Maven's left walked in one tall man who flipped the switch near the doorframe. Fluorescents on the low ceiling overhead flickered until most stabilized, but one bulb continued to twitch intermittently. The man stood in front of the faded blue wall beside the door. Sam and Maven waited for him to speak, but they only received his glower. Not nearly as towering as Talmadge or Sam, his stature was still impressive. He rested his hands in front of him, lacing his bulky fingers together. Maven noticed his flawless dark skin and symmetrical features. In her stupor, she couldn't help but think if it weren't for the rancor across his face, she would have found to him be quite handsome.

Disengaging from his stare, Sam and Maven found each other's bewildered and frightened faces. They sat roughly ten feet apart, facing one another in stainless steel chairs. No rope or cord touched them, but their wrists and ankles were bound to the arms and legs of the seats. Clearly, either the man by the door or someone nearby was a Flyer. Looking down, they saw the metal feet were bolted into the cracked, dingy, once-white tile floor. Maven's arms tested the invisible constraints, but Sam subtly shook his head in admonishment.

Hasty footsteps echoed through the open door.

Without slowing, another fairly tall man turned the sharp corner from the hallway and cut between the chairs. Nearly meeting the wall opposite the door, he halted and spun around. His floppy, brown hair slightly caught the wind as he turned. A wide smile stretched across his thin face. Happy, pale blue eyes sparkled from underneath his thick eyebrows.

"Maven, my dear! How are you?" His voice trilled with excitement as he clasped his hands together.

Her forehead creased. At a loss, she looked to Sam and then back to the man who spoke.

"Beg your pardon? You don't remember me?" His face fell, and he shook his head exaggeratedly.

It was then, seeing his profile, the sharp point of his nose and his frowning mouth, that Maven identified him as the man who had spoken the words to her in her vision at the cemetery.

"I am profoundly insulted. I know you are up there in years, and it may have been a century or so," he spoke slowly as he walked the short distance to where she sat and started circling her, "but surely you haven't forgotten the first man to court your friend?"

Stopping in front of her, he crouched down to her seated level. His eyes followed his fingertips, grazing the skin of her face as he carefully tucked a loose curl behind her ear. Maven jerked her head away from his touch. He picked up another curl in front of her chest and twisted it between his fingers. Looking away from his hand, he found her expression hardened and jaw tightened.

"How is Sabine these days? I understand she's here with you," he smiled lasciviously.

It was then Sam who strained against his bindings. For what appeared to be the first time, the man in front of Maven recognized another presence in the room. Still crouched, he twisted his neck to see Sam. Only giving Sam a moment of his attention, he turned back to her and gave a disapproving frown.

"Honestly, Maven? A human?" He sighed and stood.

Wandering over to the other chair, he loomed near Sam.

"Even as base of a being as you are, there's no need for my rudeness. All the Gods' creatures and such," his tone belittled. Putting out a firm hand, he said, "My name is Kendrich. I believe you've already met my cousin Talmadge? Blond, tall, seemingly disagreeable man? Anyway, it is a pleasure to meet you, Sam."

Ferocious eyes stared back at him.

"Oh. Right." Remembering their held wrists, Kendrich bent down a little, picked up Sam's index finger, and shook it playfully. Walking back to the middle of the room, he continued.

"Sorry about the fastenings, but my partner

Harrison here," he pointed to the other man still poised at the door, "felt it was necessary. Now, Maven, you will have already noticed that you, also, cannot break your ties. I understand that, for you, this must be enormously frustrating, but I find it endlessly fascinating. Would you like to ask me how?"

Smiling again, he glanced enthusiastically back and forth between Sam and Maven. He raised his eyebrows in anticipation. He was given no encouragement and received despicable stares from both.

"I understand Maven's silence; she already knows. But you, Sam?" he turned, surprised at him. "You're not even the slightest bit curious about how to quell a shrew as powerful as Maven?"

Not speaking had almost begun to feel like a game to them at that point. Both remained mute, but Maven's expression raged. Somewhat pleased with her upset but irritated as they continued to ignore his words, Kendrich looped around to behind her seat. He stood directly in Sam's eye line.

"You see, Sam, what I did in the cemetery, was something..." he spoke as he placed a hand on either side of Maven's head, "like this."

A quick jolt of light came from his palms and shot into Maven's skull, and a short, shrill cry escaped her throat. He set his hands back to his sides. Maven sunk a little lower in her chair.

"That was merely a small demonstration, of course, as I already Sealed her talents," Kendrich made certain he maintained Sam's attention. "That's a trick an old friend of Maven's taught me, actually," he said as he placed a hand on either of Maven's shoulders.

Leaning as far forward in his seat as he could manage, Sam's shoulders rose as his breath grew heavier, and his heart beat faster. Maven shook her hair out of her face and found Sam's worried eyes. She gave him an unsteady smile to let him know she was fine, but they still said nothing.

"I see I'm boring you," Kendrich hissed. "Let's get down to business, then, shall we?"

He motioned Harrison towards Sam.

"Now, Maven, we tried to Read you and Sam while you were unconscious, but it appears you had already placed a Shield over your minds, you clever girl. We both know how long it takes to penetrate those. Seeing as how I can't possibly trust you enough to Unseal your powers and have you remove the Shields yourself, I have decided to go about this the antiquated human way. Well, our version of it," he explained to her almost sweetly as he sauntered to her side.

Sam's face stared unflinchingly at the massive brute near him.

"Maven," Kendrich asked as he trailed a finger from her shoulder to her wrist, "where are they?"

Across the room, Maven locked eyes with Sam. They both understood what was about to happen, but only she knew the irrefutable ending. Even if she gave up the location of everyone else, she had already Seen how their time in that room finished. There was nothing to do but let it play out, even though it broke her heart to do so. With the men surrounding them, they were unable to use words, but they still expressed precisely how they felt. Sadness, regret, and an immense love shone from their faces.

"Where are the others, Maven?" he asked again, too softly.

Keeping her and Sam's eyes hooked, she still said nothing.

Kendrich nodded to Harrison. Understanding, Harrison swiped a single finger a few inches through the air, causing Sam to growl in pain. In that one swift movement, Sam's nose was broken and bloodied. Both Maven and Sam turned to Kendrich. Their rage was palpable.

"Something to say?" he asked calmly. He shrugged. "Again," he said to Harrison.

Another small, swift gesture from his hand and Sam then had a deep cut down his lower lip. Maven shook her head, helpless.

"Anything?" Kendrich raised his eyebrows and held a hand to his ear.

Sam gathered the blood in his mouth and spat in the direction of Kendrich's shoes. Looking at Maven, Sam winked. She forced a smile and winked back.

"Again," Kendrich growled.

That time Harrison slowly closed his fingers into a half-fist. They heard a bone snap. Kendrich's eyes burrowed into the side of Maven's face as he awaited an answer, but nothing could possibly tear her eyes away from Sam.

"Again. Again. Again!" Kendrich barked.

Maven's chin quivered through her clenched jaw as a tear fell from her eye. She fought against her unseen restraints. She refused to look away as bruises formed around his nearly swollen shut eyes.

"Do you not love him?" Kendrich seethed as he bent down to Maven's ear. "Again."

She counted every cut and gash scattered over his cheeks, and nose, and lips.

"This man you Bonded with. Your supposed eternal partner. He means so little to you that you would gladly watch his suffering without a word to the contrary?" His hot breath was hitting the side of her face. "Again."

Unaware that her wrists were bleeding from her struggle, she watched as the blood ran from each wound down his neck to his chest and soaked through his shirt.

"Raise his head. Show her," Kendrich commanded.

On the verge of unconsciousness, Sam's head hung low. Harrison extended a finger, and, without touching his chin, lifted Sam's face up for her to see.

"One last chance," he hissed in her ear, "before your human dies in a very human way."

Even though Sam's eyes were closed, Maven mouthed the words *I'm sorry* to him.

"Remember, Maven, *you* are choosing to let him die," he spoke placidly.

Kendrich stood at the back of her chair and pantomimed what he expected from Harrison.

Standing behind him, Harrison snaked his hands around and firmly gripped either side of Sam's face.

"Do it," Kendrich commanded.

CHAPTER FIFTEEN

Harrison gripped Sam's face tighter and flexed to snap, but the rumbling at his feet stopped him. Still holding Sam's head, his eyes darted around the room frantically. The walls shook, and the ceilings trembled. Dirt and dust rained down from above and at every joint. Relenting his clasp on Sam, Harrison scanned Kendrich's face and identified a snarl of vexation. Kendrich regarded the quaking room with disgust.

"This is such inconvenient timing," Kendrich muttered.

With his fingers open and slightly curled, Kendrich placed his palms up and near waist level. A vivid blaze whirled in his hands. He studied each of the walls suspiciously as the room all but rocked off its foundation. Maven's watch never left Sam's drooped, swaying head. The booming thunder underfoot roared then suddenly stopped. Kendrich and Harrison looked at each other. A dull cracking noise came from the far wall, and all eyes flew towards it.

"Shi--"

Kendrich didn't have time to end the word before two massive, circular hunks of concrete ripped from the far wall, launched across the room, and crashed clean through the wall with the door, sandwiching both he and Harrison in the rubble. Although covered in dust, still sitting firmly bolted to the floor were Sam and Maven. Maven tried to blink away the flecks of dirt on her lashes to see Sam, but only more fell in. Rushing in from the dark outside through the giant, gaping hole, Eldon, Sabine, and Lila climbed over the crumbled concrete and mangled rebar to their friends. Lila and Eldon reached Sam as Sabine met Maven's side.

"Get up," Sabine yelled at Maven. "Get up!"

Maven looked up at her with a desperate expression. She jerked at her bindings, but Sabine didn't understand. Eldon and Lila struggled with moving Sam's arms, too.

"Tal!" Lila yelled back to the opening.

His hands remaining at the ready, Talmadge was at the damaged passage at once. His head swiveled around in a frenzy.

"They're bound," Lila spoke quickly and motioned to their hands and feet.

An abrupt flick from his finger and they were released. Maven ran to help the others with Sam. Unconscious, they could barely lift his massive body from the seat. Even with Eldon under one arm and Maven under the other, they could hardly manage to support his entire deadweight.

"Talmadge, we can't," Eldon groaned through gritted teeth as they labored under Sam's mass.

Tearing his survey off the mounds of debris, Talmadge looked to the others struggling. With one hurried hand, Sam was raised a few inches off the ground. They could easily guide his body then.

"Come on!" Talmadge shouted.

Sprinting, they all took off down the alley away from the tear in the building. Waiting around the corner was a dark blue minivan. The doors opened before they reached it. Talmadge got behind the wheel with Lila in the passenger seat. Sabine climbed in the far back as Eldon helped set Sam in the middle row. Maven climbed in next to him, and Eldon slammed the door as he slid in beside Sabine.

"Go!" Eldon called to the front.

Talmadge, without a key, turned the engine over. Never touching the steering wheel or pedals, the car hurled forward. Without slowing, the van rocketed into traffic. Horns blared, and fingers flew as Talmadge corrected and came alongside the other vehicles.

Speeding down the road, he didn't stop for a single red light. Narrowly avoiding collisions, Talmadge looked at the backseat from the corner of his eye.

"Where do we go?" He asked Maven.

Another horn blasted in Maven's silence as they shot past glaring headlights.

"Maven!" Talmadge yelled.

Ignoring everyone and everything around her, Maven turned on the small overhead light and kneeled, crouched above Sam's lifeless body. Placing her fingers on his bloodied neck, she felt an irregular, thready pulse. In the dark, she tried to find a spot on his face that wasn't already wounded. She patted the side of his cheek and shook his shoulder, willing him to wake up.

"Why don't you Heal him?" Sabine questioned, distressed from the back seat.

"Where should we go?" Lila called to her from the front.

"Maven!" Talmadge roared again.

She paid no attention to any of their words. Maven's breath heaved in her chest as she stared down at Sam. Her face grimaced as a thought came to her. Slightly hesitating, she slapped Sam across the face. Sabine gasped as the others sat stunned.

"Maven, don't!" Sabine threw herself forward and grabbed at Maven's hands, but Maven shook her off and shoved her back into her seat. Reaching back, Maven slapped Sam again.

"Maven," Eldon whispered his shock.

Balling Sam's shirt in her fists, she shook him. Again, she hit him hard across the face. Sam's eyes rolled around in their sockets. Holding his head upright with both her hands, she inched towards Sam. Blinking furiously through turgid lids, he focused on Maven's face. Breathing through his mouth, he took short, stuttered breaths. Her eyebrows stitched together in resolve. Slowly, she turned his head to Eldon and Sabine in their seat, towards Lila and Talmadge in the front, and then back to her face. He nodded in understanding. Sam weakly reached a hand to the back seat causing Sabine to frown in confusion. Frustrated, Maven shook her head and motioned Sabine forward with her fingers. Her stern face kept both in the back seat frozen in place. Maven grumbled and seized Sabine's arm. She roughly placed it in Sam's, and he feebly held it. Maven stabbed a finger into Sabine's chest, and then pointed back at Sam. Sabine's open mouth and blank expression infuriated Maven. Again, she pointed from Sabine to Sam, but then she held their hands together. Tears built as her eyes pled with her to understand. Sabine's eyes bulged open and then slammed shut as she finally got it.

"What is going on?" Lila shouted, twisted around in her chair.

In the back of the van, a tenuous, pinkish light flowed under the skin from Sabine's heart. It trickled down her arm and through her hand. Slipping up Sam's fingers, it climbed his arm until it met his chest and touched his own heart.

"My Gods," Talmadge whispered while looking at the sight from the rearview mirror.

Sam flimsily felt for Maven with his free hand. She took his hand between both of hers and held it to her cheek. An unstable light started in their palms but quickly fired from behind the slits left of Sam's opened eyes. Right in front of them, the hunched and broken body of Sam luminously transformed into Maven. Where Maven had just knelt, Sam sat hovering over Maven's small, injured frame. Each and every wound that had appeared on his body, in fact, lay on Maven's. The only blood on him then was from the cuts around his wrists from struggling while watching Maven get beaten and that of Maven's on his hands that held her to his cheek.

"It was her," Lila gasped. "It was her the entire time."

"We need a hospital!" Sam shouted angrily to Talmadge.

"No," Maven spoke, barely audible.

"Mavey, we need to. You need a doctor. You're hurt," Sam explained to her gently.

"No!" Maven's beaten face contorted in pain after she shouted.

"She's right. We need to get somewhere safe, Sam," Talmadge said, unconcerned from the driver's seat.

Sam stared back at him affronted.

"She can Heal herself," Lila spoke calmly. "But we need another place to hide, Sam. We can't go back to your apartment. Do you know of anywhere we can go?"

Closing his eyes and taking a deep breath, he ground his teeth. "Lila, can you Search for my friend's house?"

"What's the full name?" she asked.

"Derek Wilkes, Jr. Upper West Side," he added, unsure of where they were exactly.

Lila's eyes closed as she Searched. "Got it," she replied.

Turning around, Lila directed Talmadge through the darkened city streets. Giving his full attention back to Maven, Sam was amazed to see that the smaller of the cuts on her face were already gone. She and Sabine's hands held the other tighter.

"Here," Eldon tapped Sam's shoulder. "Swap seats with me."

Sam shook his head. He had no intention of leaving her, even if it was just from the back seat.

"I can help her from her other side," Eldon offered.

"Right. Of course," Sam acknowledged his suggestion.

Reluctantly but rapidly, Sam switched seats. He looked on as Eldon took Maven's left hand into his. The same light as Sabine's flowed from beneath his skin and into Maven. Briefly closing his eyes, Sam said a quick prayer to anyone listening, and then found Maven's bruised face again.

CHAPTER SIXTEEN

The van slammed to a stop in front of the row of brownstones. Everyone started climbing out of their doors.

"Did you steal this car?" Sam asked no one in particular as he carefully cradled Maven in his arms.

"We weren't stealing," Sabine started, still holding Maven's hand.

"Yes, it's stolen," Lila cut her off.

"Get rid of it," Sam said softly.

"What do you mean?" Eldon questioned.

"Park it a few blocks over. Drive it into the river. Set it on fire. I don't care. Just get it away from us and the attention it'll bring," he ordered as he took the steps to the door.

Talmadge got back behind the wheel.

"Get everyone inside," he spoke to Lila when she attempted to sit in the car, too.

Begrudgingly, she shut the door and watched Talmadge drive away into the night. Taking the stairs two at a time, she met the others at the top of the stoop. On the doorknob was a locked keypad. She looked up to Sam for direction.

"8572," he said without looking at her. "Punch in the code, and the box will open. Get the key and unlock the door."

Lila followed his instructions and got them through the door. Once inside, she locked the handle and deadbolt behind them. Eldon switched on lights as they went. Sam carried Maven into the study on the right and laid her down across the overstuffed brown leather couch. Immediately, Sabine knelt beside Maven as Lila stood behind the sofa, each taking a hand. Sam hovered over their shoulders. Nervously watching their lights pour into Maven, he was apprehensive as he saw her blood-painted face cringe in pain.

"I think you're making it worse," Sam interjected.

Eldon, Sabine Read, *Keep him calm.*

"Sam, they know what they're doing," Eldon spoke while taking Sam by the elbow and backing him up a couple of feet.

Suddenly, they heard a loud pop come from inside of Maven, and she let out a cry.

"You're hurting her!" Sam yelled and took the two steps back towards the women.

"Get him out of here," Lila called without opening her eyes.

Pushing, Eldon slowly edged Sam to the entryway and slid the door shut behind him. Wrought with worry, Sam paced in front of the study.

"It's going to be a little while. You might want to sit down," Eldon suggested from the doorway of the living room, which sat across the short hall from the study.

From the other side of the door, they could hear another howl from Maven. Shutting his eyes, Sam froze. He listened to a moan followed by a gasp. He reached for the handle.

"You'll only be in the way," Eldon said composedly. "They are three of the most competent witches you'll meet, Sam. Let them do what they know. They'll tell us when they're finished."

Warily, Sam left the door and collapsed on a couch in the living room. Blood still on his hands, he rubbed his forehead with the back of his arm.

"What happened out there?" Eldon quietly inquired, his gaze intense. "How did Maven change places with you like that?"

"I have no idea," Sam shook his head in frustration. "One second, we were on our way back to the loft, and the next thing I know, I'm outside of my body and completely helpless, watching her almost die. She made it so I couldn't speak. I would have said something, told them anything they wanted to make him stop."

"Whose place is this?" Eldon asked sedately.

Sam glanced at him. He could tell Eldon was attempting to keep his mind off the other side of the door, but Sam's thoughts still raced.

"It's a buddy of mine's place," he replied. "It's a rental he's trying to sell. I helped him stage it with some of my paintings and..."

He trailed off at the sound of pain across the hall.

"Which ones?" Eldon continued.

"What?" Sam asked, looking back to him from the study door.

"Which ones?" Eldon said again as he twirled a finger around the room. "Which paintings are yours?"

"Um," Sam rubbed his forehead again, "one above the fireplace in the study, one in the dining room, the hallway, each of the bedrooms upstairs..."

That time, he trailed off at the sound of the front door opening and closing. Standing, Sam took a step towards the entryway. Talmadge came around the short wall separating them. He turned his head at the sound of the girls in the study then took the step down into the living room.

"The car's gone," he said as he leaned against the wall and crossed his arms.

Sam instantly closed the gap between the two of them. Banging Talmadge's head into the wall, Sam held him in place with one fist twisting his shirt and his other forearm in his throat. Talmadge made no move to resist.

"What did you do?" Sam yelled.

"I parked it miles away and Flew back. Calm down," Talmadge groaned through a squeezed windpipe.

"No!" Sam lifted him far enough away from the wall just to slam him back into it, "What did you do to get us taken? You sold us out to your cousin!"

"What are you talking about?" Talmadge questioned with a furrowed brow.

"Kendrich," Sam seethed and pressed harder with his arm.

"Kendrich?" Talmadge met his eye. "Are you certain?"

"I think I remember the name of the man who forced me to watch as he had Maven nearly beaten to death!" Sam growled through his teeth.

Eldon placed a hand on Sam's shoulder.

"Why would I help you get caught only to turn around and save you?" Talmadge wheezed.

"Sam, I've known Tal almost my entire life. He

wouldn't do anything to hurt any of us. He doesn't even have to stand here and take this from you," Eldon attempted to mollify the situation.

"Wizard or not, Talmadge," Sam whispered, "if she dies, I *will* kill you."

He tossed him to the side and walked to the other end of the living room. Clearing his throat, Talmadge rubbed his neck.

"Great. Now, I need Maven to Heal *me*," he choked out sarcastically to Eldon standing near him.

Sam turned to have another word with Talmadge, but the door sliding to the study made him forget the comment altogether. Carefully walking across the landing, Lila and Sabine escorted Maven on either side as she slightly limped. Her left arm wrapped across her body and held onto her right ribs. Sam gleaned what the crack he heard earlier had been from. The cuts and gashes across her face were all wiped away, and her nose was straight again. Her swollen eyelids then only had faint bruises at their edges.

"What's the commotion out here all about?" Maven asked, still a little short of breath.

She eyed Talmadge, who was staring at Sam, who never took his gaze off Maven.

"Nothing," Eldon mumbled. "Guy stuff."

"Okay," she let it go. "So, who do I have to thank for saving our lives?"

"Eldon was the one who found you," Lila boasted. "I couldn't get a lock on you or Sam, because of your insane body switch, but Sabine and I boosted him once he got a trace."

"Is that right?" Surprised, Maven weakly forced a smile at Eldon through the pain. She hoped it didn't come across as depreciating.

"Yeah," Eldon shrugged then rubbed the back of his neck. "I got lucky. Lila would have gotten there eventually."

Maven took the single stair down from the entryway into the living room and took a step towards Eldon. Gingerly, she placed her right hand on the side of his beard and kissed his other cheek. He smiled down at her meekly. Taking his hand, she had him help her to the couch. She sat on the center cushion, but everyone else stood. They each regarded Maven carefully. Looking to Sam, she patted the seat next to her, but he didn't budge.

"Come on," she motioned her head.

He swallowed before sitting down. She gently picked up his hands and inspected the bloodied and broken skin around his wrists. With her fingers hovering over his cuts, a quick flash made them disappear.

"Are you okay?" she asked.

"Yeah," Sam quietly scoffed. "I'm not the one who-
_"

"I'm fine," she cut him off, making sure he met her eye as she spoke.

"Mostly," he commented on the bruises, and limping, and hand still on her ribs.

"I'll finish mending as we talk. There are more important things than healing my soreness right now," Maven assured him.

Closing her eyelids, Maven set her hands facing up on her knees. A deep green glow emitted and dashed from her fingers. Bolts crawled across the floors, up the walls, around the ceilings, doors, and windows. Covering every surface in the home, they ceased as she opened her eyes.

"Will that keep us hidden?" Sabine hoped.

Maven nodded. Glancing around the silent room, she took in the cautious faces who risked their lives for others.

"I told you to run," she spoke matter-of-factly.

Their faces creased.

"You can't be serious," Lila scoffed, surprised.

"I am. Quite," Maven responded.

"How about we ignore your ingratitude and discuss the fact that you Read to us, all of us, from Gods' know how far away," Talmadge threw out, leaning against the wall.

"And how *did* you do that insane body swap?" Lila nearly repeated herself.

"What did you just do to the house?" Sam asked.

"Why did they take you? What did they want?" Eldon chimed in.

"Why did you leave in the first place, Maven?" Sabine's question conveyed a sting.

Each question lapped over the other. Maven again beheld the faces of those who risked their lives for hers and Sam's. She noted as she looked to him that his eyes requested all the same answers. She took a moment and a breath.

"I left, with every intention of coming back, to leave a message for help," she began.

"A message for whom?" Talmadge questioned.

"To allies in the area," she said. "To the warlocks."

Maven glimpsed each of their disbelieving faces.

"What are you trying to say?" Sabine asked, more confused than ever.

"I'm saying the history is wrong," Maven claimed and braced for their resistance.

"I think you need to lie down and finish recovering," Lila advised as she sat at Maven's other side.

"I am speaking very soundly," she replied with an appreciative smile.

"Okay, let's say that warlocks weren't completely abolished during The War. Why in all the realms would they have allied with a witch such as yourself?" Talmadge wasn't even attempting to contain his incredulity.

"The answer to that is the answer to all your other questions, actually," she replied.

They awaited her response.

"Because I am one," she answered.

"One what?" Sabine's tone begged for clarification.

"I'm a warlock," Maven stated simply.

No one spoke. Her words mystified them all. They each peered around the room to the others' faces looking for some sort of consensus about her declarations.

What is wrong with her? Sabine Read to all, excluding Maven and Sam.

Do you think her head is still injured from the trauma? Lila proffered an explanation.

Maybe she's in shock? Eldon suggested.

I am neither concussed, in shock, nor am I crazy, Maven smoothly Read to every mind in the room.

Everyone gawked at her on the couch, but Sam stared with both his eyes and mouth wide open. The experience of being Read jarred his frail composure.

"I have your attention," she spoke aloud. "Good."

Eldon and Sabine lowered onto the loveseat opposite the couch. Talmadge remained inclined against the wall.

"Almost everything you know about The War is a lie," Maven started. "It's true that the warlocks came to be within a single generation, but it wasn't until several generations later that conflict arose. It's also true that we individually possess nearly all of the known talents, but we most certainly did not lose our empathy and reasoning. The opposite happened; they were amplified along with everything else. You know that to be true. Through me, through my dad. You've felt our compassion firsthand."

She scanned their expressions. All sat stunned, except for Talmadge; he carried a look of burgeoning resentment.

"Our abilities were considerable," she continued, "but they weren't our greatest gift. As Creators, our capacity to Heal also evolved. On their own, bodies regenerated cells as quickly as they naturally depleted."

"Meaning what exactly?" Sam questioned, but he already thought the answer in his head.

"Immortality," Talmadge murmured.

"To an extent, yes," Maven replied. "I, as you all just saw, have a mortal body. Injury hurts us just as easily as the rest of you, and we can die. But, having said that, if no harm befalls us, or if we can Heal quickly enough..." Noting they all grasped the concept, she allowed her words to lag.

"How old are you?" Lila eagerly asked.

"I was sixteen when The War started," Maven admitted.

Most of them breathed a sharp intake of air in response.

"Wow," was all Lila could manage.

"What does that mean?" Sam, utterly lost, was again unsure he wanted an honest answer.

"That was almost four millennia ago," Sabine interpreted for him.

"I stopped keeping track after I turned 3,000," Maven spoke plainly then swallowed.

Sam's jaw slacked, but he briskly collected himself. He blinked then nodded.

"Continue," Talmadge prodded from the edge of the room.

"What you also weren't told is that we didn't start the bloodshed," she carried on. "We had nothing to gain by it."

"Then, who?" Eldon inquired.

"The witches and wizards of that time's Elders Circle," Maven prepared for the backlash.

"Lies," Talmadge proclaimed.

He pushed off his perch and stood tall. His resentment had bloomed into full-blown anger.

"It's true," she countered. "Liam was on the Circle, then. He served side-by-side with them until the moment they turned against us."

"I've had enough with your deceptions, Maven!" Talmadge yelled at her and took a step forward.

Sam rose at her side.

"I'm not lying, Tal," she remained cool and seated. "Those witches and wizards came to be known to us as The Warring Families. It was them and their kin who fed off of each other's greed and jealousy. They were the ones who conjured up the siphoning. They thought if they stole our energies, they would be the ones to live forever. They started the fighting. We only protected ourselves."

"I'm warning you," Talmadge whispered as he took another step.

Maven placed a hand on Sam's leg to prevent him from moving forward.

"Those families, who stripped warlocks of their powers and left them for dead, were once people I loved and cared for. It was my father's *best friend* who betrayed us. A man I had known since birth, Talmadge. I called him Uncle Nils," she said as her voice started to crack.

Her last words halted Talmadge's stride.

"What did you say?" he breathed out.

"But that was a nickname. You would have known

him better by his full name: Niklas," she pronounced the name deliberately. "Your ancestor."

"Impossible," Lila shook her head, but her tone betrayed her word.

"This isn't some fiction I'm spinning to hurt you," Maven directed her words to Talmadge. "My family, my people, were hunted for centuries to the brink of extinction. We fled and scattered ourselves to the farthest corners of the realms in hopes of staying hidden long enough that any hints or whispers of our legacy would die out before we did. If we didn't exist, we could stay alive. But then we wanted to go back to Loremara, to our home. Liam and I thought a few thousand years had been long enough."

After a long, pregnant pause, Sam cleared his throat.

"You said they 'thought' they would live forever," he stated.

"Yes," she tore her look from Talmadge to look at Sam. "For lack of a better term, it didn't take."

"How so?" he asked.

"It's like a kidney," she suggested. "Your own will last you until your body expires. But if you needed a transplant, even one coming from a healthy, living donor would only give you another twenty years of use. It would sustain you, help you function, yes. Eventually, though, even that one would give out."

"What happened to The Families?" Eldon questioned.

"The ones who succeeded in draining warlocks added years to their lives. Some lasted for centuries past their expirations. Over time, they all met one fate or another. From what we gathered throughout the years, they had covered their tracks. The stories passed down even to their own children were of heroes slaying the evil demons," Maven's face twisted at the memory. "History is written by those who win," she added to no one in particular.

Witnessing her dejection, Sam's temper boiled.

"Am I the only one who sees the connection?" he steamed. "A great-grandson of your world's Hitler has conveniently been at your hip the entire time you've been running!"

Talmadge's expression incensed.

"It was your family then, and it's your family now. Kendrich, *his cousin*, was the one who almost killed you trying to figure out where the other warlocks are!" Sam's voice boomed as he threw out the information he had pieced together.

Lila and Maven both stood up from the couch. Everyone was surprised when Maven turned and used her body as a barrier in front of Talmadge, but no one more than Sam.

"He is no more responsible for another wizard's actions than you are," Maven defended quietly.

Behind her, Talmadge's face sunk with guilt. He crept back to the wall and leaned against it once more, facing away from the group. Lila walked to his side and wrapped an arm around his waist. In front of Maven, Sam's expression was harder to read. More than anything, he looked shocked.

"Maven, how did you know," Sabine warily cut through the tension. "How did you know to switch bodies with Sam?"

"I Saw it," Maven answered with a heavy sigh.

"What?" Eldon's eyes got big. "You mean... you're a Seer? I thought they died out."

"They basically did. Only warlocks ever had the gift of Sight, and at the end of The War, most with the talent had been killed for it," she replied.

"If you can See what's to come, why don't you do it now?" Sabine questioned.

"Because that's not how it works. And I only just inherited it from Liam. I didn't even realize that was what happened until we were in the cemetery, and I Saw a vision of Sam... about to die," Maven finished.

"The burn on your hand," Sabine inferred.

"Yeah. It finished healing when we were on our way back to the apartment," Maven explained.

"You knew?" Sam eyed Maven carefully.

The look on her face was response enough.

"So, what about the other warlocks," Sabine carried the conversation along.

"I left word for a rendezvous point and time," Maven said. "Hopefully, they'll be able to help us."

"When?" Eldon asked.

Maven closed her eyes and stretched her neck. She had suddenly hit a wall of exhaustion. Scanning around, she found a clock on the wall. It wasn't quite one o'clock in the morning, but depleted and bone-weary bodies riddled the living room.

"Look, everyone, I know there is still a lot we need to discuss. We'll finish it tomorrow," Maven called out. "Sam, are there enough beds for everyone?"

"There are four bedrooms," he gradually nodded. "Two upstairs, two more on the top floor."

"Good," she replied. "We'll sleep here tonight."

"Is that a good idea? Will we stay hidden?" Sabine worried from the loveseat.

"Trust me, we are safe now," Maven answered her with a serious, asserting tone. "Right now, let's all try to get some sleep. Please."

At that, Maven left them all mulling in the living room and climbed the stairs.

CHAPTER SEVENTEEN

On the top floor, Maven had taken the smaller of the two bedrooms, choosing it for the window facing the backyard and the one-person balcony that extended out from it. Sitting with her back on the side railing, she gathered her knees to her chest. She pitched her head back to stare at the sky. Even though it was the middle of the night and no clouds obstructed her view, Maven could only count a handful of stars. Listening to the light traffic drive through the neighborhood, she had forgotten how foreign the human realm could feel.

She closed her eyes and breathed deeply in an attempt to quiet her thoughts. There was no escaping the next day's proceedings, but that night, she didn't want to think about those things. In fact, she didn't want to think at all. Not about tomorrows or yesterdays, anyone or anything, but just that calm instant in the quiet moment. Then, there was a soft rapping at her closed door. She smirked at the impeccable timing of the person on the other side of the knock.

It's open, she Read.

Not getting up from her seat, she saw Sam peek his head through the opening. He glanced around the room but couldn't find her.

"Maven?" he whispered puzzled.

Out here.

She smiled and gave a short wave as he found her to the right and through the window. Nimbly latching the door behind him, he walked over, knelt in front of the opened frame, and rested his arms on the sill.

"I'm not sure I'll get used to this Reading thing," Sam, shaking his head, still spoke softly.

"Sorry," she replied and rubbed a finger across her lips.

He opened his mouth, but Maven held her hand up to impede his objection.

"Sam, I really am," she said with painstaking care. "I am. For not telling you the truth when we first met. For leaving. For coming back. For causing you pain. For getting you involved and putting you in danger. For every single stupidly selfish thing I've done and said. I truly am sorry for hurting you."

Sam looked up into the apologetic face that implored his forgiveness.

"Will you come inside, please?" he requested firmly.

Pushing himself up from the ledge, he walked deeper into the room while Maven crawled in through the window. She closed the glass and drew the curtains. Watching him lightly pace along the rug covering the hardwood floor, a knot started forming in her gut. She knew she could Read him without him knowing, but they were his words to give not hers to take. He stopped a few feet away from her and turned.

"Maven, I don't want your apologies. They're appreciated, but I don't need them. The only thing I ever wanted from you was *you*. When you left," he winced at the memory, "I experienced a personal hell that I never fathomed existed on Earth."

Concentrating on the floor, she nodded while she replayed her own memory of that time.

"It took a year and a half before you agreed to go on a date with me. It was six months into dating before you even let me kiss you. From the day we met, it took me almost four years to build up the courage to ask for an answer to the question I had wanted to ask since the moment I first saw you. Then, you took off," he recounted.

Her eyelids drew together at the guilt she felt from his words.

"It was eight years, two months, three weeks, and six days before you showed up again," he said slowly.

With eyes closed, Maven nodded again.

"I guess what I'm saying is," he sighed, "you're a girl worth waiting for."

Maven froze, and her pulse stuttered.

"The things you listed do not matter to me in the slightest, except for one," he deliberately paused until her eyes met his. "You came back."

Reaching into his pocket, Sam pulled out her engagement ring.

"I brought this with me to chuck at you when I thought you snuck off again," he flashed his dazzling smile.

Maven laughed nervously but still couldn't find her voice.

"In your realm, we're married?" he asked tentatively.

"Bonded," she scarcely breathed out the cherished word.

"Bonded," he repeated. "Still?"

"Always," she answered earnestly.

Sam took a step forward and held out the ring between his index finger and thumb. It was dwarfed in his hold. Maven raised a shaky hand to meet it. His fingers barely grazed her skin as he placed the ring on her left hand. Staring down in disbelief, she shifted the ring side to side to watch it catch the light.

"Thank you," she beamed up at Sam brighter than any diamond.

"Don't thank me, yet," he warned.

With her hand still midair, her eyebrows raised with apprehension.

"I never should have made you close off our Bond," he rushed out.

That time, Sam held his hand to stifle Maven's objection.

"I did it because I wanted to hurt you. It's that simple," he chewed his lip at the admission. "And, now, I want you to lift it. Or open it, or unlock it, or whatever. For both of us."

"Sam, I told you earlier, I have no way of knowing how you'd handle--"

He cut her off.

"Maven, enough. You can protect me and everyone else here in ways I never knew possible, and you have. But *you* aren't something I need shelter from, and this isn't yours to keep from me. I want it. This is our Bond, mine and yours. I need this. I'm done being kept at arm's length, Maven. You've been strong alone for long enough." He wasn't demanding, but it also wasn't a request.

"Are you certain?" she tested.

"Please," he implored.

Closing the short gap between them, Maven placed her right hand over her heart and her left hand over Sam's. She bent her neck back to meet his gaze. The brilliance began to shine beneath her palms, then swirl and pulsate. A small heat built in their chests. After a moment, she felt his heart pound under her touch, and his expression grew severe. Closing his eyes, Sam grimaced and tilted his head to the side. Worried, Maven started to remove her hand from his chest, but his hand flew up and held it tightly to him.

The air whirled around their bodies, and all focus of the outside world was shut out. They were cocooned in a cyclone of spinning light. It began as a radiant gold then faded through each shade of orange, pink, and then a blinding white. Sam gripped Maven's hand tighter and tighter as his pain built, and the heat in their chests scalded. Finished, the light faded, and the heat from her contact dwindled. Less than a minute had passed with Sam's face wrenched, but it seemed much longer to them both.

With their hands still on his chest, Maven stared anxiously at Sam's pinched face. A second later, he was upright and focused on her eyes again. The flood gates came crashing open. Every thought elicited an emotion that reverberated between them. Every memory launched a sentiment that they echoed from the other. Maven thought about the phone call from Liam the night she left, which made her think of her dad. Her agony was Sam's agony. Sam recalled recognizing her face at his door, their talk in his room over her box of things, him shaving. They both smiled somewhat sheepishly. Before he realized he was doing it, Sam remembered watching Maven take the beating that he knew belonged to him. Their hearts lurched and stomachs dropped at the aching helplessness. Looking at their grip, Maven realized that was the first moment they had willingly held hands with each other since the night he proposed. She flashed through every night together preceding that one. She replayed every laugh and tickle, each smile and kindness.

It was then that Sam closed his eyes and loosened his grip on their hands. Leaning down, he pressed his forehead against Maven's. The love that they each transmitted for the other fought for priority. His freed hand looped around her lower back. With the other, he laced his fingers through her hair near the nape of her neck. Gently gripping, he pulled her head backward. Looking into each other's eyes once more, a suggestive, crooked grin crossed Sam's mouth. He pulled her face up and kissed her hard.

Their lips never leaving the others', Sam backed her against the wall. His hands moved to hold either side of her face. Maven clung to his torso until she gathered together the hem of his shirt. Guardedly, she raised it a couple of inches. She had not yet dared to fully believe what was happening. Sensing her hesitation, Sam leaned back to see her face better. His eyes begged. With her hands still on his shirt, he raised his arms high and waited. Maven smiled and pushed the fabric over his head.

Immediately, his hands were back on her cheeks as he kissed her fiercely. Her fingers outlined the muscles of his arms and across his back. Slinking down her sides, his hands then gripped the bottom of her shirt. Without missing a beat, she raised her hands over her head. In one deft motion, she saw the wad of cloth sail across the room. She couldn't help but laugh at the sight. Looking down at Maven's bare midsection, Sam noticed the familiar scattered scars on her skin.

"These aren't really from having your appendix removed, I take it?" He gently ran a finger over each one.

She shook her head, solemnly. "War wounds," she admitted. "They weren't Healed quick enough not to scar."

Feeling her dolefulness connected to the memory, Sam had an overwhelming urge to comfort her. He pulled her body to his.

Wait, she Read between fervent kisses.

Under unspoken protest, he paused. One hand gripping her tightly, he pressed a stiff arm on the wall above her head to stabilize himself. He stared down at her headily through his lashes and licked his lips. A pleased look crossed her face as he felt both her excitement and her amusement towards his impatience. She lifted his reluctant hand from her ribs. Maven swiped her incandescent palm over his own. Watching him, she waited for his reaction. Looking down, he saw a simple, wide, silver band encircling his left ring finger. He stood still. The ostensibly effortless symbol of devotion built tears behind his eyes. A landslide of her adoration cascaded down him. With that hand, he ran his thumb across her lips. Her tender expression, coupled with his ring against her cheek, caused a tear to escape his brim. Maven brushed it away with her fingertips. Stretching high on her tiptoes, she lightly skimmed her lips across his before she pulled him into another deep kiss.

Grabbing her hips, Sam picked her up easily. Her legs wrapped around his waist and her arms around his strong neck. His hand gripped under her thigh, and the other was tangled in her hair again as he steered them to the bed.

MAVEN'S HEAD rested on Sam's chest. He absentmind-edly played with her long, messy hair while she traced the line of his collarbone back and forth with her finger.

"What about werewolves?" Sam asked.

"Real," Maven replied, "but not exactly what you think. They're called Phasers, and their powers are linked to the moons. And they're not just wolves; they can shift into any type of creature found under a realm's moon."

"Zombies?" he continued animated.

She stifled a scoff. "None that I've ever found, no."

"Vampires?" he carried on.

"Nope," she answered, then pressed her lips, swal-lowing the urge to mock.

"No?" Sam's eyebrows rose.

"No! You, as a species, are obsessed with the 'undead.' There are no such things as vampires, zombies, Frankenstein's monster, or his bride," she laughed. "Dead is dead, pal."

"Fine," he chuckled. "What about dragons?"

"Now, *those*, believe it or not, are real."

"C'mon! Seriously?" he exclaimed.

Maven smiled at his excitement. "Seriously. In fact, they used to be a part of Tartooc. But, as humans have a slight tendency to do, they were hunted nearly to extinction. It was witches and wizards actually who helped relocate them to another realm."

"Wow. Dragons... and witches... and warlocks..." he breathed out as he let the concepts sink in. His free hand found Maven's resting on his chest. Picking it up, he studied her fingers and thought about the light and power that continuously flowed from them. "How do you do it?" he asked.

"Do what?" she questioned back.

"All of it. All the... magic. I know you called it energy, but what does that even mean?" he ardently inquired.

Maven propped herself up on her elbows to look at his face. She paused a moment to reach for the best words. "Honestly, it boils down to belief."

"Oh, that's all, huh? Infinite cosmic abilities for the low, low price of a can-do attitude?" he teased.

"You're making fun of me, but it's true," she smiled back at him. "You and I live in the same universe, Sam. The same rules that govern my realm apply here and everywhere else in between. Granted, I have been around a bit longer, but the only difference between you and me is that my people know the power of belief. Every single thing in creation, in the history of ever, is energy, right? It's all pure vibration. You are, I am, the stars in the sky, and that chair in the corner. Even your thoughts have their own vibration, and every thought that you have, intentional or not; is sent out into the universe with its powerful attraction. Our thoughts become our beliefs, again, whether they're intentional or not. What I do, what we all do, is harness that intent. Your world even has a saying that perfectly explains it: mind over matter. We do that."

"But it has to be more than that. I mean, you have to have the capability as a species before your thoughts, your beliefs even allow you those certain gifts and talents, right?" Sam tried to draw out her simplification.

"Humans are no less capable than witches and wizards or even warlocks. We've all come from the same line. Physically, you can't tell us apart. Certainly, we've evolved, but it's been of the mind. The difference is you've grown up in a world where you were told that magic doesn't exist. Anything you witness as phenomenal is reduced to a being a trick or a fluke. Worse yet, if individuals express themselves as having a special gift, they're not only ridiculed and dismissed, but some have been hunted, persecuted, even killed. It's understandable that you'd think yourself incapable, but that doesn't make you right. What's more, your perceptions of your given circumstances greatly affect your thoughts, which shape your chosen reality. But the thing is, and this is *the* thing, you don't believe you have control over any of it. You do, though. It's just a matter of changing your beliefs."

"You make it sound like it's so easy," Sam countered slightly dissatisfied. "A person just has to change their *entire belief system*, forget every single reaffirming life experience, and simply choose to see their reality in a completely brand new way."

"Who says it's hard?" she replied with an unapologetic shrug.

"I can think of a few billion people who might back me up on this," he answered. "It's complicated for me to entertain much less believe, and I've seen you do it!"

"All of life is a series of choices," she continued. "If you can choose your intent, your belief, your sincere expectation... I think you'd be shocked to find what you're truly capable of."

Sam merely stared at her in wonder as he felt her patience and sincerity with every word she spoke.

Maven smiled fondly and kissed him. "You'll get there," was all she said before laying her head back down onto his warm chest.

"Get where exactly?" he questioned as his hand found itself strumming up and down her spine.

"You'll get to the point where you believe in yourself more than you believe in me," she replied simply and sensed his mix of astonishment and disbelief. "Personally, I don't know why you're surprised. You always seemed pretty magical to me," Maven stated through her smile.

"Me? How so?" He asked, somewhat incredulously.

"I'd never felt the type of immediate chemistry or connection that we had," she said thoughtfully. "It felt more like... recognition. And that seemed like a magic even I didn't dream existed."

While lost in thought, Sam once more continued to twirl her soft curly hair between his fingers.

"Maven?" he spoke after a brief quiet.

"Hmm?" she replied.

"I love you," he said.

"I love you back," she answered through a wide grin.

"I would have waited through an eternity for you," he confessed sincerely.

"I know the feeling," she related frankly. "I very nearly did for you."

In that quiet moment, Maven found her peace.

CHAPTER EIGHTEEN

The midday sun's rays were beating through the edges of the curtains covering the window by the time Sam started to wake. Rolling over from his side, he reached out to place a hand on Maven but only found rumpled sheets and a dented pillow. Her absence jolted him back to reality. Sitting upright, he scanned the empty room, and a flash of panic ran through him. He sprung from the bed and scrambled for his clothes on the floor.

Whoa, buddy. Take it easy, Maven's voice Read to him.

Unsteadied by the abrupt access of his mind, Sam sat back down on the bed. He could feel her uneasy calm but knew she wasn't in any kind of jeopardy. Not sure of how to respond, he sensed the lull in their communication. Maven picked up on his uncertainty.

It's just like a normal conversation, she coached. *You can still think whatever you want but focus on the words you want to be delivered. Try to imagine yourself actually speaking those sentences.*

Sam's eyelids crept shut as he concentrated. He pictured his mouth forming the words he wanted to send.

Where are you? he asked, looking around the room again.

Nicely done, she mentally applauded. *We're in the kitchen. Are you hungry?*

Starving, he answered flirtatiously.

From two floors up, he could tell she was smiling.

Well, if you would like to drag your lazy butt out of bed, we're eating lunch, she replied.

Not what I meant, he inwardly mumbled as he stood and picked up his jeans from the floor.

I heard that, she informed.

You were absolutely supposed to, he laughed.

Dressed, Sam descended the stairs to join the others. In the kitchen, he found the three women talking as they ate their food. Maven sat on a barstool at the counter with her back to him but turned her head over her shoulder before he made a noise. Lila and Sabine stood next to each other on the opposite side of the dark granite and followed her gaze. He happily nodded hello while he walked into the room. The smile

Maven already had pasted on had been fooling the other two, but Sam could feel her internal turbulence. Reaching the stool, he swiveled her seat around to face him. Leaning forward, he placed his hands on the cool countertop on either side of Maven. Their noses were a few inches apart.

"Uhhh, hi," Sabine chirped playfully.

"Good morning, ladies," Sam spoke to them but didn't take his eyes off Maven.

"Good afternoon," Maven teased.

Grinning as he felt her turmoil abate slightly with his presence, he inclined his head a little farther towards Maven. She didn't budge a millimeter. He could tell she was allowing him the lead. Spying over the top of her hair, he readily discerned from Lila's and Sabine's slack-jawed expressions that she hadn't shared any of the details from the previous night. Enjoying their surprise, he tapped his fingers across the smooth surface. Hearing his ring clinking on the stone, Maven's smile finally touched her eyes. Her cheer over the dull sound led Sam to plant his lips against hers in a long, drawn-out kiss.

A long whistle came from across the room. They disregarded it. A deep voice cleared his throat. Sam pulled apart from Maven and looked to his right. Both of the other men had entered the kitchen.

"I didn't realize this was an appropriate time to be

making out," Talmadge mocked Sam with his own words.

"It's always the right time to kiss your girl," Sam quipped, uptight at his very presence.

Talmadge ignored Sam's quote. He stood at the counter farthest apart from the group and folded his arms, but when Lila strolled to his side, he automatically opened them to her. Eldon ducked beneath the two men's icy glares at each other to get to Sabine. Sam only looked down after absorbing Maven's growing apprehension. Suspicion, dread, and fury stormed inside of her, but, beyond the slight flush in her cheeks, her bland exterior deceived any who saw. Without needing the stoke, Sam realized she didn't trust him either, and his anger grew.

"You shouldn't be here," Sam spouted.

"I think out of everyone in this room, you might, in fact, be the odd man out," Talmadge argued.

Opening his mouth to hurl his wrath, Maven placed a hand on Sam's stomach. Glancing at her, she cautiously shook her head.

Please, don't, she Read.

Maven, he needs to be handled. If you won't deal with this, I will, he replied hotly.

The directionality of her irritation suddenly spun around to Sam. It caused him to take a long step backward.

"May I see you upstairs, please?" she snapped as she leaped off the stool and left for their room without another word.

Stunned, he looked to Eldon for some form of understanding or even solidarity.

"Witches, man," Eldon shrugged his shoulders.

"You should probably go talk to her," Talmadge recommended indifferently as he cleaned his nails.

Sam's rage boiled, but his concern for Maven was greater. Fuming but silent, he walked out and followed her footsteps back to the top floor. The door to their room was half-open. Once inside, he shut it behind him. Maven darted back and forth across the floor. Her emotions were so numerous and frenzied that he had to lean his back on the wall for balance.

Are you trying to piss off Talmadge? Provoke him? You know he could snap your neck by blinking, right? she Read without looking at him.

I'm trying to help us, he replied weakly.

She halted mid-stride. Seeing his feeble expression, she strained her eyes while isolating her thoughts. Sam visibly strengthened with her effort to compartmentalize. Still leaning, she stood in front of him and laid her forehead on his shoulder.

"I'm sorry," she sighed.

"Stop apologizing," he spoke softly as he stroked her cheek. "Are you okay?"

Without answering, Maven's head shot up and instinctively looked to the window. Walking over, she used one finger to peek out behind the curtains. Sam felt her heartache. Shaking her head in disbelief, she stared outside.

There he goes, she Read as she let out a punch of air.

Taking action, Maven ran to the bed. Ramming her arms into her jacket sleeves briskly, she picked up and shoved Sam's jacket into his hands. Pushing him towards the door, her resolution steeled over him. With her drive immediately tenacious, he was ready to act.

We're leaving. Now. Quietly, tell the others it's time to go. I'll meet you back downstairs, she Read quickly, leaving no room for argument.

Releasing his arm, Maven started to the window, but Sam grabbed her wrist and yanked her back to him. Hastily, he kissed her then unwillingly let her go. She ran back and separated the curtains. He opened the door to head down the stairs.

Sam?

"Yeah?" he asked aloud.

Keep her inside, she stated soberly.

He understood. As he watched Maven climb over the sill, Sam braced himself for a battle with Lila.

CHAPTER NINETEEN

Standing motionless on the balcony, Maven watched his tall frame hike the last length of the long, narrow yard. Nearing the edge of the lawn, he ducked beneath the low-hanging branches of a large hardwood and disappeared from view. Regardless, her eyes bored through the dying leaves as she affixed her mind to her target. Despite her emotional chaos, her thoughts were steady. Waiting, she hoped against hope for it all to be an atrocious misreckoning on her part. But then, in the subtle breeze, she sensed precisely what she anticipated: a beacon. Rejecting the stinging hurt, Maven fortified her heart. Effortlessly, she Flew off her perch and landed silently on the grass behind her unfathomed enemy.

Inside, Sam skipped half the stairs as he rushed back down to the others. Barreling into the kitchen, he found Sabine and Lila finishing their lunch. They knew from his approach that something was very wrong.

"What is it? What's happened?" Lila immediately asked.

"Where's Maven?" Sabine spoke on top of her.

"She's fine, but she said it's time to go. Right now. Sabine, go tell Eldon," he drilled out his words.

Not needing further explanation, both girls headed towards the steps. Unseen by Sabine, who hustled to the second floor, Sam blocked Lila's advancement. Without thinking of anything apart from warning Talmadge, she attempted to sidestep around him. He moved with her. At a loss, she glared up at him.

"Move," Lila barked.

Sam's face frowned with pity, but his stance didn't sway. Her eyes burned.

"Move!" she yelled and tried sliding passed him again.

Being quicker than he expected, she got by half-way. He reached out and loosely gripped her thin wrist.

"I'm so sorry," he spoke in all sincerity as he maneuvered her other arm into his free hand.

Laboring madly to break his hold, she understood

the meaning of his apology. She started to cry hot tears of indignation.

"He didn't do what you think," she wailed. "He loves her, Sam! He would never do anything to hurt her, and she knows that!"

Lila's faithful words and blatant suffering just about shattered his resolve. He wanted to console her, but he knew nothing he said could possibly comfort her when he was the one thing preventing her from defending her Bonded partner from Maven. All at once, Sam's fix on her skin released as his body was tackled into the far wall.

"What the *hell* do you think you're doing?"

Noiseless, Maven stood unnoticed under the tree limbs. Discreetly, she cleared her throat.

"Eldon," she addressed him as he whipped his head around in alarm.

"Gods, Maven. You scared me. I didn't hear you walk up," he spoke, agitated.

"That's probably because I didn't walk," her voice was frigid.

"Oh, right," he inferred her words.

"You know what's impressive?" she asked rhetorically. "You found Sam and me, even when Lila couldn't pinpoint us."

He looked embarrassed at her transparent denunciation.

"Do you think that could have had anything to do with the fact that I Shielded myself from Searching when I was a teenager and Sam over a decade ago?" she questioned with feigned curiosity.

The awkward quiet fell immediately between them. Maven settled evenly in her stance. Eldon shifted his weight from one foot to another. Inspecting him thoroughly, she scrutinized every inch of his body. She found his handsome features repugnant. The twinkle that normally reflected in his blue eyes fell dull and flat. She was grateful for how rapidly her profound affection for her friend consumed itself. In its place was an eager hostility.

"You definitely were unpredicted," she spoke unexcitedly. "They chose well."

His face showed very little surprise at her comment.

"Or did you volunteer?" she inquired.

PUSHING himself up from the cold tile, Sam tried to shake out the cloud in his sight and the buzzing in his teeth, but that seemed to make both worse. Dancing in front of him were four blurred sets of Lila and Talmadge. He blinked until only one couple came into view. He groaned as he stood.

"Touch her again, and you'll know what your spleen tastes like," Talmadge's threat rang in Sam's already ringing ears.

"Where's Maven?" both men asked simultaneously.

Talmadge looked up from examining Lila's reddened wrists. "What do you mean? Is she not upstairs?"

"She went out of the window in our room. I thought she was going after you for being a traitor," he spoke candidly with no time to mince words. Motioning to Lila, "She told me to keep her inside."

"She specifically said me?" Lila was dumbfounded.

"She said..." Sam stopped himself realizing the mistake in his assumption. "Where's Sabine?"

Folding her lashes, Lila Searched.

"Better question: Where's Eldon?" Talmadge countered.

"I can't... I can't find any of them," she faltered.

Anxious, all three took off for the stairs. At the landing, Talmadge Flew to the top story as Sam and Lila ran to the second. Separated, they looked through every room. Lila found her in the master bedroom at the back of the middle floor.

"She's here," Lila called out to the others.

Stationed at the bay window, Sabine was riveted to the view in the backyard. She squinted. Sam and Talmadge joined Lila at the door.

"I can't Read Eldon," Sabine turned to them with a worried scowl, "and he's... terrified."

The three faces at the door glanced at each other with disheartened knowing looks. Sabine was bothered by their hidden understanding.

"Stop. What aren't you saying?" she demanded.

None of them knew how nor wanted to articulate the thought, yet each stepped forward to shoulder the responsibility. Lila, however, spoke up first.

"Sabine, it was Eldon," she delicately answered as she walked to her friend.

"What was Eldon?" she asked defiantly.

"He was the one who led Kendrich to us," Sam replied much more placidly than he felt at the memory.

"You don't know that," Sabine breathed heavily.

"But Maven does," Talmadge gently returned.

"So, that makes it law?" she yelled.

They understood her outrage; none of them could bear the thought of their own partner being the cause of so much malice. But they knew Maven, and even with the holy mess of recent events, they trusted her implicitly.

"No," Sabine shook her head with denial. "No!"

Pushing passed Lila, Sabine charged towards the door. Again, Sam made himself a barrier between a witch and her love. She shoved him as hard as she could over and over without him moving. Frustrated at the wall of a man, she started to slap and kick and punch at any part of his body she could make contact with. Sam took every blow freely. As she pounded her fists against his chest, she started to weep. Her beating died down with every sob. Soon, she was fighting for her breath. Talmadge came to her side. Cautiously, he placed his arms around her in a hug. Sabine drooped into his embrace.

ELDON's and Maven's eyes briefly shot to the middle window of the house then back to one another.

"So, you do feel. You just don't care," she spat. "Why, Eldon?"

Her question physically pained her.

"Maven, I didn't know," Eldon spoke simply.

"Didn't know what?" she flared. "What information could you possibly have not known that would excuse *anything* you've done?"

"Any of it," he pleaded. "I didn't know the truth about The War, about The Families, the warlocks. And I had no clue--"

"So, what?" she stopped him short. "You just Read out a signal of our location to let the others know it's bad to have genocidal tendencies?"

"I had no clue, Maven," he continued, "no clue that they were going to kill Liam."

Without lifting a finger, she Flew Eldon into the solid, brick fence. "You..." she hissed, "do not... say *his* name."

Climbing back to his feet, Eldon began again, "I swear I didn't know they were going to kill him, Maven! I swear!"

"But they did!" she yelled. "And you *still* helped them! You still led them to this realm, to Sabine, to me, to your best friends. After they *beat me* within an inch of my life, you still sent a beacon to bring them here. There's nothing you can say that justifies any single one of your actions."

As she spoke her last word, the fear in Eldon's eyes shone. In a panic, he took off sprinting back towards the house. Maven shook her head in exasperation. She lifted her hand in midair, and Eldon halted in his tracks. With a flick of her eyes, Eldon was again slammed against the fenced wall.

Splayed out against the brick, he couldn't move any

of his appendages. His bearded chin writhed under the ghostly bridle across his neck.

"Maven," he croaked out through a tightened larynx, "I'm sorry."

"Better yet, you say nothing at all."

Bringing her middle finger and thumb together near Eldon's throat, she pulled them back through the air. A string of pale pink light came from between his lips. Flicking her fingers off to the side, the light splattered like water droplets and vaporized before hitting the ground.

You know what's next, she confirmed his suspicion.

Slamming her angry eyes closed Maven Read Eldon's memories. Starting with the most recent of her face as she stole his voice, she flipped through his private moments and thoughts in reverse. Every secret, every whisper, every cohort, and hidden agenda seeped from his mind and was duplicated into her own. Days, months, years whipped by. Each answer she found only left her asking another question. Needing more, she didn't relent. His life zoomed by in flashes. Maven realized his motive for the drive of his participation went further back than she anticipated. Decades merged into centuries. She had never Read so much of a single person's life. Her mind spun dizzyingly, but she continued reaching further into his past. Suddenly, she was at the end, which was Eldon's beginning. Her eyes blazed as they shot open.

"All of this," she snarled through heavy breath, "because you felt weak? You didn't have *enough* power? You want for nothing in Loremara! With all the humble creatures in all of the endless realms, and you still thought you deserved more! You mistook your greed for entitlement, you miserable, cowardly wizard bastard."

Eldon's face was pallid and drained from her Read. The little give in her bindings allowed his head the tilt slightly to the side. Maven emptied the space between them. Edging her face near his, she clenched her fists. Wanting nothing more than to destroy him, she had to consciously bottle her rage.

"Well, if you thought you were weak before..." With her mind, she caused Eldon's left arm to rotate and straighten until his fingers stretched out as if to shake hands. Palm to palm, she firmly gripped his hand.

Eldon shook his head and looked away, understanding her intent.

"Your people may have invented the siphon," she whispered, inches away from his face, "but it was mine that perfected it."

Keep away from the windows. Do not let her see this, Maven Read to Sam, Talmadge, and Lila.

A searing bright light shot out in every direction from under the tree. The ground rumbled deeply and rapidly built into a booming roar. Suddenly, a giant blast blew through the neighborhood. Glass shattered, and car alarms blared as the ground shook. Then, as quickly as it came, the light was gone, and silence befell the backyard.

The scream that Sabine let out pierced Maven to her soul. Releasing Eldon's hand, she wiped away her fallen tear. His head lolled limply. Wistfully, she floated his body down to lie on the grass under the tree. Steeling herself once more, she trudged back to the house.

In the living room, she found silent despair. Despite the fact that it was covered in shards of glass, Sabine sat on the couch crying. Hovering around her were the other three. Sensing Maven, Sam turned and instantly had his arms wrapped around her. His relief at her presence was immense.

"Are you okay? What happened? What was that?" Sam rattled off his questions.

"Did you kill him?" Sabine spoke clearly even through the hands that hid her face.

Maven dropped her touch on Sam. "No," she delivered tightly.

"Where is he, then?" she asked between stuttered sobs.

"Eldon stays behind," Maven replied as she maintained her tenuous composure.

Sabine broke down.

"We have to leave. This will draw everyone's attention, human or otherwise," Maven spoke authoritatively.

The room's concentration was on Sabine's sorrow, but none were unaffected by the betrayal of Eldon.

Maven tried to swallow her guilt. "We need to go," she urged.

Even without their acting empathy, the anguish in each person rebounded through the room. Talmadge scooped Sabine up off the couch. Following the others' lead, he carried her away in his arms.

CHAPTER TWENTY

With Maven guiding, Sam followed while Lila and Talmadge, with Sabine in his arms, brought up the rear. Crowds were already forming along the sidewalks as they hurried away from the home and down the street. Weaving through the people, they heard murmurs about earthquakes and blown transformers. Keeping a brisk pace, the group was a couple of blocks away by the time police cars zoomed passed them with sirens blaring. Everyone kept their heads forward and their eyes down.

Eventually, Sabine's composure returned, and she quietly wormed out of Talmadge's clutch. She fell in line behind him, using his body as a buffer between herself and Maven. Even with countless thoughts and questions in their minds, no one spoke for quite a while. The sun arced its path across the sky as Maven wordlessly serpentined her way through Manhattan. Wanting to keep moving and in as public of places as possible, she avoided subways and any empty streets. Perceiving Maven's desire to be left alone but also her overwhelming burdens, Sam would occasionally place a hand on her shoulder to remind her of the support behind her. It wasn't until they neared the bridge hours later that Sam caught up to her while stopped at a crosswalk.

"We're going back to Brooklyn?" he asked.

"Yes," she replied as she watched the illuminated orange hand transformed into a white body.

Taking Maven's hand as they crossed the road, Sam let her know he was through giving her space. She gladly accepted it. On the other side of the street, he paused at the corner of the building and waited for the others to gather.

"I think we should stop. Get something to eat maybe," Sam suggested. "Talk about what's next."

"Shouldn't we keep moving?" Lila's face panned around paranoid.

"If you couldn't Search for one of us in the next room at that house, I doubt they could find us out here, right?" Talmadge directed the last word to Maven.

Maven nodded. "I Shielded the rest of you when I placed the Protection after we landed."

"Okay, then. Let's find a restaurant," Sam encouraged.

"I don't think anyone is particularly hungry," Maven voiced.

"Good. I'd rather we all get a drink anyway," Sam answered and started down the street in pursuit of a bar.

A block later, they all filed into a dive. The low ceilings, dark décor, and dim lighting made the mostly-empty space feel oddly comforting. It smelled of booze and whatever cleaner had recently been used to wipe down the tables. An old country song with too much twang played low in the background. Choosing a booth at the back of the narrow room, Maven slid in on one side of the deep red, cracked vinyl while Lila and Sabine took up the other. Talmadge grabbed a chair from a nearby table and sat at the end. Sam came over with a tray of glasses and two pitchers of beer. He poured each of their drinks.

"Is that how you knew? That it was Eldon, I mean," Talmadge picked up from their brief conversation outside.

"Yes," Maven took care to avoid Sabine's face. "Well, when I assumed I knew."

"When were you certain?" Talmadge continued after taking a hefty swig.

Despite the obvious tension, Maven knew answers were necessary for everyone's sake.

"He tried sending out a signal of where we were from the backyard," she replied plainly.

"Tried?" Lila questioned.

"I had done a kind of reverse Shield on him. It kept his talents available but confined to closed quarters," Maven explained.

"When?" Sabine whispered without looking up.

Maven tensed at the sound of her. "Last night. When Lila said he had been the one to find us."

"But when?" Sabine asked again. Her eyes remained on the same spot in her lap.

"When I kissed him," Maven admitted. "I needed to touch him to Create it."

Sabine said nothing.

"Why didn't you just Seal off his powers right then?" Sam wanted to keep the conversation moving.

"Because I... I wanted to be certain, to give him a chance to prove me wrong," Maven's tone was brittle.

"What did you do to him?" Sabine's ordinarily soft voice bristled.

"I stole his voice... siphoned his gifts... Shielded his memories," Maven paused, "and Read his life."

"You Read his *life?*" Lila spoke up, stunned. "His entire life?"

"Yes," Maven could only manage to look at the stained water ring on the wood table.

Sam put his hand on her knee.

"What I don't understand," Talmadge started but chewed his lower lip as he decided on the right words. "Forgive me, Sabine, but how did you not know?"

Everyone except Maven stared at Sabine, awaiting an explanation. Still not looking at anyone, she stood up.

"You don't need me to explain. You Read his life," she muttered without addressing Maven directly.

Walking away, she disappeared into the women's restroom. Expectantly, they looked to Maven.

"They, um," uncomfortable, she stammered, "they weren't Bonded."

"What?" Talmadge's head jerked backward. "Of course they were. They've been together for almost seventy years!"

"No, it wasn't... they didn't," Maven squirmed with sharing someone else's intimate details. "They hadn't consummated their union."

Sighing, Talmadge said, "Eldon led me to believe they had."

"He lied about a lot of things to a lot of people, Tal," Maven told him.

"Clearly," was all he replied.

In the bathroom, Sabine washed her hands and splashed cold water on her face in the cleaner of the two sinks. Patting her skin dry with paper towels, the door opened noisily and squeaked closed. Looking in the mirror, she saw Maven's reflection standing a few feet behind her. Turning around to face her, Sabine's throbbing misery flamed. After a moment, she abruptly crossed the floor and slapped Maven across the face. Maven hadn't flinched or made an effort to prevent it. She only lifted her hand and rubbed the back of her fingers over her cheek. Out of respect, or maybe guilt, she didn't Heal the sore area.

"You should have told me," Sabine choked up as she stepped backward.

"Sabine, I--" Maven started.

"Do not apologize to me," she cut her off.

"I wasn't going to," Maven said circumspectly. "I did what I know was best for the group, what needed to be done to keep us safe."

"Why are you in here, then?" Sabine blustered.

"Because I wanted you to know that no matter what happens between us, and no matter how much you hate me right now," Maven took a breath to steady herself, "I will still be there for you. Always."

"You should have told me. Before." Sabine disregarded Maven's words altogether.

"I couldn't risk it," Maven's troubled eyes expressed her ever-present internal dilemma of who to tell what and when.

After a long break, Sabine finally said, "I understand that you did the right thing. I do. But I still don't know how to forgive you for it."

"I know," Maven sadly acknowledged and nodded.

At an impasse, they both swallowed back immeasurable emotions.

"There's more you need to hear, though," Maven spoke as she turned and opened the door.

Sabine walked through without another prompt, and Maven followed. Making their way back to the booth, their friends watched on conspicuously. Taking their seats, Sam eyed Maven's red cheek. She felt his curiosity above his concern but addressed neither.

"What I stopped explaining when I left to get you," Maven filled in Sabine, "was how you were kept unaware."

"I know why," Sabine implied what they already knew. "And I'm an idiot."

"No, you don't, and no, you're not," Maven stated. "Both Kendrich and Eldon targeted you because you're close to me, but you're also the most impressive Reader of any witch or wizard I have met. Ever. What you're not realizing is that the cause for your hesitation in completing your Bond was, in fact, your intuitive talent."

"How so?" Lila asked for Sabine, who didn't want to accept the compliment.

"She picked up on something that was off with Eldon," Maven explained. "He knew but had no way of hiding it. He never even needed to before Sabine. When I Read him, I kept finding impaired memories and diluted interpretations. Someone else had clearly Shielded certain happenings. I knew his motive was to gain more powerful gifts, but I couldn't get an understanding of what initially spurred him into it all. That's why I went back through his entire existence. And what I found... Eldon is a Second Son."

Unimpressed with her explanation and not comprehending the stupor it put the others into, Sam asked, "What does that mean? I'm gathering more than he has an older brother."

"It has nothing to do with siblings, you're right," Maven confirmed. "A Second Son is a child that's born from a witch or wizard that has previously already Bonded with another."

"I thought you mated for life?" Sam's eyebrows crept together.

"Exactly," Talmadge shook off his astonishment. "They've always been a myth."

"Like warlocks?" Sam sincerely wondered.

"No," Maven responded. "We had a place in their history then disappeared. In all my years, I've never known a soul who knew of the existence of a dishonored Bond much less a progeny of one. Sam, look at us, this." She pointed to herself then him. "Knowing what you do now and feeling it wholly, how easy would it be to leave me and have a child with another woman?"

Sam could not move beyond the emotion that her question stirred, much less fathom the words to express it. Feeling his near-delirium, Maven held his hand under the table.

"Impossible, right?" she asked gently.

He only nodded in response.

"And that's after a *day*. Imagine after a lifetime," Lila added thoughtfully.

"Who? Who could possibly ever...?" Talmadge aimed his muttered question at Maven, but his eyes were lost on Lila.

"That's the real kicker," Maven answered, piqued. "He supposedly died when I was just a few hundred years old, but it turns out Niklas was around at least long enough to father Eldon."

CHAPTER TWENTY-ONE

"What? How could that even be possible?" Talmadge gripped his glass so tightly it looked like it was on the verge of fracturing.

"That's what I intend to find out," Maven responded as she removed the drink from his fingers.

Scanning the room, Maven found a clock behind the bar. "We need to get a cab. The rendezvous is in less than an hour, and we don't have time to walk."

"Where is it at?" Sam asked as they all slid out of the booth and stood.

"Prospect Park," she answered.

OUT OF THE taxi and once more on foot, Maven marched towards their intended meeting place.

Holding hands, Sam was next to her. Lila and Sabine were in the middle with arms linked, and Talmadge tailed them all. The sun began its slow decline towards the horizon. Its light glittered between the multi-colored changing leaves above them on either side as they made their way along the paved trail. The beautiful autumn weather accounted for the multitudes of patrons that day scattered around the park. The large attendance ebbed Maven's anxiety, but she was still wary of each person they passed. Sam lightly squeezed her fingers and smiled down at her for morale.

They descended as the path turned into several stairs. At the bottom of the steps stood a monument encircled by a low, swirling wrought-iron fence. A white, polished granite column stood high over their heads on top of a marble pedestal. Fixed atop the column was a bronze Corinthian capital with a marble ball resting above it. Sam recognized the memorial that honored the Maryland 400. As they studied it, each absorbed its haunting inscription:

Good God! What brave fellows I must this day lose.

From the monument looking out, they saw they were standing on a little hill. There was a small clearing in the trees that showed other trails across the grass from them. One continued out towards a short bridge that crossed the lake. Another led left and right through the park. Maven made no motion to move.

"What exactly are we hoping to gain from meeting with these warlocks?" Talmadge asked as he shoved his hands into his jacket pockets.

"Information," Maven replied absentmindedly as she scanned their surroundings.

After a long silence, Talmadge understood she wasn't going to offer any explanations she didn't deem necessary. "Now, what?" he questioned.

"Now, we wait and hope someone shows," Maven returned.

OVER AN HOUR LATER, everyone in the group, except Maven, grew restless. Even Sam, who could feel her confidence, couldn't sit still. Nearing sunset, they finally voiced their concern.

"I don't think anyone is coming," Lila expressed.

"No, they're not coming," Maven agreed, standing motionless.

"Then, why are we still here?" Sabine's tone bordered on chafed.

"Because they're already here," she replied. "They arrived before we did. They've been sussing us out."

At her clarification, they each stood and gathered

closer to one another. Slowly turning and glancing around, none of them could see anyone else in the near distance.

"Don't worry," Maven assured them. "They aren't going to hurt us. They want to make certain you're not here to hurt them."

In the fading light, a silhouette could be seen crossing the bridge in their direction.

"Wait here," Maven spoke as she started across the grass.

"Maven," Sam objected, but she continued down to the trail.

They watched as she met the then visible man halfway. He and Maven embraced. Sam's initial reaction was jealousy, but sensing her calm for the first time beat it back completely. On the hill, her friends impatiently viewed her silent interaction. Even in the distance, they could see Maven lift her left hand near the man's face. He held her hand midair then rolled his head exaggeratedly. After a moment, she took his arm and led him back towards the monument.

"These are my friends, Talmadge, Lila, and Sabine," Maven pointed to each as she went down the lineup, "and this is Sam. My partner," she bragged through her smile. "Everyone, I'm pleased to introduce you to my very dear, very old friend, Cassius."

Standing a couple of inches taller than Maven, he

had an average build. He had handsomely quaffed wavy, chin-length, black hair and golden olive skin, which made his turquoise eyes pop even brighter. His full lips vied with Sabine's but did not smile at Maven's introductions. Seeing his face then recalling their hug, Sam's jealousy hoisted slightly. Maven notably removed her hand from Cassius's elbow. Beyond that, no one budged. Cassius eyed them suspiciously as they reciprocated in kind.

"Bonded to a human and standing side by side with witches and wizards," Cassius shook his head. "You have always been a uniquely remarkable warlock, haven't you?"

"I take that as a compliment, Cash," Maven replied graciously.

"Might as well," he sighed. "Shall we get indoors before the bugs start to bite?"

"That sounds excellent," Maven answered him. "Don't panic," she spoke to her group.

Before they could ask why, eight other men and women surrounded them. Cassius extended a hand for Maven to share the lead with him, but she declined and stood with her friends. Shrugging, he showed the way as they were herded through, and then out of the park.

CHAPTER TWENTY-TWO

Several blocks away, they were ushered through a side door under a neon blue sign that read "Shahzad Repairs" and into a large auto body shop. Cassius steered them past several cars in a varying array of conditions. The garage smelled mildly of oil and rubber. It was so quiet that their footsteps echoed off the high ceilings. At the other end of the vast room was a door that merged into the front offices and public entrance. Off to the side of the door, a set of stairs led to a private area with broad windows that overlooked the entire lower floor.

"Isolde?" Cassius glanced around the bodies in front of him.

"Excuse me," a small voice came from behind Sam, and an even smaller hand touched his back as she spoke.

Sam sidestepped, and he was amazed to see a short, Asian girl that he hadn't even noticed before. Looking at her, he was taken aback. Everyone surrounding him appeared youthful, but her face seemed downright young.

"Thank you," she replied sweetly as she walked to where Cassius and Maven stood at the foot of the steps.

"Izzy," Maven breathed relief as she bent down to hug her.

"My darling Mavey girl," Isolde's voice held a personal comfort for Maven that Sam was curious to know more about.

"Where were you hiding?" Maven grinned widely down at her friend.

"Through the looking glass," Isolde returned the smile.

"If you wouldn't mind, would you please make our guests comfortable upstairs, and then join us in the conference room?" Cassius requested as the two released each other from their tight hold.

"Of course," Isolde answered cheerily.

She gestured politely for Maven's companions to head up the stairs. Their uncertain eyes looked to Maven for guidance.

Go ahead, she Read to the four of them. *There is a great deal I need to discuss with my people, but I'll be up soon.* Still hesitant, she added, *Believe me, we are, without a doubt, the safest we have been since landing in Tartooc.*

Trusting in her words, Talmadge acquiesced and began climbing the steps. They filed by, their shoes clanking against the metal, with Sam bringing up the rear. Behind his back, Isolde pointed to Sam and looked at Maven. Biting her lower lip and fanning herself with one hand, she then gave a conspiratorial, approving thumb up. Maven couldn't contain her guffaw, causing Sam to turn. Isolde composed herself before he saw. Maven winked at him as Isolde shooed him up the stairs.

The warlocks made their way to a beige conference room on the bottom floor. Depositing themselves into high-backed, black leather chairs around the long, oval table, Maven chose a seat close to the door. She recognized three more faces of past acquaintances: Noah, Andros, and Odette, that she knew to have been friends of her father's. Her respite was short-lived at the thought of all the news she must deliver. Immediately identifying her bereavement, the nerves of all those near her strained.

"What has happened?" a slender brunette she didn't know asked fearfully.

"No," Cassius spoke from the table's head. "We'll wait for Isolde."

The only sound in the room was a faint click as the thermostat turned over. A tense minute later, Isolde entered and took the empty chair between Maven and Cassius. She gave a sharp nod indicating the discourse should commence. Without another word, they all reached for the hands of those on either side of them. Maven closed her eyes as each set of clasped palms kindled. Concentrating, she Read them her memories beginning as her father's home came into view just those two nights ago. With the other warlocks boosting her ability, she rapidly replayed every detail from his death and up to the moment they met them in the park, excluding only those private moments with Sam. A collective gasp convulsed through the room as they finished reliving her retrospection.

Before opening her eyes, Maven anticipated the scene. A river of tears flowed around her through lamenting whimpers. She loosed the hand to her right, but Isolde did not disengage her left. Looking up at Maven, her wet, brown eyes channeled a staggering amount of love and woe. In turn, every person offered their sincerest and most heartfelt condolences. Refusing to cry again, Maven only briefly nodded as she cleared her throat.

"So, as you can see," Maven choked out, "we have some serious issues at hand."

"Is this an uprising? Or possibly a handful of

witches and wizards that could be dealt with ourselves?" Andros asked.

"How did Niklas live until just a few hundred years ago? Undetected," the same brunette questioned.

"Does he survive still?" Odette added.

Maven held up her hand to deflect their questions. "You have all the information that I do. I'm here to see what *you* know," she spoke.

"There have been rumors, nothing more than whispers mind you," a man Maven found familiar, but couldn't place, began, "of disappearances of warlocks throughout the ages since The War."

"How have I heard nothing of the sort?" Maven was aghast at the man's claim.

"You know how it's been since the Purge. With the last of the warlocks dispersed across all the realms and continually Jumping every few centuries to remain hidden, there was rarely any evidence that one had been somewhere in the first place and never any proof that one had been killed," the man replied.

"Maven, the majority of people's families haven't even been found yet. It's hard enough to search for warlocks we know to exist," Cassius explained.

"I'm well aware of the losses suffered," Maven's voice rasped. "What I don't understand is why you all chose to keep Liam and me in the dark. It very well may have cost my father his life!"

"After everything you two had survived, we wanted to spare you both," Isolde answered delicately. "Idle chatter and gossip weren't worth nullifying the lives you had rebuilt for yourselves."

"Izzy... you knew?" Maven doubted every syllable as she uttered them.

"It was my decision not to tell you," she responded firmly.

Maven had no words. She wanted to scream her frustrations and upturn the table and storm out, but she knew that anything done on her behalf by Isolde had been done solely for her benefit. It took time, but she controlled her breathing. Her melancholy stayed, but her anger was spent. Still holding her hand, Isolde rubbed her thumb over Maven's fingers.

"What's next?" Noah asked from the other end of the table.

"There is only one option: Jumping," Maven said solemnly. "The human realm is no longer safe to any warlocks or their allies who remain in it; they're on the hunt here. They at least have the small numbers I Read in Eldon's memories, but he clearly wasn't told much. We can only assume the worst from here on out, and I believe them to be amassing forces. It's time we come out of hiding and do the same."

As THEY DEPARTED the conference room, Maven found Sam sitting on one of the floral armchairs in the reception area outside its doors. She had felt him come downstairs after she had been told about the information that was kept from her. He stood as she said goodbye to all as they exited the building. Cassius and Isolde were the only ones who stayed.

"We'll be up in a second," she spoke to the warlocks.

Maven, what about him? Isolde Read her question carefully.

Does he know? Cassius asked, sad for his friend.

Not yet, she replied cautiously. *I'll deal with it.*

"You were upset," Sam stated his reasoning for being present while watching Cassius as he reluctantly walked away.

"Very," Maven said as she wrapped her arms around his waist and set her head against his chest.

Placing his arms around her, too, Maven relaxed into his hold. Sam could tell that was the calmest she had been since arriving in his world, and an irrational part of him was jealous that it came after spending time with Cassius. He could feel Maven smiling at his emotional response.

"Are you laughing at me?" he kidded.

"Yes," she nodded.

"Why?" he held her back to regard her expression.

"There was never any romance between Cash and me. Plenty of love but all of it platonic. Plus, he's not my type," Maven exaggerated her batted eyelashes.

"Oh, please. He's so pretty he's everyone's type, even mine," Sam snorted.

Maven laughed. "Trust me; I'm not his either. Besides, don't you think if he had been interested, he would've made his play sometime in the last, oh, three thousand years? Well before I Bonded?"

"I don't understand how anyone male, female, warlock, human, or otherwise could resist being attracted to you, Maven, but I'll drop it anyway," he answered genuinely.

She grinned at the sincerity she felt at the compliment, and he bent down to kiss her.

"How do you know them, Isolde and Cassius?" Sam asked.

"Cash and I grew up together. He's not even six years younger than I am, so we dealt with a lot of the same stuff at the same time before, during, and after The War. I didn't meet Izzy, though, until a few centuries after we left Loremara. She had lost her daughter, and I had lost my mom. We kind of adopted each other," she said reminiscently, "She really stepped up for me. Over the years, I went to her for everything. She was the one who convinced me to take a chance on you, actually."

"I knew I liked her," Sam smiled.

Beyond his joke, Maven felt his gratitude for Isolde's presence in her life.

"It blows my mind, though," he shook his head. "She really looks like a teenager."

"She's almost 1,200 years older than I am." Maven laughed at his shocked face. "Like I said, pal, it's all good genes."

Studying his handsome features, she was suddenly sad and hugged him close again. She wanted to forget everything else in all the worlds that had gone on and continued to happen. Soaking up her angst, he held her tighter.

"What's wrong?" he asked quietly.

"There's something I have to tell you," she whispered as she lost her fight against her tears.

CHAPTER TWENTY-THREE

Cassius and Isolde entered through the door with a plaque that read "Employees Only." The front room upstairs, where the other three awaited Maven's and Sam's return, was a break room. To the left, there was a single long counter with cupboards above and below. A microwave, coffeemaker, and fridge were the only appliances. The rest of the room was filled with a few circular tables and folding chairs, a beaten-up couch against the far wall with another door, and a worn-in recliner.

Talmadge stood as they entered. "Where are Maven and Sam?"

"They're downstairs. I think they needed a minute," Isolde silenced Cassius before he could reply to the brusque question. "We haven't been properly introduced. I'm Isolde. Izzy, if you like."

"I'm Lila," she spoke as she crossed the linoleum to take Isolde's hand. "That's Sabine," she pointed as Sabine meekly waved from the couch.

"Talmadge," his tone was much friendlier while his hand engulfed Isolde's. "Do you know how long they'll be?"

"I can't be certain, but I wouldn't think for too much longer," Isolde answered truthfully.

"Thank you," Talmadge replied.

"Maven has spoken very highly of you all over the years. She's very fortunate to count you as her friends," Isolde carried the conversation.

Cassius rolled his bright eyes and shook his head behind her as she spoke.

"Something to add, Cash?" Isolde asked sternly without turning around.

"Fortunate, Izzy? A lot of good it did her," Cassius blurted as he leaned against the countertop.

"Beg your pardon?" Lila challenged.

"Look what trusting your kind has gotten her, both then and now," Cassius defended.

"I think that's enough, Cassius," Isolde looked at him as she spoke then.

"No. Look at their faces, Izzy. They don't know a thing about her, and yet they claim to be Maven's nearest and dearest," he called out.

"We know her," Talmadge said coolly.

"You only know the bare minimum of what she's allowed you," Cassius corrected.

"What do you mean?" Talmadge earnestly inquired.

"Do you know how many lives she's saved, mine included? Do you know that either during The War or directly because of it, Maven lost every single member of her family? Aside from Liam, and now even him. Do you realize what she risked by bringing you here to keep you all safe? So, as you might understand, I am more than a little surprised not only at her willingness to trust any witch or wizard but especially at her *love* for a descendant of the one who actively laid waste on her life. Quite a testament of the woman, wouldn't you agree?" Cassius steamed.

Talmadge, Lila, and Sabine said nothing. They only absorbed his words as each grew lost in their thoughts.

A few minutes later, Maven and Sam entered the noiseless room.

"Whoa. You can almost smell the tension," Sam commented as he leaned against the wall between the door jam and the window.

"Everything alright?" Maven's eyebrows raised. She stood at the counter near the refrigerator.

"It's fine," Isolde answered.

"Well, let's get to it, shall we?" Maven dove in.

"The only feasible option is for everyone to leave Tartooc."

"Jump?" Talmadge voiced the question that all three thought.

Their concerned eyes were aimed at Sam, who gave a half-hearted smile.

"Maven, humans can't Jump," Lila urgently reminded her.

"Yes, I know," Maven swallowed down the hot grip at the back of her throat as she avoided everything except the floor. "He and I have already talked about it."

"What does *that* mean?" Talmadge wondered loudly.

"It means," Sam looked to Maven, "I told her to Jump with you. She needs to help take care of this, to finish it."

"But, Maven..." Sabine whispered from her seat.

"This was my decision to make, everyone," Sam interrupted. "Let's leave it at that."

Concluding the resoluteness of his immovable tone, no one pushed the issue. Still, it didn't prevent their hearts from weighing heavily.

"What else?" Talmadge offered the question in abatement to the room's growing bleakness.

"You three will go back to Loremara. I hate to involve you any further, but I am asking you to spread the truth about The War as far as it'll reach and to as many that will hear it," Maven implored.

"Of course," Talmadge didn't hesitate to say.

"Anything we can do, we will," Lila spoke from her partner's side.

"Of course," Sabine quietly echoed from the back of the room.

"Thank you," Maven sighed, "but it won't be as easy as that. Even having your memories Read will do you very little good, considering no tangible evidence of the warlocks innocence lies within them. You're going to meet resistance and a lot of it, especially from the Families." Her eyes settled on Talmadge at her last word.

"I'll make it known, Maven," Talmadge resolved.

She knew he would do everything within his power to do so, and she appreciated him greatly for that.

"Where will you and the warlocks go?" Lila asked.

"That, I'm afraid, I can't tell you. For your safety and ours, it's better that you don't know any more than you already do. If the wrong person were to Read your thoughts, we'd be finished before we began," Maven reasoned.

Sabine joined the others. "When will we see you again?" she questioned uneasily.

"I don't have an answer for that either," Maven dismally replied.

"Weeks? Years? Decades? Can you give us an estimate?" Lila's fret painted her entire body.

Maven shook her head. "I honestly can't say when it'll be safe for you to be near me again. Any of you."

Sabine and Lila looked to each other then to Sam, but Talmadge didn't stray from Maven's face.

"When?" Talmadge spoke gravely. "When do we Jump?"

"Since Maven destroyed the one you came through, our closest site is a few hours' drive upstate from here," Isolde explained.

"Why don't you make one here?" Sam inquired. "Why not Create one right now?"

"Building a Jump isn't that simple. It averages about a decade to cultivate that much energy between realms. It's not like opening a door; it's more like building a freeway from here to the moon," Isolde explained.

"The others are attending to what they must and readying for departure. Once they've returned, we'll caravan up," Cassius told them.

"We will most likely leave here very early morning. Through that door, there are a couple of bunk beds. There are this couch and recliner in here and also the couch and chairs downstairs. I know it's not ideal, and as impossible as it might seem, try to get some sleep at some point. We all have taxing days ahead of us," Isolde mothered.

"We'll be downstairs if you should need us," Cassius directed to Maven before he and Isolde took the stairs.

Awkward glances shifted around the room quickly. Speechless as they were, the numerous emotions from all colored each of the faces making them. It was a leaden moment before anyone spoke.

"Hours," Lila whispered. "We have hours left together."

Everyone's shoulders sunk a little deeper at the acknowledgment.

"Maven," Talmadge said quietly, "may I have a word with you, please? Privately."

"Let's walk," she replied as she motioned her head towards the steps.

As they exited, Talmadge closed the door behind them. At the bottom of the stairs, Maven slowly led them back across the long shop. She could tell he was having a difficult time choosing his words, which was so out of character for Talmadge that Maven was put even more on edge.

"I know it's a loaded question, but I'll ask anyway," Maven tried a smile. "What's on your mind?"

"I have always been proud of my lineage," he began. "The stories we were told growing up... Maven, those witches and wizards were my heroes. How they stood strong in the face of adversity, fought away those who preyed on the weak. I was proud because it was in my blood. I identified my family, past and present, as a major part of who I am."

She wanted to interrupt to relieve him of his guilt, but she knew that Talmadge was generally a man of few words. What he spoke, he needed to be heard, for his sake, if not for hers as well.

"Knowing what I do now, though, I've realized a lot about myself... and you." He stopped walking and faced Maven. "I know they're only words, and I know they'll never set things right or undo the wrongs, but on behalf of me and my line, I am eternally sorry for what those who came before me did."

"They're much more than words, Tal. Thank you," she breathed.

"I'm so sorry about your family," he added.

"I'm sorry about yours, too," she returned.

"One thing I did know long before any of this, Maven, was that we might not be blood, but you *are* my family. All those proud feelings I had were accurate, just misplaced; they belong to you. You're my hero... You're my sister," Talmadge spoke so earnestly he had to wipe away what almost became a tear.

Maven stepped forward and locked her arms around him. He held her steadfastly in return.

"Talmadge, I'm not sure I'll ever be able to fully explain neither the space you helped fill in my life nor my gratitude for having you for a brother," Maven answered heartfeltly.

"This feels a lot like a goodbye, kid," his voice cracked.

"No, it's not," she muttered with a cheek against his chest.

"It's not?" he sincerely questioned her.

She took a step back so she could look him in the eye.

"No," she repeated. "Goodbyes are forever. This is just a... see ya later."

"Well, I can't do this twice, so let me say it now." He cleared his throat. "I love you, you frustratingly brave, impetuous warlock."

"I love you, too, you overbearing, overprotective, meddlesome wizard," she replied with a smile.

"I'll see you soon," he spoke the promising words as he placed a hand out in front of him.

"Soon," she said as she extended her hand.

And they shook on it.

CHAPTER TWENTY-FOUR

From the break room window, with Sabine beside them, Sam and Lila observed their partners below as they made their way back across the garage arm in arm.

"Did you know she introduced me to Talmadge?" Lila asked reverently.

"I didn't," Sam looked at her.

"Ironically enough, Liam had tried to set them up first," she grinned at the memory. "But I guess they always knew they were meant to be mates of a different sort."

Sam watched as her smile faded into a hollow sulk.

"I am... beyond sad for Sabine, and Talmadge, and myself to be parted from our friend," Lila said softly, looking up at Sam, "but I mourn for the loss you and Maven will suffer."

"If there was some way we could bring you with us, I hope you know we would, Sam," Sabine took Lila's hand as she spoke.

Staring down at their faces, he was grateful they couldn't sense his feelings like Maven could. Their sincere sympathy was almost enough to wreck him. He was surprised that after only a couple of days, and despite their rocky introduction, he had genuinely grown attached to Maven's friends. He reached out and pulled both of them in.

"I know you would," he responded.

The door opened behind them, but they didn't turn.

"I thought I warned you about touching her again," Talmadge half-joked as he eyed their three-person hug.

"Worth it," Sam gave half a crooked smile as they released their embrace.

"Whatever they said, don't believe them," Maven kidded. "They would say anything to steal hugs from Liam, too."

"It wasn't stealing when he gave them willingly," Lila smirked.

"Ugh." Maven wrinkled her nose at the comment, which caused most of them a chuckle. "Alright, witches. You're up." She pointed to Sabine and Lila then headed for the door by the couch.

They followed her into the back room and shut the door. The tension between Sam and Talmadge was gone, but there was still something Sam wanted to say.

"About before, the arm in the throat, the things I said," he began.

"Don't sweat it," Talmadge stopped him. "It was honestly the first time I had respected you. So, don't apologize."

Sam nodded his understanding. "I also wanted to thank you. For saving us. And for being there for Maven when I couldn't."

Then, it was Talmadge who nodded his understanding.

IN THE SMALL, square room, two sets of bunk beds were nestled in the corners and sat a few feet apart. Lila and Sabine sat on one and Maven on the other. The springs lightly squeaked as they got comfortable.

"I know this isn't a conversation any of us expected to have, but like I told Tal, this isn't permanent. We'll see each other again," Maven attempted to smooth the distress before it built.

"Have you Seen us all together?" Lila desired.

"No," she answered.

"Then, you don't know," Sabine replied somberly.

"I have hope," Maven insisted. "I may not have answers or a deadline for you, but I will always have hope. I have learned a lot of hard lessons throughout my life — one of them being that it goes on. Despite every horrible thing that may or may not happen, whether we like it or not, with or without us, life goes on. And whether we spend those inevitable days miserable or happy is an active choice we're allowed. Tomorrow is coming and every day after, and I choose to spend those days with the deliberate hope of seeing my friends... my family again."

"I am going to miss you so much," Lila cried as she stood.

"Me, too," Maven rose to hug her.

After a moment, Sabine got to her feet as well. The other two opened their arms to her.

"I choose hope, Maven," Sabine whispered.

LATE INTO THE NIGHT, the five exhausted friends started to yawn and stretch their tired muscles in the folding chairs of the break room.

"I know we're all fighting it, but I think we should take what sleep we can get before we have to head out," Talmadge suggested halfheartedly.

"I think we should just have a slumber party," Lila joked.

"Oh, that there was a bed big enough," Maven teased.

Chair feet scraped the linoleum floor as they all reluctantly stood. Looking behind him, Talmadge flicked his fingers, and they heard the metal frames of the bunk beds clink together.

"You and Sam take the beds. We'll sleep downstairs," he spoke as he scooted his chair underneath the table.

"No, there are more of you..." Maven countered.

"Just, for once, don't argue," Talmadge cut her off.

"I don't always argue," Maven scoffed.

"You, right now, are arguing about not arguing." Talmadge raised his eyebrows in anticipation of her rebuttal.

Maven opened and closed her mouth as he proved his point.

"Thank you," she mumbled her resistant, albeit amused appreciation.

"C'mon," Talmadge motioned for Lila and Sabine.

A round of tired "good nights" was muttered out as they divided towards the two doors opposite each other.

As Maven latched the door shut, Sam ducked his head and sprawled out his bulky frame diagonally on the joined bottom bunks. He kicked off his shoes over the edge. Schlepping out of her boots, Maven crawled over the squeaky springs to lie next to him. Resting her head near his shoulder, she used his arm as her pillow and let out a long, billowy sigh. Bending his arm, he picked up one of Maven's curls and started twisting it around in his fingers.

Long night, she stated as her body melted against Sam's.

He didn't respond as he distractedly played with her hair. Maven lifted her head to see his face in the dimness.

What's wrong? she inquired at his contemplative quiet.

I can't help thinking you should Jump with them, he answered, both discouraged and with remorse.

She rested her chin on his shoulder. *I'm sending them home because it's the safest place for them. Having the truth spread about The War and the warlocks will eventually be vital, but for now, it's nothing more than an errand to keep them busy and out of harm's way. I wouldn't have them go if I thought for one second they'd be in any danger.*

No, I know that. Sam slightly angled his head to see her better. *I mean with all the other warlocks. I'm* scared *you'll regret staying behind when there's so much at stake elsewhere.*

Trust me, Sam, there is still more than plenty to be done here. It could take us decades or longer to locate and warn all the warlocks that reside in this realm, she Read truthfully.

I understand how paramount it is that everything coming up goes according to plan. I know what it could cost you if it doesn't. And I also know you wouldn't forgive yourself if you thought there was something more you could have done to prevent any wrongdoings from happening. I just... I don't want you to end up hurting worse than you already do or resenting me because of your decision to stay, as he spoke, his eyes searched hers for any hint of misgiving she might have.

The hardest decision I ever made, she explained, *was leaving you. The easiest has been choosing to stay. I'll do what I can from this world. If I am ever truly needed, Isolde will send word. But my place is here with you. Besides, this could go on for centuries, and I am going to spend every single second with you while I can.*

Maven could feel his rigidity unwind. Sam puckered his lips. She leaned over, met them with a sweet peck, and then rested her head back on his shoulder.

We should sleep, she advised.

Yeah, you're right, he agreed with a wide yawn.

They laid unmoving in the stillness with their sore eyes half-open.

"Forget it. I'll sleep when I'm dead," Sam said aloud as he rolled towards a giggling Maven to kiss her again.

CHAPTER TWENTY-FIVE

It seemed to Maven that as soon as she had fallen asleep, she was being nudged awake. Her eyelids felt like sandpaper as she tried to lift them.

"Babe, wake up. It's time to go," Sam's gruff morning voice whispered as his hand gently shook her ankle.

In the dark, her eyes struggled to focus against the harsh light beaming in from the opened door of their makeshift bedroom. She rolled over and found Sam at her feet. He was already dressed and sitting on the ledge of the mattress, tying his shoes.

"What time is it?" she grumbled.

He smirked as he remembered how grouchy Maven could be on little sleep. "It's almost two A.M.," he answered.

Feeling his amusement, she kicked him with her foot, which made him laugh.

Maybe I should *Jump with the others,* she threatened sleepily.

Sam grabbed her ankle and quickly slid her across the bed to where he sat. *You wouldn't dare,* he Read as he leaned down to kiss her good morning.

You're right. I tried that once. Couldn't make it stick, she teased in return.

Sitting up, Sam grabbed her shirt from the floor. He tried to toss it in her face as he stood, but she caught it midair with her mind and Flew it slowly to the bed.

"C'mon. No one likes a showoff," he shook his head.

Despite his words, Maven could feel how impressed he actually was. They both grinned.

"Get dressed," Sam asserted. "I'll be downstairs with the others. Waiting."

Closing the door to offer her privacy, he had slipped one arm in his jacket when he saw a dash of light at his feet from under the door behind him. Before he could turn around, he heard Maven exiting. Looking back, his eyes followed her as she walked from one side of the room to the other. She was fully dressed, and even her hair was tidied.

"C'mon. No one likes a rubbernecker," she imitated his tone.

"Mavey baby," Sam said with arched eyebrows, "I know I said you were worth waiting for, but I much prefer this."

"So, to be clear, some people *do* like a showoff?" She smiled as she held out her hand.

Crossing the floor, he accepted it. "Right now, I even love an exasperating one."

Taking the stairs down, they found the drowsy faces of their friends in the front office of the shop. It was clear that no one had gotten much sleep, if any at all.

"Good morning, all," Isolde called out from the front entrance.

Her chipper demeanor was welcomed by some and begrudged by others.

"Morning, Izzy," Maven reciprocated sluggishly.

"We're all set to go, if you are," Isolde glanced at each of them to check as they nodded their replies. "Okay, then."

At that, she turned and walked out the front door with the others in tow. Parked in front of the building were three identical black SUVs with dark tinted windows. Isolde climbed into the passenger seat of the opened door of the nearest vehicle.

"Is this everyone?" Maven questioned from the sidewalk.

"It is for now," Cassius answered from the driver's

side. "Some went on ahead earlier, and others will come later. Let's not tarry, Maven."

Climbing into the far back seat was Sabine, Maven, and Sam. Lila and Talmadge took the middle.

"How many are we, Cash?" Maven asked as the car pulled away from the curb.

"Including you five, there are seventeen of us traveling tonight," Cassius replied, looking at her from the rearview mirror.

Don't worry, Mavey. Our numbers are strong, Isolde Read from up front. *This is only the beginning.*

At Isolde's word, Maven didn't think on it longer.

"How far is the drive?" Lila wondered.

"It'll be a few hours," Cassius responded.

"You should all get the sleep now you didn't get earlier," Isolde again mothered kindly but fussier.

She was met without resistance that time. Their fatigue had finally caught up to them. As much as they could, everyone sunk down and got comfortable in their seats. Snug under Sam's arm, exhausted though she was, Maven couldn't shut her eyes. She watched as Cassius steered the vehicle towards Manhattan. Underneath the intermittent streetlamps, she committed to memory the entwined outline of Lila and Talmadge before her and Sabine's fragile profile leaned against the glass window on her left. Through the tunnels and past the tolls, she even attempted to memorize Isolde's elbow that occasionally poked out on the arm of her seat and the sliver of Cash's forehead visible in his mirror.

Headlights whizzed by on the interstate. A mild rain had begun drumming against the SUV. The tempo of the windshield wipers was hypnotic. They had crossed two state lines before Maven's head started to bob. When it fell, she jerked it upright. Sam stirred at the movement. He surveyed her as she fought and shook off sleep each time she started to doze. Touching her shoulder, she startled before gazing up at him with glassy eyes. Without any cue, he felt her unlock their mental dialogue.

What are you doing? His quizzical face spoke as loudly as the words he Read in her mind. *You need to rest.*

I'm trying to remember, she said in a haze.

Remember what? He asked.

Everything, she replied thoughtfully. *Every little thing.*

For the first time, he sensed a nearly imperceptible speck of incertitude amongst her conviction of seeing her adopted family again.

They'll be here when you wake up, Sam tenderly articulated his thought.

Surrendering, Maven settled into his side and

promptly passed out. Her dark hair curtained her face. Not wanting to risk waking her, Sam let it be. Tilting his head back towards the cool window, his mind raced. He started thinking about not only every person she had lost in her life but everything she had and was continually giving up for others. His love for her swelled. He couldn't imagine what he had done to deserve her, and he wasn't quite certain he did. But he privately pledged every day going forward to be worthy of his incredibly fortunate luck and his unbelievably wonderful wife.

CHAPTER TWENTY-SIX

As the SUV slowed, Maven started to rouse in her seat. The tires crunched the gravel beneath them as they turned off the road. She jolted awake as she took in her surroundings. It was barely dawn as Cassius parked the car. The rest of their procession pulled into the stalls next to them.

"We're here," Isolde said as she and Cassius climbed out of the car.

"Did you know this was where we were coming?" Sam asked Maven curiously.

"Yes," she hid a sly grin behind her stretched arms.

"Have you been here before?" Lila questioned.

"Yeah, I grew up and went to college in Ithaca. We drove through it about twenty minutes ago," Sam answered Lila then eyed Maven. "And this is where we met."

"Really? How interesting," Lila commented.

"Mmhm. She had said she was here visiting family, but now I'm thinking maybe that wasn't the real story," Sam calculated.

"Partly real," Maven corrected. "I *was* visiting Izzy and others in New York, but this is where my dad and I had landed from Loremara."

"So, when we met..." Sam quickly put the pieces together.

"I had been in Tartooc for about five minutes," she replied.

"Wow," Talmadge spoke with his back to them as he tied his shoelaces, "that seems incredibly..."

"Kismet," Sabine finished for him.

"That's what Liam said, too." Maven smiled.

Cassius knocked on the window. When they looked, he motioned for them to join their party. Though uneager, Lila and Talmadge reached for their door handles.

"Wait," Maven said before they unlatched their doors.

Pausing, the leather squeaked as everyone turned in their seats to face her. Closing her eyes, Maven's hands started to gleam. In turn, each of their palms glistened luminously, including Sam's. The light from their skin paled a few seconds later.

"I left your Search Shields up. I think, for the time

being, it's better that you can't be readily found by anyone else," Maven explained.

The emotions of all those around them began to sink in again. As they plunged in and easily settled back into their empathy, they began to truly appreciate the gift of their connection to one another. Sam, however, was a little overwhelmed.

"You're okay," Maven placed a hand on his knee.

"How am I feeling... everyone?" he asked disoriented.

"Through our Bond," Maven spoke calmly. "This is it wholly and unfiltered. You feel what I feel, and I feel everyone. Take a few breaths, and don't fight it. It'll sink in, in just a second."

While witnessing Maven as she tended to Sam, the other three in the vehicle finally sensed the affection between the couple. They had each assumed that their connection was strong, but they could feel in that moment that the love amid their Bond rivaled that of even the oldest couples they knew. Sam felt their observance but couldn't understand their awe.

"What?" he questioned.

"It's just..." Lila trailed.

"I think 'kismet' might have been an understatement," Talmadge joked but meant it sincerely.

"Meaning what?" Sam's curiosity piqued once more.

Come on, honey. Let's get a move on, Isolde Read to Maven from out of view from the car.

"I'll explain later," Maven patted his leg. "We need to get going."

"Same tune, different lyrics. My life with a warlock," Sam amused.

They clambered over the seats and out the doors. It looked and smelled like the rain had just finished but could start again at any moment. The crisp, misty morning air brushed their skin and tingled in their lungs. The sky was overcast, and a scanty fog hung near the tops of the trees. A moderate roar could be heard. Peering around, none in their caravan remained at the cars. They sensed them not far off and followed towards the sound passing a sheltered sign that read their location: Taughannock Falls. Down the damp stone steps, they met their party and the source of the noise.

At the bottom of the stairs, the group of adults and children were immersed in the panoramic view of the towering waterfall as it crashed into the gorge below and the even taller cliffs that guarded it. Surrounding it, and them, was a medley of deciduous and evergreen trees. Vivid greens, yellows, oranges, and reds painted the landscape in stark contrast to the grey sky above and the slate of the cliffs' stone below. Even moss growing on the lower half of the outer cliffs was sprinkled with the same mix of autumn colors.

"This realm certainly does have its graces," Sabine regarded in admiration.

"It certainly does," Maven said, taking in their setting and Sam's hand at the same time.

"It is absolutely breathtaking, but please tell me we don't have to Jump from that waterfall," Lila voiced her aversion.

"No, not from the falls," Maven assured her with a smile.

"No? Really?" Sabine hoped alongside Lila.

"Really," Maven replied.

"Oh, thank the Gods. That thing has to be almost two hundred feet high," Sabine spoke, looking back to the scene.

"Two-fifteen, actually," Sam informed.

"Where do we Jump from, then?" Talmadge asked.

"Do you see the arches broken into the rock to the right of the fall?" Cassius pointed to the area.

"Yes..." Sabine's tone was less than thrilled at the question.

"We Jump from above there," Cassius continued.

"What is it with you warlocks and heights? I'm beginning to resent it," Lila groaned.

"Cash, don't be a jerk," Maven laughed. "Above the arches and far to the right, there's a field across the street. The Jump is *there*. We just take the trail from here then cross. It's less conspicuous."

Sabine and Lila both laid a look on Cassius that bordered on annoyed, but many of the others, their friends included, hid entertainment.

"Shall we?" Noah's voice came from the edge of the assemblage.

They found his face as he stood from his seat on the stone banister of the overlook. He offered a tepid smile, feeling the majority's reluctance at the inevitable. His eyes found Maven, and she mirrored his halfhearted expression.

"I know," he added sympathetically to the group before he headed in the direction of the North Rim Trail.

Although staggered, the entire party fell in line with the path. Lastly were Maven and her friends. As they walked, the scattered multitude of trees soon extended high above their heads. On the left was a chest-high chain link fence to protect hikers from the steep cliffs on its other side. The trail was mostly flat with some small rolling inclines and was lightly littered with fallen leaves and pine needles.

"What did you study in your schooling?" Talmadge asked Sam, breaking the collective hush.

"History," Sam replied. "Actually, there's a pretty cool story attached to these falls."

"Pray tell," Cassius sarcastically chimed in from several feet ahead.

Ignoring him, Sam continued, "There's an old Iroquois legend about the local Cayuga tribe capturing a few Delaware braves. Long story short, one of the braves and a Cayuga maiden fell in love. They fled one night for the Delaware's hidden canoe, but someone noticed and sounded the village's alarm. They ended up in a hopeless chase, knowing that the brave would be tortured to death if they were caught. Once they realized they weren't going to make it, they embraced and leaped off the ledge of the falls."

A couple of the children lagged behind their parents to hear his story.

"What happened then?" The younger brunette girl breathed out her worried question.

"Well, the legend goes on to say that the villagers, mourning the loss of their maiden, returned in the morning to the base of the waterfall to collect their bodies. But their remains were nowhere to be found. Do you remember those arches in the stone?" Sam asked the girl.

She energetically nodded while staring up at him with wide, brown eyes.

"Evidently, the Great Spirit sympathized with the couple's love and had opened that 'door' you see to the right of the falls and ushered them safely into another realm..." he faltered at his own word.

Maven nudged him. "Tell her the ending."

"They, uh, they were ushered safely into another realm where they could remain youthful lovers... forever," Sam finished hazily.

The little girl let out a heavy exhale. "Good," she said, relieved.

"Tell her what else the Great Spirit is known as," Maven encouraged as she attempted to hide another sly grin.

Sam smiled and shook his head as he replied, "The Creator."

"Ohhhh, so a warlock saved them," a young boy presumed.

Looking to Maven, Sam knew the boy had guessed accurately.

"You're not saying their Great Spirit was a warlock, are you?" Sam asked, incredulously.

"No, no, no. Totally separate entities. In that instance, though, their word for Creator overlaps with our own," she explained. "There was a warlock living not far from the Cayuga. He felt the tribe's disturbance, and when he neared the cliffs to investigate, he saw the couple leap. With his attempt to Fly them gently to the water below, he knocked loose a piece of the rock wall."

"Creating the 'door' in the cliff," Sam related.

"Exactly," Maven said.

"You all knew that story already," Sam stated, understanding Cassius's earlier sarcasm.

"Some of the children hadn't heard," Cassius humored.

"So, he's your *good* friend?" Sam, referring to Cassius, questioned her judgment.

Maven laughed. "He's really never like this. I think he just finds all this added testosterone in my life *intimidating*," she shouted her last word to make certain Cassius heard.

Intimidated? By a wizard and a human? I think not, Cassius Read amused to Maven.

No, not by a wizard and a human. But I think my oldest friend might be intimidated by my best friend and my partner. Just maybe, she mused in return.

Partner, he chewed the word over in his mind. *I do wish we could have celebrated that properly.*

We will, Maven replied certainly. *There's not a chance I'd let you get out of throwing that party.*

Cassius mentally sighed. *When will we catch a break in these lives?*

When we're meant to, Cash, she answered. *No one ever promised us that life would be easy or fair, but that doesn't mean it's not worth every ounce of hard work it takes to get through it.*

Gods, you're annoyingly positive, he retorted.

Hopeful. I'm annoyingly hopeful. I'm lousy with the stuff, she teasingly corrected.

That, too, Cassius responded. *Well, at least promise me I'll see you again.*

Of course. We both know you can't keep yourself out of trouble, and aren't I always the one saving your hide? she joked.

Cassius and Maven laughed out loud at the memories they Read back and forth of their centuries of antics. Even though he couldn't hear their conversation, Sam's uninhibited Bond allowed him the knowledge of its happening along with its tone, in addition to feeling Maven's reaction to it. He realized that there could be privacy but no secrets between them. With each new aspect that he learned about Maven, her people, and their Bond, the more amazed he was that she had picked him to Bond with. Sensing his bordering deprecation, Maven looked up at Sam.

"You chose me, too," she stated simply, and then resumed Reading with Cassius.

Faster than anticipated, they came to the sharp bend in the trail. From there, anyone else could carry on towards the Upper Falls, but for their group, it was time to get into position. They wordlessly walked the short distance off the trail to the edge of the trees that neared the road as the clouds overhead began to drizzle once more. Sam squinted into the distance of the angled open field. He saw nothing through the intermittent raindrops except grass and trees and more grass, but, as he turned to say precisely that to Maven, something caught his attention.

"Is... is that it?" he asked, again squinting.

"What do you see?" Maven cocked her head to the side and raised her eyebrows.

"I don't know. Kind of an iridescent... shimmer, I guess? Along the edges of a pretty big circle," Sam answered, but it still sounded like a question.

"How can he see that?" Talmadge inquired.

"I have no idea," Maven breathed out her reply. "Izzy?"

"I've never heard of such a thing either," Isolde spoke, impressed.

"Should I not be able to see it?" Sam questioned nervously.

"No. Not only are all Jumps Protected, but humans aren't capable of seeing them," Cassius responded, equally impressed.

"I guess this one is," Maven beamed both proudly and unnerved.

"Well, no matter to us now." Cassius turned and began Reading to the warlocks.

"What's he saying?" Lila asked next to Talmadge.

"He's making sure everyone knows the correct

realm to Jump to. Now, he's telling the families with children are to go first," Maven interpreted.

They watched on as the warlocks carefully aligned themselves with their invisible target. Checking up and down the empty street for clearance, the first three poised. A second later, they were blurs streaking through the air and across the field. Sam barely had time to avert his eyes to the Jump before they broke the barrier. All that was visible was a translucent ripple through the air. Quickly, two more small families Jumped.

The last child remaining was the young brunette girl who turned out to be the daughter of the unknown brunette woman from the warlocks' earlier meeting. The woman was kneeled down, Reading with her daughter. She smiled and nodded, and then the little girl ran to where Sam stood.

"Thank you for the story," she placed her hand out in front of her as she spoke.

Sam squatted down to meet her eye line, and his hand swallowed hers as he accepted it. "You are more than welcome," he replied.

She curled a chubby finger, motioning for him to lean in closer. He did.

With their faces a few inches apart, she Read in a whisper, *I hope you and your maiden find a secret realm to be in love in.*

A broad smile swept across his face. *Me, too,* he whispered back. *You stay safe.*

Without another word, she kissed his cheek and ran back to her mother. Sam hadn't finished standing as they Jumped.

"That little tart," Maven joked. "What was that about?"

Before he came up with a response, Sam felt his stomach drop. Suddenly, he was blanketed in a dizzying feverish chill. As abruptly as it came, it was gone.

"Are you okay?" Maven asked anxiously. "Did you stand up too fast?"

Sam flipped around and stared into the woods behind them.

"What's going on, Sam?" Maven felt him tense under her touch.

"Kendrich," he growled. "He's on his way here."

CHAPTER TWENTY-SEVEN

"You must be kidding," Cassius said as he spun and looked through the trees himself.

"Sure doesn't feel like he's kidding," Talmadge differed, studying Sam and his demeanor.

"Everyone who can, Search," Isolde commanded.

Cassius's, Isolde's, Noah's, and Lila's eyes darted back and forth underneath their tightly shut eyelids. Their brows furrowed as they Searched in every possible direction as far as their reaches allowed. Maven, however, continued to examine Sam, who was positioned unblinkingly to the south.

"I can't find anything!" Lila exasperatedly shouted.

"Here, give me a boost. Talmadge, Sabine, you help, too," Isolde directed.

The wizard and witches took the steps towards the focused warlocks and paired up. Linking hands, the considerable reach of the warlocks was extended. After a minute, though, they all still came up empty.

"I wonder..." Maven said to herself with an inquisitive calm.

Slipping her hand inside of Sam's, her long, thin fingers spread his bulky, tan fingers apart as they intertwined. Maven firmly seized her grasp. Right away, the faint, rosy light smoothly streamed from her heart and down into their united palms. Having given up their Search, everyone else intently traced the flow as it gridlocked in their hold. The glow started to pool. Maven's focus built in tandem to the obstructed energy.

"It's not possible. He's human," Isolde tried to comfort Maven's failing efforts.

"Shhh," Talmadge quietly hushed her.

"I need you to work with me, Sam," Maven's voice strained through her concentration. "You have to let me in."

At that point, she illuminated from her fingertips to a couple of inches below her elbow. Her forehead started to perspire, and her skin was slightly blanched. Sam's face strained, and a bead of sweat dripped down the side of his cheek. The exertion they radiated began to splinter. Sabine moved to Sam's free side and gently set her small hand on his forearm. She could feel the heat through his skin that emanated from Maven's potent power.

"Sam," Sabine spoke patiently, "close your eyes."

His reservation and fixed gaze refused for him.

"You won't lose your connection to Kendrich. I promise. That's not how these gifts work," she addressed his fear directly.

Accepting her word, Sam dropped his eyelids, but the burden of his effort still creased his expression.

"Relax. Breathe," Sabine instructed.

His broad shoulders slightly eased as he breathed deeply.

Concentrate on Maven, she serenely coached. *Not her touch but her intent. Just like you are accepting our conversation now, you have to allow her to help you. A Read is through your mind. A boost comes from and to the heart. She is literally giving you a piece of herself. Direct your attention inward.*

As Sabine talked, Sam's focus stayed, but his composure returned. Feeling his body temperature cool, she lifted her hand from his arm.

Let her in, Sam, Sabine Read again. *You trust her. You love her. Utilize that trust and love to yield your control and unbind your heart.*

Ultimately, Sam understood. Giving a great sigh, he provided an avenue of access. Maven closed her eyes to guide the flow before it flooded him. Her eyebrows stitched as she restrained the light to a steady seep. With the energy managed, she peeked at their hands. The astonishment she felt matched that being projected by every other person there. Her eyes tracked the line from her chest, down her arm, up Sam's, and to his heart. The impediment had fully drained, and there was a free, even flow between them. She could hardly believe what she was witnessing.

Eyes still closed, Sam adapted to the new sensation coursing through his body. The boost amplified everything; everything he felt internally and everything he sensed externally. He wanted to get lost in his thoughts about Maven but instead consolidated his newly strengthened effort on his earlier alarm. His eyes dashed side to side under his eyelids. Suddenly, Sam's view shot high passed the trees and into the sky. Below, he saw the land laid out somewhat ghostlike as both a map and a satellite image. Where Maven and the others stood far beneath him, he could distinguish their colorful individual energies, including his own.

Scanning the local area, he recognized innumerable other spirits, but each flickered white and weak in comparison. He again aimed his gaze to the south then adjusted it to the southeast. The landscape rocketed away under him as he hovered fixedly above. Like nothing, Sam had pinpointed his mark. Several vibrant sources of energy caused the barreling earth to come to an abrupt standstill. Not knowing how, he recognized Kendrich without even being able to see his face.

Noting their location and course, the setting dissolved around him until he saw nothing but the blackness behind his eyelids.

No one said a word, and some held their breath when they watched Sam's eyes come to a rest in their sockets. He felt Maven's boost slip and withdraw. Reeling slightly as he opened his eyes and adjusted back to the ground beneath his feet, Sabine grabbed hold of his other arm to help Maven to steady Sam. He blinked until his sight was no longer blurry. As he regained focus on Maven's face to deliver Kendrich's position, he was met with her awe.

"Where are they?" Noah asked as he stared captivated at Sam.

"They're just out of Jersey, but they're Flying here fast. They must have left New York when the first family Jumped. It's maybe a matter of twenty, twenty-five minutes before they arrive," he answered knowledgeably.

"Impossible," Isolde whispered as she placed a hand over her rapidly beating heart.

"I assure you, it is possible, and it is happening," Sam replied sternly.

"No," Maven squeezed their still held hands as she spoke, "she means you, Sam. Although, I think we can all agree that 'impossible' is now seriously overused and wildly inapplicable. You, a *human*, not only perceived a wizard from here to Manhattan, took aid from a warlock and Searched, but you found them through their Shields. What has been beyond the bounds of possibility in our extensive lives, you achieved in a few minutes. I think you might be some kind of species loophole or phenomenon..."

Lost and unsure of what to think, Sam decided to process the information and experience later.

"Kendrich," Talmadge swiftly readdressed the issue. "What's the play?"

"I think it should be the same as before. You all Jump," Sam answered firmly. "I'll take one of the cars out of here."

"We're not about to leave our talentless friend here to die," Talmadge retorted.

"Talentless?" Sam repeated, acting insulted.

Talmadge shot him an unapologetic look. "You know what I mean."

"We couldn't risk leaving the Jump active after we left now anyway," Noah added. "If it stayed open, they could trace each of the different realms in which the warlocks landed."

"For your own safety, you need to escape this realm," Sam insisted.

"If you are still imagining a scenario in which we leave Maven and yourself behind to collapse the site, I am afraid you are mistaken," a recomposed Isolde declared.

"Iz," Maven expressed her rebuke with only the name.

"Don't cast your blame on her," Cassius defended. "The instant your companions fully sensed your Bond, they knew you were never abandoning Sam again."

"And how would you know that?" Lila questioned him pointedly, already knowing the answer.

"He's been Reading the three of us since the park," Sabine beat Cassius to his response.

"Very good, miss," Cassius genuinely complimented Sabine. "A warlock can never be too careful these days, as we all learned yet again yesterday."

Cassius realized too late the cost of his cavalier statement for her and the others. At just the implication of Eldon, the friends winced, and Sabine's heart lurched. She dodged her eyes to the ground in anticipation of any pitying glimpses.

"I'm sorry," Cassius spoke contritely. "I've worn a thick skin for maybe too long, but that's no excuse for my callousness."

"So, if you're not going to Jump," Sam continued with the task at hand, "what do you plan on doing?"

"How many were there, Sam?" Isolde asked.

"Eight, I think," he answered.

"Well, we are slightly outnumbered," Noah clearly expressed his opinion, "but we have four warlocks and the most powerful Flyer since his savage, criminal ancestor."

"Thanks." Talmadge pursed his lips together as Noah slapped his back while wearing a grin.

"But we don't know which or how many of them might have siphoned off other warlocks' gifts," Isolde considered.

"I do," Sam said matter-of-factly.

"How?" Isolde inquired.

"I don't know," he replied honestly. "I could just tell from their emissions, and the only one who had was Kendrich."

"Could you tell..." Maven cleared the words stuck in her throat. "Do you know where..."

"I don't know who he took the powers from or when. I'm sorry," Sam answered her incomplete questions. He placed an arm around her shoulders and kissed the top of her head.

"Were you able to discern which talents each of them had?" Noah wondered.

"I think I might if I Searched again. I just need to know what to look for," Sam spoke hopefully.

"We know their numbers, and we'll know they're strengths. We also have the element of surprise; these witches and wizards have no clue they'll be running into an ambush. If those are our odds, I'll take them," Cassius cast his vote.

"I think it's time someone in my family joined the right side of the new history anyway," Talmadge affirmed his choice. Although, all noted his trepidation.

"I'm not sure what it is precisely, but I have a sinking in my gut. I think we should destroy this Jump and move on to the next. Immediately." Isolde twisted her hands as she voiced her wishes.

Knowing they could not contribute if it came to a battle, Lila and Sabine stayed quiet, but their fear spoke for itself. The group's attention fell to Maven. Having had the most experience with similar situations, she was aware her vote would carry a heavy weight. She considered each of their expectant faces along with their capabilities, thoughts, and concerns. Tilting her head back, she looked to Sam and peered into his brown eyes. Smiling down at her lovingly, he broadcasted nothing but trust and his full, unconditional support of any decision she made. She turned back to their small collection of audacious individuals.

"I'm sorry, Izzy, but I'm sick of running," Maven said. "I say we stay, we fight, and we end this."

CHAPTER TWENTY-EIGHT

After being walked through two more thorough Searches, Sam was able to discern that in addition to Kendrich's siphoned powers, there were four Flyers and one Creator joining him. Yet he was unable to get a read on the remaining two.

"What do you mean 'indecipherable'?" Cassius questioned, frustrated.

"I'm not sure," Sam answered, equally as strained. "They're both clearly a witch or a wizard, but I can't make out any talents whatsoever. And one of them seems... hollow."

"Eldon," Sabine and Maven simultaneously drew the same conclusion.

The groups' tenuous grief played out silently with the echo of the crashing falls behind them.

"So," Talmadge cleared his throat. "How do we do this?" he asked.

"They're coming to trace the Jump. We should hide in the surrounding dimension." Cassius quickly turned into tactical mode. "We'll position ourselves in teams on either side of the field for the best advantage."

"What do you mean 'dimension'?" Sabine's head swiveled towards Maven. "How much do we not know?"

"It's not a matter of not knowing but not having the capability yet, Sabine," Maven replied. "Searchers come closest to utilizing dimensions; their minds are transported when they Search, but to be physically able to open one isn't within the current talents of witches and wizards."

"How do you get to it?" Lila asked eagerly.

"You Create a Pull; it's like a personal door into the dimension. And if we each make our own Pull, we end up separated, like different rooms off the same hallway," Isolde quickly explained.

"That's how you surrounded us in the park," Talmadge inferred.

Cassius nodded in acknowledgment.

"We'll have to Yoke them fast. If we can't gag a least a few of them right after they land, we can kiss our upper hand goodbye," Noah added.

"Yoke?" Sam questioned Noah's word choice.

"Harnessing their powers, he means," Isolde clarified. "It's quicker than a Seal, but it also leaves their gifts locked to them and available to others."

"Like animals?" Appalled at the term, Sabine poorly hid her disgust.

"Yes, exactly like that," Cassius brusquely answered.

"Why exactly do you know how to do this?" Talmadge warily inquired.

"It's a long story, Tal," Maven anxiously cut the query short.

"You'll have to fill me in some time." Talmadge glanced from warlock to warlock with reserved criticism.

"Why not attack with guns blazing as soon as their feet hit the ground?" Sam asked, perplexed. "Just siphon their powers completely and eliminate the threat."

"Because there might be innocents involved. One power-hungry wizard could easily cause a feeding frenzy that's affecting them all. We need time to Read them individually to figure out who is an active part of this and who has been swept away by someone else's malice," Isolde answered.

"Noah, Cassius, you'll each Create your own Pulls.

I'll hold Sam, Sabine, and Lila in mine. Tal," Maven continued with logistics, "you'll pair up with Iz. She'll keep you both hidden, but, and this is important for you four to know, once a witch or wizard is brought through, your powers won't work. Talmadge, you'll only be able to cover us when Isolde opens her Pull. After the strike ends, then we'll meet back in the field with those witches' and wizards' talents bound."

"Can't you all stay hidden? Won't your powers reach them from there?" Sam's voice started to lace with concern as their reality began to sink in.

"No. A warlock's gifts do function cross-dimensionally, but we need physical contact for the Yoke," Maven explained. "We'll all remain unseen while we're in the dimension, but we'll have to transition back and forth to bring someone else through our Pulls. The Yoke only takes a minute to place, but it's, obviously, least risky to do when they're powerless. And we'll alternate; as one of us is Yoking, another can be Pulling someone else through, while another still will run interference. This is our best, least aggressive attack option."

"What's to stop them from killing you on sight?" Lila spoke up somberly.

"No one is going to kill us. At least, not yet," Cassius's tone was annoyed but not with Lila.

"How can you be so certain?" Sabine asked.

"They want us alive, Sabine. You can't siphon a dead warlock, now can you?" Maven replied simply.

"Come on," Noah evaded the immediate tension that set in from Maven's sentence. "Let's get into position."

They left the security of the trees and crossed the empty street into the field. As they neared the Jump at the end of the clearing, they split off into their assigned groupings. Noah and Cassius took to the left as the others spread out and finished forming the semi-circle of vantage points.

"Can't I stay with Talmadge and Isolde?" Lila asked quietly, but her tone pleaded.

"Izzy's Pull is going to be open more often and for longer than any other's, in order for her and Tal to provide cover," Maven tried to reason. "You'll be over-exposed."

"Also, you're defenseless. If you were dragged into this, you'd be in danger as well as putting us into more harm's way to help you," Isolde sullenly agreed.

"They're right," Talmadge added. "If I thought you weren't safe, Li, I'd lose my mind. You'll better off with Maven." His tone equally pleaded with her to accept his justification.

Rather than wasting more time with an argument she knew she'd lose, Lila launched herself into Talmadge's arms. He held her tightly to his chest.

Watching on, the field echoed loudly all of the unspoken emotions each person emitted. Some cast out anxiety, some steely determinations, others cold fear, but everyone broadcasted some degree of gratitude for those at their sides. After too short of a moment, the couple relinquished their hold on each other.

"This will all be over very soon," Isolde placed a consoling hand on Sabine's shoulder but spoke to them all.

Separating again into their designated positions, everyone took one last look at the faces around them.

"Don't be a hero," Cassius called out to Maven with a smirk.

"Don't be a fool and make me have to be one," she jokingly returned, in reference to memories they shared.

"Watch Izzy's back, Talmadge," Cassius directed the sobersided order from several yards away.

"I will," Talmadge answered solemnly. "Maven, watch theirs," Talmadge spoke as he motioned to Lila, Sabine, and Sam.

"I will," She promised.

"Ready?" Noah glanced from each apprehensive face to the next. "Let's step through, shall we?"

Cassius gave him a firm nod in agreement. Each warlock placed a glowing hand in front of their bodies and drew them with slight resistance across the air as if draping a heavy, albeit invisible curtain. As they did, their Pulls appeared to the others. Shimmering in their holds, it seemed as if a black and white filter had been placed between where they stood and the scene behind it. Sam leaned around Maven's Pull and saw the exact same outline of trees in their everyday colors then back in front of the door she had Created.

"It looks even wilder inside," Maven informed their curiosities. "After you," she motioned to her friends to enter the gateway.

Hesitantly, Lila gave Talmadge one last reassuring smile before she stepped through first. A soft whirring suction was heard as each person disappeared one by one into the tears of the fabric between the two dimensions. Soon, only the warlocks remained in the field.

See you on the other side, Maven Read to each of them with a confidence that bolstered their individual resolves of that very fact.

May all the Gods be with us this day, Isolde Read lovingly.

I'm sure they are, Maven returned with just as much care before they each turned and entered their Pulls.

The curtain closed after Maven's foot cleared the opening. The ghostlike world was eerily beautiful. Everything around them in the field retained the same shape and outline, but each living organism shone brightly with a different colored energy. Even the air sparkled as tiny microorganisms floated around them lazily. Absorbing their new surroundings, the witches and Sam noticed that any manmade thing in view was a shade of black and grey, including their clothes. But each of them bore a distinctly glowing outlined aura; Lila's a soft blue, Sabine's an amethyst purple, Sam's a flickering white, and Maven's a deep, leafy green. Even though their other companions could not be seen in their separate Pulls, there remained a hazy connection to them still.

"This is what you see when you Search?" Sabine, in awe, asked Lila.

"Yes, but... nowhere near as beautiful. When we Search, most everything remains grey except for that specific object we're looking for, and even then, it's honed in on a small area. This..." Lila trailed again, "is much more powerful than I imagined."

"It's amazing," Sam agreed.

Once more blown away by Maven and her capabilities, he felt somewhat less apprehensive about the impending confrontation. Sensing his faith in her, Maven pulled Sam close to her. Sam returned the hug so tightly he accidentally pushed some of the air from her lungs.

"Be safe," was all Sam could muster.

"I love you, too," Maven replied, understanding his meaning.

"Oh, my Gods," Sabine whispered in surprise.

"What?" Maven lifted her head from Sam's chest in alarm.

"No, it's just..." Lila breathed, "look at you two." She regarded them with a new wonderment.

Looking at one other, Sam and Maven understood their astonishment; in each other's embrace, their auras had both transformed into a singularly golden hue. Sabine touched Lila's arm to recreate the response of the physical touch of another, but their energies continued to emit unchanged. Feeling Maven's shock, they all were left stumped.

"This is new to you as well," Lila gathered.

"What does it mean?" Sam wondered.

"I... I don't know," Maven admitted.

"Another mystery for another day," Sabine kidded. "Seems we all have much to discover, yet."

"Seems we do," Maven mused with a grin.

Releasing her hug with Sam, Maven wrapped an arm around his waist. Lila joined them on Maven's other side and linked her arm around her. Sam quietly offered his hand out to Sabine, who accepted it gratefully. They stood in wordless support for several minutes until they heard a barrage of thunder building in the distance. Above them in the other dimension, the originally overcast clouds turned from a brilliant white to a murky grey and began streaking by quickly.

"They're getting close," Sabine anxiously noted.

Get ready, Cassius invisibly Read to everyone from across the field.

CHAPTER TWENTY-NINE

As Kendrich and his accomplices drew nearer, the dimension around them responded adversely. The glitter of the floating organisms fell flat. The trees' hues waned, and every remaining animal in the perimeter fled. Nature itself was taking cover.

Maven separated from the others. She inched closer to the Jump while they stood back. Their collective suspense spiked as the warlocks stood at the ready. In anticipation of their enemies' arrival, the seconds slid by at a glacial pace. Finally, the thunder crescendoed unseen above the overcast sky. A giant boom resounded as bodies of energy, each the color of dark, murky burnt orange, burst through the cloud cover and barreled toward the ground.

Before the witches' and wizards' feet touched the grass, the others witnessed Cassius's red aura shoot out of his Pull and upon the witch nearest him. His hands gripped on either side of her head before she had gained her balance, and she fell unconscious in his hold. Quicker than any could react, he Flew the two of them back through the Pull and immediately began placing his Yoke.

As soon as Cassius had cleared the field, Noah was in the air behind the turned heads of the confused cluster. Unaware of his approach, Noah grabbed a wizard. His yell of surprise alerted the others and scared an already terrified Eldon even further. The helpless wizard ran as fast as he could into the tree line and out of sight. While Noah attempted to reach his doorway, the Flyer resisted greatly trying to break Noah's hold. Through the dimension's veil, Maven watched on as both the tall blonde witch, the Creator, and Harrison raised their hands to aid the wizard as the others looked around frantically, anticipating the next strike. Harrison pulled at the wizard in a tug of war with Noah. At the same moment, the witch launched a large flaming orb directly at Noah's head.

The ball of fire zoomed through the air but erupted into a cloud of smoke inches from the warlock's face. Part of Isolde's frame could be seen through the small slit she held open. Talmadge's hand came into view as he cut across the air and broke Harrison's hold on the other wizard. With Harrison's clutch released, Noah and the wizard tumbled backward into the open Pull, which closed the instant their backs landed in the other dimension.

"Really?" Kendrich called out disgusted to the seemingly empty field. "Hiding from us like a bunch of cowards! And here I'd been told you warlocks were supposed to be fearsome and brave."

As Kendrich spoke, Maven situated herself within arm's reach to the witch nearest her. Like the others, the witch was on alert but unsure from where the next grab might come. Maven simply waited until the witch rotated her back toward her and quickly snatched her through her Pull.

"No!" their Creator erupted with a scream, propelling a flaming orb at Maven's Pull only moments too late. The orb landed in the woods and caught a tree on fire.

In the other dimension, Maven's hands were on either side of the witch's head as Sam carried her back towards Lila and Sabine. She struggled briefly before going limp in Maven's grasp. Kneeling beside the witch's unconscious body, she continued to place the bindings on her mind.

"That was close," Lila spoke quietly from over Maven's shoulder.

"She's important to that other witch," Sabine noted, pointing to the Creator. "Maybe family or a partner. Be careful of going out again, Maven. Who knows what she'd do to get her back?"

"You're right," Maven replied, standing.

In their dimension, she reached out an arm, her palm facing the tree ablaze and closed her hand into a fist, smothering the flames.

The Creator needs taking out, Maven Read to the other warlocks. *She's going to fight ugly after that grab.*

Already on it, Cassius assertively Read in return. *Noah, you're with me this trip. Let's get this over with quickly.*

Cash, one at a time, Maven urged her friend.

Without acknowledging her, Cassius and Noah were through to the original dimension and grabbing two more witches in tandem. That time, though, their adversaries were readily anticipating them. Cassius wrapped his tan hands around the side of the pale Creator's blonde hair, but she gripped his wrists firmly. He let out a growl of pain as smoke could be seen rising from under her palms. Noah gave up beginning to place the Yoke on the petite brunette witch and resorted to a headlock as the powerful Flyer fought against him. Kendrich and Harrison stood back to back, preparing for another attack. Through her opening, Izzy broke the Creator's hold on Cassius, and he quickly retreated into his Pull severely burned.

Harrison landed a heavy blow to Noah's head as

he turned to reenter his doorway, knocking out the warlock and releasing his grip on the witch. Noah fell unconscious inside his Pull, the entry closing behind him. At the same moment, Talmadge got a shot off at Harrison. The wizard grunted before his shoulders drooped. As the Flyer released from Noah's grasp tumbled and rolled across the damp grass back towards her companions, Harrison toppled forward. Maven capitalized on the wizard's weak moment. Faster than he fell toward the ground, Maven was streaking through her Pull and Flying to his eventual landing spot. She tore open a new Pull in time for gravity to complete her effort. Both she and Harrison were enveloped into the other dimension before the witch had rolled back to Kendrich's and the Creator's feet.

The wind blew gustier as the Flyer rubbed her sore neck while on her hands and knees. The Creator helped her to stand, but the other witch angrily shook off her hands. Upright, her face was enraged. Kendrich's eyes darted around the field apprehensively watching for any new assailment. Maven, alone with a blacked-out Harrison in the new offshoot of the other dimension, eyed the witch cautiously as she simply stood there. The witch's neck was red from Noah's earlier grip, but her olive-toned face smoldered from rage. Maven tried to Read her but was unable. The witch slowly and calculatedly placed her hands behind her back in a surrendering gesture.

"What are you doing?" Kendrich frantically questioned. "Put your hands up! Fight!"

The Flyer merely stood there, unflinching. Harrison began to stir on the ground beside Maven. Not wanting him to wake fully before she could place her Yoke, she knelt and grabbed his face. Monitoring the witch, an uneasy feeling grew in Maven's gut.

What is she doing? Cassius Read to Maven and Isolde. The wince to his pain could be heard even in his mental voice as he still mended his wounds.

She's conceding, thank Gods, Isolde replied relieved. *Maven, are you finished with your Yoke?*

No, just started, Maven answered, still observing the Flyer carefully.

I'll grab her, Isolde stated.

Without another word of discussion, Isolde shot through her Pull and was barreling through the original dimension. Flying as a blur above them, she evaded a fireball from the Creator and had to circle back for the Flyer. Maven completed her Yoke on Harrison. As the soft whir of Isolde cutting through the air drew nearer, Maven rose and stood face to face with the surrendering witch in opposed dimensions.

"Get your hands up," Kendrich screamed at the woman. "Help us! You don't just give up!"

Ignoring his words, the Flyer's dark brown eyes stared straight ahead and seemed to be looking right through the warlock in front of her. Then, in the instant before Isolde captured her, the witch smirked.

Izzy, don't! Maven yelled the warning into Isolde's mind, but not in time before they were back through the warlock's Pull. *It's a Mimic!*

Too late, Maven figured it out. The Kendrich that stood before her in the original dimension stumbled and hunched over, his hands on his knees. An effulgence shot out from his eyes and under his hands. The wizard's tall frame shrunk and altered itself until the witch that had just been taken into the other dimension by Isolde was standing in Kendrich's place. Disconnected from the malicious energy, the two witches' auras shifted. The light surrounding the dark-haired witch morphed from the murky orange back to its authentic yellow. The Creator's light, though, flickered between different shades of orange as she slowly sat down in the same spot she stood, looking utterly confused.

"I'm sorry," croaked the petite Flyer. She shook her head as her mind became her own again. "I'm so sorry," she offered to anyone who could hear her before catapulting herself through the Jump.

Izzy, Maven called out to her. *Izzy!*

Maven was answered with a resounding silence.

She could tell from the stillness of Isolde's mind that she was no longer conscious, and Maven hoped that was all it meant.

Tal, are you okay? Maven solicitously reached out to him. *Is Izzy alive?*

Sorry, Mavey. I hope you're not trying to reach Talmadge, as he is currently otherwise engaged, Kendrich returned her query in lieu of Talmadge.

Kendrich, Maven Read to him, seething. *I swear to all the Gods that if you've hurt them--*

One moment, please, dear, Kendrich answered, cutting her off with a cloying sweetness.

Kendrich. She called out again, *Kendrich!* Maven could feel her fury building with every second that passed while waiting for the wizard to address her again. The impending storm overhead grew restless. Thunder boomed while she paced a small patch of grass with Harrison lying at her feet.

Cassius, you better be done Healing, Maven declared anxiously, clenching and unclenching her fists.

Working on it, he returned adamantly through his distress. *Maven,* he added quickly, *a how did he learn to control that talent?*

I don't know, Maven replied, warily rubbing her hands together. *But I do know that if he is the one responsible for my dad's death, that's not the only warlock he's siphoned. Liam wasn't a Mimic, Cash. Be ready for anything.*

Maven Read to Sam, Sabine, and Lila, after still being unable to reach Noah. *Are you all okay?*

Maven, Sam leaped onto the sound of her voice in his head, relieved. *We're fine. There's a pissed off witch who has just woken up in here, but we're all safe. Are you all alright?*

I'm okay, she replied as she squatted down. She hadn't realized how allayed she'd be by hearing Sam's voice, too.

What's going on? Lila asked with aching concern. *Does that body swap thing mean Kendrich is in there with Talmadge and Isolde?*

Yes, Kendrich is in there. I'm waiting for him to contact me. Lila, Maven smoothed her tone as much as possible, *I am not going to let anything happen to Tal. I promise.*

I know, Lila quietly lied to both Maven and herself.

Be careful, Sabine uttered to her privately. *When we were courting, I would catch slight glimpses of Kendrich through a Read. Things that I didn't believe to be true and made me doubt my gift, doubt myself. He's corrupt, Maven.*

I'll be careful, and you... Maven started to echo Sabine but became distracted.

Across the field, a Pull was opening. Maven jolted back to her feet. She hoped that she'd be seeing Isolde's fingers grasping the curtain between dimensions, but she recognized a man's hand. Somehow, Kendrich had figured out how to manipulate the dimensions. Maven and the others all watched on as Talmadge was roughly shoved out of the doorway, his body outlined in a glowing indigo, followed by a grinning Kendrich. The Creator stood and walked towards the two wizards, closing the gap between them. Her flickering aura settled, again matching Kendrich's.

"Oh, Maven. Come out, come out, wherever you are!" Kendrich playfully sang out. "Be a doll, won't you? Bring out Harrison. Unbound and Unyoked, of course."

Why, in all the realms, would I do that? Maven asked Kendrich directly. *I'm considering keeping him, actually. I can see why you like the guy; he's such an obedient pet. He's even curled up at my feet right now.* With that, she Read to Kendrich the image of Harrison sprawled out unconscious on the ground, blades of loose wet grass matted to the side of his face.

"Because if you don't," Kendrich warned aloud, "I won't hesitate to kill your precious Talmadge."

Standing behind Talmadge, Kendrich flicked his

wrist. Talmadge's legs buckled underneath him, his powers apparently Sealed, and he knelt on the damp ground. Kendrich wrapped his fingers around the back of his cousin's neck, gripping tight enough to force a reluctant grimace out of Talmadge. Maven could sense his fear but also his resolution. At that moment, she hesitated. Knowing full well that Harrison was her only bargaining chip with Kendrich, Maven rapidly ran through every defensive angle of how to proceed. She knew she was cornered, and the inevitable outcome grieved her immensely. Walking away from her prisoner, she edged close to Talmadge.

Tal, Maven whispered her friend's name dearly, as she knelt in front of him, the dimension's veil separating them. *Can you hear me?*

He subtly nodded. The cold, blustery wind ruffled his soft hair. The clouds overhead finally succumbed to their own weight, and fat drops of rain started to fall in the field. Maven gently placed her hands on Talmadge's cheeks. His eyes showed awareness at the faint hint of her presence.

I'm right in front of you, she spoke quickly but peacefully as she placed her complete plan inside of Talmadge's mind. *We already said our piece earlier, but I want you to know that this is the only option. I can't see another way out of this. Not one that saves as many of us as possible.*

Okay, he replied tersely, biting his lower lip. *I understand.*

"I have all day, Maven," Kendrich yelled unknowingly above her head, "but I'm not so sure that *he* does." For effect, he wrenched Talmadge's head to the side.

Maven, don't do this, Cassius Read to her gravely. *Don't let this happen.*

I have a plan. Hold. Do you hear me, Cash? Hold, she commanded.

Tears brimmed at the corners of Talmadge's eyes. Even through their separation, Maven could feel Lila's screams at her inaction. She ignored everyone and focused on Talmadge for one final moment. Removing her hands from his face, she kissed her fingers then placed them on his lips. She stood and turned back toward Harrison as she saw Cassius open his Pull.

Cassius! Don't! Maven both Read and yelled out loud.

The warlock was in the air and Flying straight for Talmadge. The Creator formed a ball of fire between her palms. With both her and Kendrich's attention diverted, Talmadge lunged onto his stomach, grabbed the witch's ankles and pulled. Knocking her to the ground, the unfinished orb rolled out of her reach and fizzled out in the rain. Talmadge wrestled to keep his hold on her, but the Creator's ability to make her skin burn like flames quickly released his grip. Kendrich furiously sliced at the air while Cassius did all he could to evade his shots until one landed. Cassius fell from the air and crashed, gushing blood from his midsection. He writhed on the ground, feebly placing his hands on his stomach to Heal himself. Kendrich swiped both hands in front of him, annoyed, binding Cassius's hands to the soil, blood escaping the warlock's lips.

Turning around to face the open field, Kendrich growled angrily. "We only need you alive, Maven! Not unharmed."

"Oh, my Gods. No." Maven gasped in horror. It was over before she knew what had happened. She ached with the pain of her friends.

"And we don't need him at all," Kendrich declared while standing over his cousin, who was agonizing over his blistering hands.

Kendrich tightened his fist and twisted. A panicked look covered Talmadge's face as a sick crackling sounded from within him. His skin blanched, and his grasp on consciousness wavered. No one could be certain of what damage had been caused.

I'm coming out! Kendrich, I'm coming out with Harrison, but you have to let me Heal them, she Read instantly, kneeling to wake Harrison.

"No," Kendrich stated quietly and firmly.

What? Maven released Harrison's head from her grasp and stood in front of Kendrich.

"No," he repeated. "There will be no more bargains, Maven. I am weary of this exchange, and I am sick of this realm. We are through with this nonsense. Bring out Harrison, and then we are departing."

You'll leave? Hope laced her words despite her attempt at control.

"You misunderstand: you are coming with us. I came here with a purpose, and I intend to see it through. Unyoke Harrison, bring him out, and we simply Jump to our destination. At least this gives whatever is left of your companions a chance at survival. Your remaining option is to keep Harrison from me and watch on as I slowly destroy what little life these two heroes have left." His tone was bored, and his expression venomous.

Maven briefly glanced at Talmadge's and Cassius's beaten and marred bodies. There was no question of what her action would be. Hearing their groans of pain and suffering, she closed her eyes and shook her head.

Okay, she silently Read her defeat as she knelt in the cold, soggy grass.

Resting tired, shaky hands on either side of Harrison's head, she quickly unfolded the trap in which she had ensnared his mind. The rain pounded heavily into the field. Each drop firmly added to the grief Maven felt weighing on her shoulders. The wind cut deeper through her wet clothes. In the time it took to Unyoke the wizard, she was overcome with the deluge of conflicting emotions of those around her; the agony of the men dying on the ground, the fear and anxiety from Sabine, Lila's horror watching Talmadge writhe, the disgust and impatience of Kendrich, and Sam's helpless heartache knowing Maven was, in a moment, leaving him again.

Maven, Noah groggily Read from his Pull, *what is going on?*

Oh, thank all the Gods, Maven nearly wept with relief. *Look, I'm about to Jump with Kendrich.*

Like hell you are, Noah shouted.

Shut up and listen, she interrupted. *There's no time. The moment I'm through, you have to Heal Cassius and Talmadge. They're dying, Noah. And I can't reach Isolde. I don't know if she's down or... or dead. She's in her Pull. Get her out. The others are in my first Pull. You're the only one left to help. You have to do this.*

Maven, you can't go with him, he Read solemnly.

There's no choice. I'm not going to be the reason two more people I love die. No matter what, you help them. Do you understand me? She insisted. Her breathing increased in tandem to her urgency.

Harrison stirred beneath her palms. His eyelids fluttered as consciousness found him. Once his sight focused onto Maven's face, he rolled away from her touch. On his hands and knees, he raised a palm toward her, but nothing happened. Confused and still somewhat reeling, Harrison shook his head and wiped his wet sleeve to clear his face of the mud and grass.

"Don't bother; your powers don't work here," she explained as she stood.

He's awake. He's getting his footing, and we're coming out, Maven Read to Kendrich.

"Hurry." Kendrich's hateful tone coated with annoyance.

Flicking her index finger caused Harrison to stand to his feet and be held upright. Maven held him by the elbow and reached across her body. As she opened the Pull, Kendrich was ready and Flying them both out into his dimension. Standing before him, Maven's own anger immediately built.

"Bind her," Kendrich ordered, not breaking his gaze from hers.

Shaking off Maven's grip from his arm, Harrison obeyed and bound her hands behind her back. Not resisting, she stared directly back into Kendrich's amused eyes.

"Maven," Talmadge, still contorted on the ground, wheezed between struggled breaths.

Looking down, Maven saw his sorrow and anguish. Several feet away, Cassius had finally lost consciousness and was struggling to breathe.

"Come on. Let's go," Maven urged, albeit bitterly. She took a sloshed step toward the Jump, but Kendrich halted her progress.

"What's your rush, my dear?" Kendrich mockingly questioned, cocking his head to one side and raising his thick eyebrows.

"Kendrich," Maven started to panic, trying to blink the rain out of her eyes, "I'm going with you. You don't have to hurt them any further."

"I didn't *have* to do any of this," he gestured to encompass the clearing. "That's the fun of it; I'm doing this because I sincerely *want* to."

A moan escaped Talmadge as he tried to push himself into a sitting position. A sickening smile crept across Kendrich's face before he snapped his fingers together. Talmadge screamed as a matching snap came from his forearm, slamming him back into the muddy puddle under him.

"Kendrich, no!" Maven yelled. She fought against Harrison's hold on her wrists. "No! Please!"

Returning his attention to Maven, his smile turned smug. Thunder roared above their heads, and the wind grew, kicking up any loose debris around them and causing the rain to cut sideways.

"Oh, I do like that, Maven. I rather enjoy you begging," he shouted above the howling bellows of air. "Do it again," he pompously commanded.

"Please, Kendrich," Maven, without hesitation, uttered meekly. "Look around. They're dying, and I've been bested. You've won. Please, I implore you, take me and let them live."

What started as a small chuckle in the back of his throat quickly turned into maniacal laughter that shook his entire body. Maven watched on in confused silence but felt both Harrison's and the witch's enjoyment attached to Kendrich's.

"Oh, dear Gods, that is delicious," Kendrich's voice shook with his amusement. "'The most powerful warlock there ever was and ever will be,' he said! Begging me. I love it. Do it again."

"What?" Maven questioned, genuinely not understanding Kendrich's words.

Kendrich's gaiety halted. He gave another swift hand movement, and Talmadge again cried out in excruciating pain. "Beg me again."

"Please," Maven breathed immediately. "Please, please, please. I beg of you. Please stop. Please." She dropped to her knees in an act of humility, desperate to appease him.

Kendrich considered her pathetic act as he watched the steady stream of droplets escaping from the ends of her long, matted curls. He glanced back to Talmadge then over to Cassius's still body.

"Pick one," Kendrich stated.

Maven raised her head to meet his face. "Excuse me?"

"Pick which one you want to live. I'll kill the other, and then we can leave," he explained breezily and firmly planted his stance in front of her.

"Kendrich, please," Maven started to beg him again, trying to play his game.

"The time for begging is over. Choose one, so we may be finished and get out of these wet clothes. Who do you wish to keep alive? Come on, Mavey. We all have favorites. Who's yours?" he sincerely asked.

"I won't choose someone to die," Maven answered, disgusted.

"Pick one," Kendrich pressed on, having fun once more, "or I'll kill them both."

"What purpose does this serve? You've won! You have what you wanted. Finish your 'purpose,' and take me where you're supposed to. I'm through stroking your ego," she retorted.

"Very well, then," the wizard replied. His fury spilled out of him.

Kendrich turned his back to Maven, walked to position himself equally between the two men, and raised both hands high above his head. In the instant before he pulled them down to strike, Maven Flew from her knees directly into Kendrich. Harrison was a second too late with his attempt to stop her. What was intended to grip her arm turned into a gaping cut below her right shoulder. It sliced through the muscle down to her bone. Her left shoulder landed firmly into Kendrich's spine, and the crack in both of their bodies was audible. With the force of her Flight, they landed near the base of the Jump. Harrison was beside them when they opened their eyes. Maven rolled onto her stomach, still bound and unable to lift either of her arms. The searing pain sprung hot tears to her eyes.

Through the rain and mud, Maven watched as the Creator ran to Kendrich and knelt to Heal his broken body. Satisfied with her work, Harrison took the short steps to where Maven lay. With his boot, he slowly pressed down on her left shoulder. Maven screamed as she felt her already cracked collar bone fracture completely. He crouched down next to her head. Raising his finger slightly rotated her onto her side, which caused another sharp cry to escape her. Blinking through the blinding pain and the heavy rainfall, Maven could see the feral expression that possessed him.

"Normally, I would never debase myself so low as to touch you with my own hands," Harrison spoke calmly, "but you, Maven... I want to *feel* every bone in your body break."

With that, he stood and kicked her in the stomach, which launched her back across the field, landing in the cold, soggy grass a few feet away from her original Pull. She fought to regain the air that had been knocked out of her chest as Harrison slowly closed the gap between them. Her entire midsection felt like it was burning from the inside out. Maven struggled to roll to her back. Trying to Fly, she dug her heels into the mud, attempting to gain any kind of traction. As she found some breath, she gained height off the ground, but Harrison was too fast. He leaped, gripped her shoulders, and pounded her body back into the sludge landing on top of her. Another agonizing scream would have been released when she felt her ribs crack if any wind had been in her lungs. Releasing her, Harrison stood and gently waved his hand through the air forcing Maven to float upright in the air. She was eye to eye with Harrison when he closed his fingers around her neck.

You are pathetic, Maven Read to him, desperately gasping for air but unable to take a deep enough breath.

"I'm pathetic?" Harrison questioned, amused. He tightened his hold of her throat. "How do you figure?"

You're afraid to fight me fairly. You would still be asleep in my Pull if it weren't for Kendrich. Even now, you're too scared to undo my binds, she taunted, trying to ignore her entire body throbbing with stabbing pain.

A grin parted Harrison's lips. "You're under the

assumption I care about fairness. This isn't a fight. This is a beating."

Maven's heart beat faster, and her face burned with the lack of oxygen. She thought she saw stars and imagined her wrists felt loose because she had lost feeling in them. Harrison pulled back his fist with intent lacing his eyes.

"That's enough." The words halted Harrison from making contact with her jaw. "Put her down, Harrison. She's still needed," Kendrich said, placing a hand on Harrison's drawn back arm.

Harrison tossed Maven aside, causing her to limply land facedown in the pooling blood around Cassius. All she could focus on was the metallic smell she laid in and was on the verge of losing consciousness when she realized her hands were free of their constrictions. Careful to appear as motionless as possible while the wizards spoke behind her, Maven crept her right hand to the left side of her chest and began to Heal her shattered bones. As she felt her ribs snap back into place, she was careful not to take the deep breath she craved. Finally able to breathe without pain, Maven's head cleared. She noticed through her eyelashes that her left hand was lying beside Cassius's arm. Ever so gently, she placed the muddy tips of her fingers against his skin. With most of her collar bone fixed but not the gushing slice in her right arm, she ended her Healing to focus entirely on sending her mend into him as quickly as possible.

Thank the Gods you're alive, Noah spoke silently to Maven. *I couldn't get through to you. I'm going to grab you and Cassius while their backs are turned.*

Wait, Maven whispered as she felt a presence near her head and the squish of shoes in the grass.

"Let's be done here, Kendrich," the witch spoke in a surprisingly soft, albeit disgusted voice.

"In a moment, Lucinda," Kendrich replied, turning back to Harrison.

"We're already late, and this world makes me feel sick," she whined like a child.

"Will you shut up!" Kendrich yelled at the witch without looking at her. He closed his eyes and pinched the bridge of his nose in clear frustration. "We are waiting for our friend to reappear," he spoke with painstaking patience.

All the while still Healing Cassius, Maven remained perfectly still on the cold ground as the argument behind her escalated. She wondered who the young witch was but was more concerned with coming up with an exit strategy. Each scenario she came up with seemed more foolish and less likely of working than the next while both she and Cassius were still so incapacitated. She risked placing her hand more fully on his arm to form a better connection for a quicker remedy.

I'm going to cause a distraction, and you get through a Pull, got it? The urgency in Noah's voice made Maven nervous.

I can't get both of us through yet. I need more time to Heal, she explained.

I'm sorry, but we're all out of time. And I am sorry. His apology seemed too burdensome for him to carry as if he had to give it to Maven because it was too heavy for him to hold any longer.

A confused Maven didn't have to open her eyes to feel the presence of someone come through from the other dimension.

"Well, it's about time you showed up, Noah," Kendrich declared.

CHAPTER THIRTY

"We were beginning to wonder if you'd decided to back out of our deal, but here you are. I am happy to see that family does, in fact, matter to some people," Kendrich uttered in his forced, too kind tone.

Maven fumed as she understood Noah's apology. She could feel the icy rain steam as it pelted her hot, angry face. If she had her full strength, she would have stood up and destroyed the man her father called a friend. As it were, she was still hurt badly. She willed her Healing touch to course faster than was safe to bring Cassius back from the brink of death.

"I did exactly what was asked of me, just like I said I would," Noah replied through gritted teeth.

"Did you? I don't remember asking you to steal one of my best Fliers and hide him in another dimension,"

Kendrich spoke rabidly, his forced voice too much for him to fake.

"I will gladly retrieve him for you," Noah answered as he held up his hand to draw a new Pull.

"No," Kendrich waved him off of his errand. "The fact that he's been caught by an old man like you means someone misjudged his level of competency. Leave him here."

Maven could feel Cassius's body responding to the mend. She probed his mind, but he wasn't conscious enough to Read yet. The moment he was, though, she was going to be ready to go.

"You want to leave a man here, condemn him to a secret solitude, and maybe even death because he fell during a battle that you instigated?" Noah spewed his revulsion at Kendrich. "All because of what? You want some girl?"

"Yes," Kendrich stated. "What is your point?"

"My point is," Noah began yelling but was interrupted by the howl of pain Cassius involuntarily gave as he started regaining awareness.

"What the hell?" Kendrich whipped around to face the noise.

Harrison flew to the warlocks lying in a mixed puddle of mud, grass, and their blood. His survey found Maven's unbound hands, but not until they were a blur and wrapped around his ankle. Quicker than his cry for help, she had frozen him completely solid. She flew herself into a standing position and held Harrison floating in front of her as a shield attempting to hide her still unusable arm.

"What have you done?" Kendrich gasped. "He's... is he dead?"

"He's sleeping, more or less. And if you want him to stay alive, you're going to let me gather my people, and walk through a Pull, or I swear to all the Gods, Kendrich, I will kill him," Maven answered with more strength than she had left.

Kendrich paused, but then shrugged his shoulders. His hesitation was all Noah needed to attack him. The warlock's hands were on the side of his head, trying to get a firm enough grasp to place a Yoke. Lucinda Created a ball of fire and aimed carefully as the two men struggled against one another for control. Maven dropped Harrison to free her left arm to attempt to bind the blonde witch. She Flew toward Lucinda, who was still holding her flaming orb and launched it at the men, seemingly not caring who it hit. It made contact with Noah while Maven placed ties around the Creator's hands. They both watched as the flames absorbed into his body. For one moment, it seemed as if he would be fine. Then, clutching Kendrich's jacket in his fists, he staggered a step backward. The flames consumed him from the inside out, and they witnessed the warlock turn into a statue of ash.

Kendrich was still caught in Noah's grip. He broke Noah's fingers off to free himself, and the fracture, combined with the wind and rain, caused Noah's remains to melt and scatter across the field.

"Whoa," said Lucinda in a hushed, reverent tone. "I did that!"

"Yes, you did," Kendrich made his snarl seem pleasant. "As for you." He looked at Maven like he was going to eat her alive.

A familiar ripping sound turned their attention. Streaking through the air in front of them, person after person appeared through the Jump. There were already ten people and more kept landing. Fear colored Maven's face as she raced to Read the new arrivals, but it was replaced immediately by relief once she realized they were all warlocks.

Him, she shouted to the group. *Bind him before he gets away!*

The terror was transferred to Kendrich as he was surrounded and captured before even lifting off the ground.

Maven ran to check Talmadge. He was unconscious but stable. *You,* she pointed to a warlock with a free set of hands, *Remove the Seal placed on him and Heal him.*

She Flew to Cassius. She had to use her left hand to lift her right into place on either side of his still open laceration. Doing her best to ignore the smell of the inside of his body, Maven focused instead on mending the tissue, muscle, and skin. While she wove the fabric of Cassius's body back together, she placed the most recent events into the minds of the warlocks closest to her. They broke off from the others and began opening Pulls that held everyone left. Patiently, she waited to feel everyone's presence but was especially anticipating Isolde's after being unable to reach her.

She could feel the swell of emotion break through the barrier as Lila and Sabine rushed to Talmadge. But even that was nothing compared to when Sam stepped through. He was much more cautious about his approach to Maven. Unsure if he should touch or distract her while she was Healing Cassius, he simply knelt beside her quietly. She laid her head on his shoulder.

"Hey," Maven said.

"Hey," he echoed, adding a deeply relieved sigh.

"How are you?" she asked.

"Me?" He shrugged. "Oh, you know. Fine. Glad the rain decided to let up, I guess. Anything new with you?"

"No, not much. Just working on a craft project," she replied with a smile.

"Am I the craft project?" Cassius grimaced as he stared up at the two of them. "I don't know what's worse: being sliced completely open or being forced to listen to your weird foreplay." He tried to laugh, but it only made him cough and slightly tear his newly mended flesh.

"Stop that. I just made you again," Maven complained.

"You did a really great job there, too," a tall, redheaded woman complimented Maven.

"Thank you," Maven responded without taking her eyes off of her work on Cassius. "I'm not finished."

Sam could feel Maven's mood shift into neutral, which caused him to take a second look at the warlock standing above them. He didn't recognize her from the auto body shop. He thought he might introduce himself when Cassius pushed into his mind.

Would you please do me a favor? he all but begged.

Yeah, man. What do you need? Sam asked.

Will you please check on Talmadge? I feel responsible for him being injured like that, and I want to make certain he's okay before I attempt to Read any of them, he explained.

Of course, Sam couldn't help but empathize. *I'll be right back.*

Thank you, Sam, Cassius spoke his sincere gratitude.

Sam stood without a word to Maven, assuming she already knew what Cassius requested of him. Despite being soaked through, freezing, and sinking into the field with every step on his way through the crowd to Talmadge, who was sitting up and talking, Sam was grateful for the fact that most everyone had survived. His heart went out to Noah. Despite what he'd contributed to, he had given his life to protect Maven. Sam wanted to discuss everything further with Maven, but he knew it wasn't the right moment yet.

A quiet commotion near the Jump altered Sam's path from Talmadge to the small cluster of warlocks. He tried to catch a glimpse from a distance of what they were struggling with when two of the three warlocks in the group collapsed to the ground. A lone warlock was left with a raging Kendrich fighting the binds she was trying to place. Their struggle ended with him Flying her head into a tree. Between his fingers, he deftly formed a flaming sphere of blue fire. Sam ran full speed at the wizard, but he was able to shoot it off before he got within feet of him. Still, Kendrich was surprised to see a human attempting to capture him.

The ball of fire shot through the crowd even as the warlocks did what they could to push it off course or extinguish its flame. It was unstoppable and aimed directly into Maven's back still turned Healing

Cassius. The spikes of fear and calls to her made Maven turn around in time to see the blue light within feet from her face. With only her left arm to defend her, she swept her hand across the air and ducked. Everyone stood silent as they realized the orb was through her Pull.

Without any time to process what had happened, Maven connected with Sam's distress and fear. She found him hovering high above the ground near the middle of the field. Directly below Sam, Kendrich held him in place with one hand as he raised his other over his head and shaped it into a claw. Kendrich locked eyes with Maven making certain she was watching. And then he winked at her.

"No," she breathed.

Maven Flew through the cold autumn air at the same time Kendrich swiped his bent fingers through it. He Flew towards the Jump before Sam had begun to fall to the earth. Maven caught her partner and set him gently on the field below. Sam touched the grass just as the skies opened up again, unleashing a downpour. Diagonally across Sam's entire torso, from his shoulder to his hip, were five massive gouges. The blood seeped out of him as fast as his heart could pump it.

Kendrich had reached the Jump and was halfway through the portal when he realized he wasn't moving any further. In fact, he was being pulled back. He couldn't turn around because his momentum was set, and he couldn't move forward because of the hold someone had on his hand from the other side of the Jump. The struggle wasn't even between Kendrich and another person. Whoever was in the tug-o-war match was playing against the Jump itself, and nature was going to win. Kendrich was sure of that. But as the Jump pulled harder to get him through, he felt more and more resistance, so much that he felt his forearm ripping from the rest of him. He screamed as his hand left his body, but it was silent as he fell through pure energy. His hand fell to the ground in front of the Jump.

"No, no, no, no, no," Maven muttered as she kneeled over Sam's motionless body.

Ignoring the blood that escaped her own deep wound, her hands glowed over Sam's as she tried to Heal him. She ran her fingers back and forth over his arms and chest, but she couldn't feel the mend happening. Maven could see shredded muscle and tissue down to the bone, but she could feel a faint heartbeat.

"Come on, Sam. Come on! Stay with me," she shouted above him.

Lila and Sabine had joined Talmadge where he sat on the ground. The entire company in the field watched and felt Maven's desperation. Maven's heal wasn't enough to prevent the damage already done from Kendrich's assault. Sam's heart stopped beating.

"No, Sam, stay with me. Please. Stay with me, please, please, please," Maven begged.

She closed her eyes and sobbed but didn't stop her attempt to mend. Lila and Sabine wept with her. Suddenly, the heartbreak that she emitted turned into an edgy determination. Her hands blazed brighter. Slowly, the white light from her hands melted into a hot, neon gold the consistency of lava.

"What are you doing?" Talmadge questioned intensely.

Maven looked up at her friends. They sensed her intent and were scared for her safety.

"No," Lila whispered. "Please don't."

"I have to try," Maven replied to her through her tears.

"Maven, he's gone. He's dead," Sabine pleaded with her.

"I'm sorry I hurt you," was Maven's only answer to her.

The air began to swirl around her and Sam. The

energy poured from her hands directly into his open flesh. The harder she concentrated, the faster it came out. The wind picked up, and their bodies levitated off the grass. Dead leaves flew as the trees swayed, and the others covered their eyes from the mud that kicked up. Both Maven and Sam's skin started to radiate the same gold that bolted from her hands. She looked at Talmadge.

"Goodbye," he said through a choked voice.

"Goodbye," she breathed out.

Unable to locate Isolde, Maven shot a quick glance to the redheaded woman.

Protect them, she Read.

The woman kissed her fingers and placed them in the air towards Maven.

I will, she replied.

Maven closed her eyes, and a brilliant, blinding light beamed out from every pore in her skin. A heavy rumble built beneath their feet and shook the earth. A bolt of lightning and a deafening crack exploded through the field as Maven and Sam disappeared. The wind died, and the trees straightened. All that remained of them was a wisp of smoke and tiny dust particles that floated to the ground.

CHAPTER THIRTY-ONE

S ilence settled over the meadow. Stunned faces looked to each other for an explanation, but no one had any to offer. Lila and Sabine had both fallen to their knees beside Talmadge. The redheaded woman walked over to them.

"Where did they go?" Sabine asked her question but addressed no one.

"It looked like..." Lila trailed. "When she disappeared, and the dust..."

"It looked like when Liam died," Sabine finished for her.

All three felt the woman's pain at the mention of Liam.

"I'm sorry," Talmadge spoke sincerely. "Did you know Liam?"

"Yes, I knew him quite well." She smiled tenderly

at them as she wiped a tear with the back of her finger. "Forgive me. I'm Nova."

"Nova?" Sabine repeated the name. "You feel... familiar."

"She should," Talmadge replied while he stared at the woman. "Nova was Maven's mother."

Lila gasped, and Sabine's hand covered her mouth.

"Or should I say 'is' Maven's mother's name?" Talmadge asked as he stood.

"Yes, 'is' would be accurate," Nova answered as she took Talmadge's offered hand, and they all climbed to their feet.

"But Maven said you were dead," Lila said, confused.

"I think her word was 'lost,'" Cassius spoke as he joined them in the field.

"Cash," Nova hugged him tightly.

"As we said before, most warlock families were separated and scattered throughout the realms. In a lot of cases, when we say we lost someone, it's the literal meaning," Cassius continued.

They could see his swollen, tear-stained eyes matched their own.

"Then how did you know Maven was here?" Talmadge questioned Maven's mother.

"Andros. He had Jumped realms earlier to start gathering warlocks, and he happened upon us in Astonia. Once he mentioned Maven, we headed straight here," Nova responded somberly. "I just wish we would have landed sooner."

"What did she do?" Cassius asked as he swallowed down more emotion.

"She tried to give her life to Sam," Sabine replied, slightly shaking her head. "She literally poured her energy into his heart."

"Has that ever been done?" Lila inquired.

"No, I don't think so. I've never seen anyone do anything like that before, but it resembled an expiration after a siphon," Nova explained with a heavy heart.

"There's no way she survived that, did she?" Lila wiped away the new tears that fell down her cheeks.

"I don't see how," Talmadge answered softly.

He placed an arm around both Lila's and Sabine's sunken shoulders. In the distance, sirens could be heard faintly.

"We need to get out of here," Cassius spoke tersely.

"What's next?" Nova asked, wiping tears of her own.

"Nothing changes. We follow through with Maven's plan; we go back to Loremara to spread the truth, and you all build your defenses," Talmadge said determinedly.

Cassius turned and Read to all the warlocks the

new urgency to Jump and the continuation of their strategy.

"What will you do with them?" Talmadge questioned, gesturing to Kendrich's companions.

"They're coming with us," Cassius answered as warlocks started Jumping with their captives. "Until we Read their memories and determine their innocence or guilt, they'll remain with us and Sealed. Except for that one," he motioned towards the trees.

In all the chaos, no one had noticed Eldon lurking in the woods.

"Maven already shared her Read of him with us. We have no use for him, nor can he do any further harm without his talents. I think it's best to leave his fate up to you," Cassius continued.

After a moment, only their small group remained in the field. The sirens grew louder as they neared their location.

"What about Izzy?" Lila asked.

Her unconscious body had been found inside of her Pull, but Healing had yet to revive her.

Cassius brushed a lock of hair out of her colorless face. "I'm taking her with me. I'll see to her properly in the next realm," he replied calmly as he Flew Isolde's body above the ground and prepared to Jump. "Nova, are you coming?"

"No, Cash, I'll be staying with them," she gestured towards Maven's friends.

"Very well, then. Get rid of that trash, won't you?" Cassius nodded to the piece of Kendrich.

"Of course," Nova said.

With a twist of her fingers, a pink light launched from her hand and landed on the lifeless one on the ground. It quickly shrunk down to the size of a thumbnail. She placed it inside a small pouch, pulled the strings closed, and set it in her pocket.

"Thank you for everything you've done," Cassius spoke and emitted his sincerity to them all. "I hope we meet again under better circumstances."

With a quick nod, he was a blur. The ripple of the Jump indicated his departure.

"What about him?" Nova asked.

Talmadge rested a hand on Sabine's shoulder as they looked towards the trees.

Taking a deep breath, Sabine replied, "Eldon stays behind."

"Okay," Nova confirmed.

The four poised themselves to Jump.

"Let's go home," Talmadge voiced with a sigh.

Sabine reached out to Lila and Talmadge. Holding hands, they broke the barrier towards Loremara.

ABOUT THE AUTHOR

Kiron Croke is an emerging author of urban fantasy. This is her first book and the first in The Jump Trilogy.

She lives in Seattle with her husband and son.

www.kironcroke.com

FROM THE AUTHOR

I cannot thank you enough for buying The Jump. If you enjoyed the book, go online and leave a review. Good ratings and reviews are the lifeblood of independent authors. Again, thank you for your support!